Dark hair brushed her cheeks, and the scent of jasmine caressed her senses. That was it. A tiny image Aless embraced at night when wolves howled from the woods. In countless ways her mother would always be a stranger. Now she understood it was better that way.

I0614072

Praise for Laurel Thomas

"Stones of Promise is a fantastical fairy tale turned daring adventure! Every beat of tension, twist of betrayal and heat of romance tells a classic tale of good versus evil."

"A must read for fantasy lovers! The message of love, forgiveness and finding destiny will touch hearts, while the roller-coaster ride of suspense only makes readers want to do it all over again!"

Stones of Promise

by

Laurel Thomas

This is a work of fiction. Names, characters, places, and incidents are either the product of the author's imagination or are used fictitiously, and any resemblance to actual persons living or dead, business establishments, events, or locales, is entirely coincidental.

Stones of Promise

COPYRIGHT © 2022 by Laurel Thomas

All rights reserved. No part of this book may be used or reproduced in any manner whatsoever without written permission of the author or The Wild Rose Press, Inc. except in the case of brief quotations embodied in critical articles or reviews.
Contact Information: info@thewildrosepress.com

Cover Art by *Jennifer Greeff*

The Wild Rose Press, Inc.
PO Box 708
Adams Basin, NY 14410-0708
Visit us at www.thewildrosepress.com

Publishing History
First Edition, 2023
Trade Paperback ISBN 978-1-5092-4724-0
Digital ISBN 978-1-5092-4725-7

Published in the United States of America

Dedication

Thank you, Mama, for etching the love of storytelling into my DNA and for being my sweetest fan.

Prologue

Scrape. Screak. Scrape. Five-year-old Alessandra Gunter rubbed sleepy eyes and peered at a branch that brushed her window as if it called her to play. Gray dawn filtered through a checkerboard of metal rods over the glass. Yesterday, she'd been swinging on that branch, legs dangling, and chin lifted to a cool breeze.

Nasty Mrs. Blundercrest had a fit when she'd seen her. "Never again." The old woman had growled, then huffed away, her wide behind swinging like wooden shutters flapping in the wind.

A big man who smelled like oily rags had tromped into her room and nailed bars to her window that afternoon. She'd sat on the bed, hugging her rag doll, Emmy. Tears dribbled down her face and onto her neck, leaving her skin sticky as they dried. How would she see the stars at night? Or let the morning air graze her cheeks.

Aless pulled herself out of bed. She could still catch a glimpse of morning sky as it shifted out of night. She took in a breath and stepped back.

A man dangled on her branch with his long legs wrapped around it. He lifted a hooded cloak and rust-colored curls spilled out. He bowed slightly and smiled.

She walked closer, to get a better look at this mystery person in her tree.

His eyes were kind. And blue. Not blue like the afternoon sky. More like the wildflowers in the wooded

1

area just beyond the tree.

Who was this man and why was he sitting in her tree? Maybe he was a fairy. Not one she'd ever seen in books, though.

Katrina, her friend whose white apron scratched her cheeks, brought a book almost every time she carried a meal into Alessandra's room. "Here, my lovely," she'd say, in her voice that sounded like a song. "A book that will take thee far away, to another land."

Katrina held her in her lap and read when the other children were napping or in school, or whatever they did. Even after Katrina left, Aless studied the picture she loved most, willing herself into a wonderland of stones and trees that soared higher than she'd ever dreamed possible.

But this was a real person in a real tree. She lifted on tiptoes and peered back at the man who balanced on the tree limb.

He leaned forward and extended his hand to her.

How could she come to him? It was too hard. Still, she placed her hand on the bars. "Please. Don't go away."

Maybe he said, "I won't." Or maybe that's what she hoped.

The cold metal bar shifted at her touch, then fell to the ground with a crash. Her eyes darted around in fear. What if she woke Mrs. Blundercrest? She'd be angry.

With another touch, the next bar pulled away from the windowsill. Aless held it against her chest before putting it on the floor. She searched her hands for a moment. Same fingers, dirty around the fingernails. Nothing different or special about them that she could see. How could bars that seemed so strong fall away in her grasp?

The man in the tree smiled and clapped.

Were there footsteps padding down the dark hallway outside her room? Aless hurried to touch one rod, then another, as she caught and positioned them on the floor. Soon, a pile lay at her feet.

She strained at the window, pressing her hands against it as she pushed. To her surprise, it opened. A rush of fresh air swept in, like the hurried whisper of a friend.

A gruff shout sounded from the first floor. Was it the night watchman?

The red-haired man bobbed his head, introducing himself as if they met in the fancy parlor downstairs. "Hello, Alessandra. My name is Aiden. Your mama sent me."

"Where is she?" Joy bubbled up inside. Surely, Mama was coming, too. Aless hugged herself but the skinny arms that tightened against her chest were nothing like the warmth of Mama's embrace. Even the scent of rain in morning air couldn't compare to the fragrance that belonged only to her.

Tears spilled out of the man's eyes. "That pretty lady down there?" he asked. "She's your cousin. Mama said it was okay if you'd like to come with us."

Alessandra strained her eyes until she saw a young woman standing by two horses. She wore a shawl the color of night and waved at Alessandra.

"What about Mrs. Blundercrest?" she asked, with a grimace. The hateful woman searched out any wiggle that looked like fun and squashed it.

"Ah. And she's a nice person?"

Aless wrinkled her nose and scowled. "She's an

ogre."

"Would it be all right to leave without saying goodbye?"

Aless nodded. "What about my friend? Cornelius."

Aiden leaned forward and searched the room as Aless pointed at a tiny brown mouse that crept along the baseboard.

"Cornelius might be happy to stay," the man said, shifting his weight. "Perhaps he has a family here." He bent his head toward hers so that she could see his eyes before he spoke. "Would you like to come to our home —in the mountains?"

Aless nodded her head until her neck ached. "Yes. Please." She grabbed Emmy and tucked her under one arm as she climbed onto the branch. She slipped once and her heart bounced, too.

Aiden grasped her in his strong arms and scooched them both against the wide trunk until they were safely positioned, with Aless sitting in his lap. Rough fabric on his trousers was scratchy, but his arms were warm and safe.

It wasn't her imagination. Angry voices shouted from the hallway outside her room.

"Can you be as quiet as Cornelius?" he asked.

Aless climbed onto Aiden's back and held on to his neck as he clambered down the tree. Even with her body shifting against his back, the man moved from branch to branch as if the tree was his familiar home. Instead of fairy, she decided, he must be part red squirrel. That explained his hair.

There was a lot of noise, now. Mrs. Blundercrest stuck her head out of the window, her hair plastered in tight pinwheels. "Get back in here. Now, I say."

Aiden called to the tree. "Come, beloved Pine. Hide us now."

And it did. After what felt like only a few minutes, Aiden had moved her from his back into his arms. He positioned her on a limb near the base of the tree, making sure she was steady, then he leaped to the ground. With only a moment to find his balance, he held his hands out to her. "Jump, Aless. I'll catch you."

Voices shouted from her window now. Aless leaped into Aiden's arms, and he caught her. Instead of letting her run on her own two legs, though, he held her close.

"I'm not a baby," she said, gripping Emmy tighter.

"I know. Only for a bit."

Aiden shifted Alessandra against his chest and her cheek rubbed against his dark tunic, damp with sweat, as he ran.

The horses were saddled. The pretty lady sat on a gray mare with splotches of black on its coat, holding the lead of a coal black horse beside her. Aiden slowed his pace as they approached, even as lights flashed down the long stairs of the building's entrance.

Maura leaned over and took Aless from Aiden. She hoisted her on the saddle, tucking her securely inside her lap. She pulled the shawl over Aless until only her eyes peeked out of its refuge, like a little rabbit. "Hello, Alessandra. My name is Maura."

Aless craned her neck to see starburst eyes looking down at hers. "You know my mama?"

Maura's eyes filled, like Aiden's had. "I do." Her words sounded like a promise.

Aless looked back at the brown bricks, muddy against the gray sky, with towering windows on each side. Metallic flames curled around an enormous serpent that stared with glittering eyes from the watchtower.

"There she is!" A man yelled, as shrouded figures ran toward them.

Aiden jumped on the black steed whose coat shone against the gloom. At a low command, both horses began at a canter, then galloped away.

Aless cuddled closer into Maura's shawl, and the woman whispered, "Peace, child."

Lights of a city ahead flickered like lightning bugs ahead from the same road Mama used when she arrived for her visits.

Aless wasn't afraid. Well, a little. The air was crisp and the sky awash in colors all around as morning light finally arrived. She breathed in the warm scent of the leather saddle and tightened her legs as the horse galloped forward.

Suddenly, a terrible thought sped through her mind. Fear rose, as ugly and hateful as Mrs. Blundercrest. Alessandra couldn't make it go away. It screamed a question she hadn't thought to ask. One that had to be answered.

How would Mama find her? She wouldn't know where to look for her little girl.

She couldn't leave. No matter how awful staying had been. Emmy fell on the ground as Alessandra rose in the saddle, legs straining to keep her balance against the horse's stride and fighting against Maura's hold.

"Take me back. I have to go back!"

Chapter 1

Twelve Years Later

"Follow me, friends." Alessandra beckoned a small covey of kids, who hurried to bunch around her in a tight circle. She pointed at a lanky young man reclining against a tree trunk, legs extended and arms under his head.

"He's sleepy," a little girl said, her forehead crinkled. "He must be velly tired."

"Oh, no, Lucy. Rory never does anything. Quiet, now. You know how he loves surprises." Aless put one finger to her lips and tiptoed to Rory, who opened one eye, then closed it.

The noisy little mob gathered autumn leaves and piled them on top of a vibrant shawl Aless had spread on the ground. They lifted the shawl full of leaves and tiptoed to Rory, ready to empty it on his sleeping body.

"Arrrgg!" Rory rose with a mighty shout, waving his arms and grabbing at squealing children, who scattered in every direction. Only Alessandra stood her ground. In one swoop of his arms, he pulled her into a bear hug. "My captive. Finally."

Warm strength of his arms pulled her close. Alessandra felt the thump, thump of her heart. Or was it his heart? She almost rested her cheek against his chest. Instead, she rose and wriggled out of his grasp.

Lucy yelled, "They was kissin'. I saw them." The little one tangled her legs around theirs until all three fell onto the damp ground. The other children threw armloads of leaves over them as they argued.

"Were, not!"

"Were, too!"

Aless dashed across the lawn to a stone chateau whose blackened stones had witnessed raucous games and shouting children for as long as she could remember. No time like the present to exit what she hadn't given permission to appear in Rory. She wasn't sure when, with no apparent warning, he'd begun to draw her as sweetly as the fragrance of a springtime meadow. No time to worry about that now, though.

She ran into Maura, who'd opened the front door and held an armload of fresh laundry. Socks, muslin frocks, and britches fell to the ground as Maura tumbled down along with them.

"Aless!" Maura's starburst eyes flashed as she sat up, rubbing one elbow.

"She didn't mean to, Mama," Lucy said, coming to the rescue. "She's velly sorry."

Rory ran to help Maura off the ground and picked up the clothes, parceling them out to children, who stood with outstretched arms. "Inside now," he said with a growl. "Off with ye, barnacle butts."

Everyone except Lucy carried in an armful of clothes. Her eyes were on Aiden who walked from the direction of the stables. She made a beeline toward her father and grabbed his legs. "Daddy, Daddy, Rory and Awess was kissin'."

Aless looked at Aiden's unruly curls, now flecked with silver, with his youngest daughter dangling from one leg. His freckles melted into ruddy whiskers with the same sprinkling of gray. He'd worked outside all day, preparing the stables for winter, gathering extra hay, and girding up any gaps in the barns with a sticky mud concoction. Except for mud up to his elbows, he looked much like the man who'd come to visit early one morning at boarding school.

Had he really been sitting on the limb of a tree outside her bedroom window? She'd never been sure whether the image was childish imagination or reality. Aiden's wild red curls spilling out, and his hand extended as if in invitation seemed real enough. Only bits and pieces of memory remained. Except for the news Aiden brought after she was safe at the chateau. Her mama was dead.

Now there was another little girl who adored him. Lucy stood, arms raised high, begging for those strong arms. "Best be mindin' your own business, little miss." He lifted Lucy and planted her on his shoulders. "Mama will be waitin' inside."

Alessandra and Rory walked into the large kitchen, where Mrs. Ransbottom stood with a wooden spoon extended like an axe poised to chop off their heads.

"Oi! Varmits! These children won't be feeding themselfs."

Rory bowed to the indomitable kitchen ruler.

She growled and handed him a steamy bowl of potatoes, then pointed to a plate of rolls from a narrow table against the wall. "Make yerself useful, yer highness."

"Aye," said Aless, saluting the aged cook.

Mrs. Ransbottom popped Aless's behind with the spoon. "Keep to yer task, girlie."

Children scampered in from all over the chateau and gathered around a long plank table in the dining room. They plopped onto oaken benches, jostling each other, and calling back and forth as Aiden took his place at the head of the table, leaving a space for Maura beside him.

Aless returned to the kitchen for more food, then went from child to child, helping the ones who needed an extra hand. Like ordinary kids, they were noisy, full of questions, and always moving. That was the end of ordinary, though. These were Magi children. Four of them belonged to Aiden and Maura. Twelve-year-old Marcella, their oldest child, sat nearby. She had Maura's sunlit curls and easy laugh, but it was her daddy's gift that understood the trees, could read their changes and even their warnings. Next in line was ten-year-old Suzette, who had a healing way with animals, and people, for that matter. She stood on one of the benches and waved for Alessandra's attention.

Louis, with his collar buttoned up to his throat, had a mind for numbers. He could recall number sequences perfectly after seeing them one time. Then, there was Lucy, the tender one who cried when someone's heart had been hurt as if the pain was her own.

Now, however, it was Lucy who looked up at Aless with a sweet smile as she jabbed an elbow into Suzette's ribs.

Aless frowned and pointed a finger at Lucy. "Stop. Now."

"She pushed me first," Lucy said, complaining when Aless walked over with a bowl of steaming vegetables.

"She pushed *me* first," protested Suzette. "Aless, sit by me."

The girls were ready to tangle until Aless placed the

last serving dish on the table and sat between them.

Rory was already seated between Louis and Daniel. Louis straightened his thick glasses and pulled at his collar. Rory nodded at him. "Louis. How's the theorem going?"

"Did you know that equal chords of a circle subtend equal angles at the center?" he asked, eyes intent on Rory's.

"Indeed. Show me tomorrow morning in class."

Aiden stood at the head of the table and clinked his fork against his glass. "Time to pray."

The little heads bowed, popped up and looked around, then bowed again. Aless peeked up to see Rory staring at her. She closed her eyes. When she opened them again, he winked. She rolled her eyes and adjusted the shawl around her neck to hide a blush that always started as red splotches on her neck and traveled up her cheeks.

"Amen," Aiden said with a flourish.

"Amen," Aless answered in a too-loud voice that brought every eye to her.

At the end of the meal, older children gathered the younger ones upstairs for bath and bed, while the adults washed and put away dishes.

When she'd helped long enough to satisfy Mrs. Ransbottom, it was finally time. She peeled off a tattered apron and sprinted out the front door. "Come on, Rufus!" A scraggly mutt appeared from one side of the chateau, yipping, and wagging his tail. Together they raced through the meadow and past the stand of aspen to a steep rise. Alessandra felt the familiar pull on her lungs as she climbed, grabbing scrub brush and low tree branches to steady herself. By the time they reached the top, she panted as hard as Rufus, who'd raced on ahead. A sound of rushing water filled the air.

It was the roar that had first drawn her. Alessandra hopscotched across a bubbling stream that widened many feet below into a tumbling waterfall. Fine spray dusted the air and became a light shower as she approached the shelter of a giant Ponderosa pine. Gathering her skirt, she leaned against its trunk and took a deep breath. This was her place. Close enough to feel the strength of the waterfall's wild descent, but far enough not to get soaked. She peered through the haze to a range of mountains in the distance, longing to be as free as the water that plummeted nearby.

Rufus barked.

"Hush. They'll find us." She wasn't willing to share the hiding place she'd discovered years ago — or the dreams she conjured in her mind there.

The fur on the back of the dog's neck bristled. Not like everything about his coat didn't stand on end. Still, he was listening. Maybe Rory was sneaking up on them. He should know better by now. The last time, she'd shoved him so hard that he'd rolled and picked up enough speed that Aless hadn't caught him until he almost hit a tree.

A man's voice called out. "Parada!"

That wasn't Aiden or Rory or anyone else she knew. She held Rufus close. The dog's body quivered beside her as she craned her neck to see a company of horsemen who'd gathered in a clearing beside a pool beyond the waterfall. A man in a scarlet tunic signaled with one hand. Each of the men dismounted and led their horses to drink. She studied the man who appeared to be the leader. His hair was black, even blacker than Rory's, which was more like dark chocolate. This man's skin was brown like buckwheat honey. He was all angles and muscles. He looked like a runner, with long sinews that streaked down his legs visible through tight leggings. His arms peeked through a tunic that didn't look like armor.

Were they warriors? Not a kind Aless had ever seen. Still, they were fierce. And foreign. The leader looked up and caught her gaze. She couldn't move, only stare back with Rufus locked in her arms. When the man bowed, Alessandra stood, and the dog jumped out of her grasp. He ran, zigzagging through the underbrush, down the steep hill in determined pursuit.

"Stop. Heel. Now," Aless yelled, hoping the dog would obey.

He didn't. Rufus had become deaf. She tore down behind him, keeping her balance by grabbing outcroppings of small trees and brush on the way down. Rufus, who usually liked everyone, yowled as if he were defending her from enemy attack. "Get back here."

She picked up her pace, dodging trees until she finally made it to the bottom of the hill. A branch from a tree limb grazed her cheek and tore the bodice of her dress. She jerked the shawl over a gaping hole that exposed her muslin slip. One of the men with hair tied into a wild tuft on the top of his head drew a curved sword out of the scabbard at his side as Rufus neared the clearing.

"Stop. No. Don't hurt him." Aless shrieked and rushed into the open. She grabbed the snarling Rufus.

The leader lifted his hand and trained his eyes on Aless. "Your animal?" He stood for a moment among the other men, who were dressed in similar tunics. That was where the comparison ended. Even from a distance it was clear that he carried himself as one accustomed to being obeyed.

Alessandra searched their faces as each man studied her. One of them, with black hair plaited like cords that spilled over his shoulders, stared with wide-eyed curiosity. Another wore a turban wrapped in vibrant silks around his bald head. His massive neck extended into his shoulders like a tree trunk. The tufted one leered at the hole in her bodice. She tried to pull the shawl, which had drifted around her shoulders, but Rufus kept struggling against her hold.

The young leader approached. The closer he came, the more handsome he was. He stopped short when the dog growled. "Ah. He protects you," he said, with an accent Aless didn't recognize. She took a deep breath to calm the staccatos of her heartbeat, then adjusted the shawl again. "He's usually friendly. Not very smart, but friendly."

The man bowed. "My name is Tareq. These are my men." He pointed to each one. The warriors fidgeted, awkward with the introduction. "This is Akeem, the wise. Basir means seer and so he is. And Heydar, the lion."

Heydar took her in with a hungry gaze as he leaned over the mane of his horse. Amulets around his neck clanked and an emblem of a coiled serpent emblazoned his silken tunic.

Her belly quivered at the serpentine image that was somehow equally familiar and foreboding.

"We've traveled all day," Tareq said. "Is there shelter nearby?"

"We live…the chateau. My…Aiden and Maura have stables for your horses. And for you and your men.

I mean. We have room for you all." She was stuttering like a ninny. "Only a mile south. You'll see our home just past the meadow."

Tareq bowed again. "How kind of you. We'll follow as soon as our horses have finished drinking."

She couldn't curtsey with her arms wrapped tightly around Rufus, and school-girl giddiness had taken her words. Finally, she cleared her throat, hoping her voice didn't squeak. "I'll tell them you're coming."

She attempted a dignified exit, but it was hard to drag away a dog the size of a small horse. Tareq's gaze followed her when she looked back. Although the other men attended to their horses, Heydar's attention was also on her. Fear shivered in her belly, and she hurried away.

It was almost dark by the time the chateau appeared; its stone walls illuminated by torches already lit at the entrance. Rufus scurried to the back of the property where Mrs. Ransbottom left him scraps each evening. Shadows grew long from the trees, and the air was frosty. She ran to meet Aiden, who was leaving the stables.

"I met men. I mean. I met a group of horsemen. They — I don't know where they're from. I told them we had stables. That they could rest here."

Aiden looked confused. "Peace, child. We have plenty to share. Let's go inside. It's getting cold." He put his arm around her shoulders, and she leaned into him, smelling horses and hard work.

As they walked, Aless peered through flowering trees to the view that welcomed her every night she returned from the waterfall. Lights flickered in long windows on the first floor, where the adults gathered around the massive fireplace, finding cozy seats with books or card games. It was the time when children were not only in bed, but also asleep. Quiet. With no responsibilities. Perfect.

"You're out of breath." Aiden gave her a brief squeeze before they went inside. "Did Rufus find a rabbit to chase?"

She looked into his kind eyes. "It was strange. You know Rufus — the worst guard dog ever. But he snarled and went after the men. I thought they'd…"

"All bluff, no brains."

Aless remembered the glint of Akeem's blade and wondered what would've happened if she hadn't run into the clearing.

Inside, Rory sat at a small table playing a card game with Mrs. Ransbottom, who peered up at him as she tapped one foot on the floor. Aless knew the look. He'd already bested the woman, and they'd just started the game. It wasn't fair. He'd memorized the cards.

At seventeen, she and Rory were the same age and had both arrived at the chateau twelve years ago. Rory had come with his grandmother, Nona, from Sanctuary. They'd been friends since that time, proven by almost constant rows over a contested race or tree to climb that never kept them from returning to each other for another adventure.

Rory's long frame slouched against the dainty upholstered chair. They'd been the same height until a couple of years ago. His chest had broadened from a narrow waist, and his starburst eyes gazed into hers with a new heat. She wasn't sure what to do with the rush of longing she'd felt when Rory held her that afternoon. She looked away, determined not to notice a smile that curved his lips.

Rufus ambled into the room and let out a half-hearted woof.

"What are you doing here, smelly beast?" she asked, hands on her hips.

"I let him in. Come, play Whist." Rory stood up and brought another chair to the table. One of his eyebrows shot up as she sat. "What's going on? Your face is flushed."

"Lower that eyebrow and I'll tell you," she said. "We have visitors coming."

Aiden stood in the foyer, taking off muddy boots and placing them by the door. "Aless met a group of equestrians outside the waterfall. They're coming here to rest before they go on."

"Horsemen. Odd that they're in the mountains. Wonder what brought them up here." Rory rubbed faint stubble on his chin.

"We've had a few travelers stop by unannounced. Hard for most to find us, though." Maura entered the room, wiping her hands on her apron. She plopped into a chair by Rory and groaned as she lifted her feet onto a nearby ottoman. "Tired feet."

Rufus growled a low rumble.

"Hush, now. What's wrong with you?" Aless massaged the ruff around the dog's neck. "You'd bark at your shadow, silly mutt."

Rufus rushed to the window, growling as if a mountain lion prowled outside. A man's voice shouted a command over hooves that clattered on granite tiles. Aless heart jumped as quickly as her legs as she ran to look outside. "It's the horsemen. They're here."

Aiden put his boots on as Rory went out with Aless at his side.

Rufus wiggled out behind her. The dog hadn't

changed its mind about the men. He charged into the middle of the riders, baying.

The majestic stallions Aless had seen by the waterfall reared and threatened to bolt.

Aiden ran out the door, laces dangling on hastily clad boots. He shouted to her and Rory. "Careful! Watch for those hooves."

Aless gripped Rufus around the belly and half-dragged, half-carried the raging mutt into the chateau. When she returned outside, Aiden and Rory were helping the men calm their steeds, as Maura watched, silent, from the doorway.

Aless didn't have to know the language to know that obscenities spewed out of their visitors' mouths.

From inside, Rufus took up his command at a window, barking like the ferocious guard dog he'd never been. The horses danced in fear, eyes wild and ears back, until Mrs. Ransbottom's head appeared in the window and Rufus disappeared.

The horses settled, prancing their hooves against the tiled pavement. Tareq spoke a low command to the three men. He dismounted and bowed low to Aiden. "Sir, my name is Tareq Kaurem. My men and I have been riding for days. I fear my horse is lame." He looked at Aless and bowed again.

In one long stride, Rory appeared at Alessandra's side. His stance hardened and his face turned grim.

"Aless told me she'd met you and your men." Aiden glanced at Rory. "We have room in our stables and plenty of hay. You're welcome to stay with them. Follow us."

Lanterns became pinpoints of light in the darkness as the men led their mounts to the stables. Aless went upstairs, got ready for bed, and tried to sleep after all the excitement. Visitors at the chateau, and foreign ones, at that. Tareq's composure was impressive when the horses strained against their riders who were powerful men themselves, but small compared to the massive steeds. Her first impression had been right. Tareq was obviously the leader. The other men looked to him in the middle of all the chaos.

Her cheeks flushed as she remembered the exotic man, especially the way his eyes had followed her at the waterfall. She flumped her pillow and smiled. Until Heydar's leer appeared like a dark shadow and followed her into fitful sleep.

Chapter 2

Aless's head bouncing against the pillow pulled her awake. Lucy's brown eyes peered down, and soft puffs of warm breath brushed Alessandra's cheeks.

"Awess, wake up. We have company! Big men. Brown men! They have horses. And they're coming for bweakfast." Lucy ended with a flourish of chubby arms, gloating over inside information.

Alessandra came to attention in seconds. Sunlight peeked through the latticed windows. She'd overslept. Again. "Out, out," she said to the child. "I'll meet you downstairs. Run, now! Save me a seat."

Lucy flew out the door. "She sits by me! She said so."

Looking into the mirror, Aless frowned at chestnut locks that never failed to resemble an abandoned bird's nest each morning. Running the brush through her hair with one hand, she pinched her cheeks with the other. She looked for and found her favorite blue muslin gown. Slipping it on, she cinched a belt at her waist. After one more critical look in the mirror, she hurried out the door.

The chatter of children gathering in the dining room drifted up the stairs. Holding on to the banister, she took the steps two at a time. Dashing toward the kitchen, she ran head-first into Rory, who backed away and swept his arms out before him. "Breakfast is ready, your ladyship."

Aless ignored him and hurried into the kitchen,

where Maura shouted commands like a field general ordering her troops. "Toast, Marcella. Yes, now. Alessandra. Oatmeal, please."

Aless grasped a bowl of steaming oatmeal in both hands and headed to the dining room, where the children were gathered in a bunch around Tareq. Children jumped up and down, pushing each other to get close to the men who held their arms close to their sides and sat at attention at the table.

Except for Heydar, who fingered a lock of Lucy's hair.

Tareq glared, and the man dropped his hand.

"Tell us another story, sir." Lucy perched in front of Tareq, searching his face. "You's bery handsum."

"Thank you, kind lady. And who are you? A fairy princess?" Tareq's command of their language was fluent. He appeared at ease in the presence of the children, especially Lucy.

"No, silly. I'm Lucy."

"Ah. I've traveled far and never seen a more likely princess — of the elven variety, of course."

Lucy hugged herself. She looked up and saw Aless standing with the oatmeal in hand.

"This is Awess. She's my sister."

Tareq looked up with ebony eyes, and Aless's face grew hot at his gaze. She pointed at Lucy, then made a broad sweep of her hand over the others. "You're being very nosy. Children, take your seats and let our guests eat."

"No fair." The children scattered and took seats around the table, still fighting over those who sat nearest the warriors.

Aless returned their leader's smile. "We don't get

visitors often. Perhaps if you tell them where you're from and what brought you to the chateau."

Tareq turned to his men and translated in their language.

Something fearsome passed over Akeem's face. The bands of fabric wrapped around his waist didn't conceal the outline of a small dagger. Basir's long plaited hair drifted past one eye and his lips twisted over an assortment of yellowed teeth.

Heydar's black eyes flitted from his leader to Alessandra, then Lucy.

Finally, Tareq spoke. "My men and I are part of an equestrian tribe east of here — many miles. We've come to seek a city called Sanctuary."

Lucy clapped her hands. "I know, I know! That's where Awess lived. Long, long time ago."

Tareq looked quizzically at Alessandra.

Aless said, "I was born in Sanctuary, but I haven't lived there since I was a child."

Maura had entered through the kitchen and stood behind Aiden at the head of the table. Her head was bowed, and starburst eyes studied the floor. Her normally pink cheeks after meal preparation were pale. She caught a breath, as if the air inside had suddenly become scarce.

Aiden stood. "We're happy to meet you all. Now, for prayer. Then we promise the questions will end and you can eat."

Aiden bowed his head. "Father, thank You for another day together. We offer our gifts in faith that they shape our world with Your goodness. Amen." He scanned the children's faces.

Lucy's mouth was full, and she'd already raised her hand.

"No," he said. "Remember. Our guests must eat."

Aless, who sat across from Tareq, watched him taste the oatmeal with the trace of a grimace.

"Here." She picked up a bowl of honey. "This makes it better." She put a spoon into the bowl and circled its amber syrup over her cereal, then handed Tareq the honey and spoon.

He did the same. Taking another bite, he smiled and nodded.

Akeem and Basir sat, staring at their bowls. Mrs. Ransbottom had deftly filled them with the steaming porridge, then moved on to fill the children's dishes.

Basir glanced up at Tareq.

Akeem studied the oatmeal, as if unsure it was edible.

Heydar, on the other hand, lifted the bowl to his mouth and slurped it down in two gulps. He plopped the now empty bowl on the table and belched.

The children stared at him, as if in surprised admiration.

Lucy picked up her own bowl and chugged it. Then slammed it to the table with gusto as she mustered up a loud burp of her own. She looked at her mother, who studied her own breakfast with great interest.

Tareq smiled at Lucy, then Aless. "Our culture, and our food, are very different." He gestured to the three men. "At our homes, families sit on the floor around a large dish of rice, meat, and vegetables. We have no utensils. Except for these." He held up his hands. "We eat the same way when we're traveling. Only much simpler fare, of course."

Louis watched with wide blue eyes. Then nodded. Picking up his bowl, he positioned it at his mouth and slurped the cereal. Marcella did the same thing, until finally, each of the children had guzzled their oatmeal and plopped empty bowls on the table.

"See how we honor your tradition, Tareq," Aiden said, with a polite nod in their direction. "The children are happy to share your culture."

He, Tareq and Alessandra laughed, but Maura said nothing. It wasn't like her to be a stickler for table manners. Although, this did appear to be a new low for the children, who raised their hands for more cereal.

As soon as Mrs. Ransbottom complied, each one gulped and dashed bowls down hard enough that the table shook. Their worthy kitchen steward looked on with a red face. The corners of her mouth quivered, as if stifling a belly laugh.

The adults were studiously quiet, except for Heydar who'd taken a large bowl of oatmeal in the middle of the table, poured the contents into his bowl, and emptied it into his mouth. Another belch. He wiped his mouth with a grimy hand and exchanged a look with Basir and Akeem.

Freedom from table manners moved into pandemonium. The children chattered, laughed loudly, and slapped each other on the shoulders, as adults exchanged glances.

When the meal ended, Aiden approached Tareq. "Come with me to the stables?"

Tareq bowed first to Maura, then Aless. "Thank you. It isn't often that we enjoy a family meal. Excuse us, please."

As his men stood, Aless smelled a whiff of pungent smoke. Had the men started a fire the night before? Perhaps they'd needed to cook their dinner, though the scent wasn't like any meal she'd ever eaten. She shrugged it off. Over-active imagination.

The oaken front door opened to the whinny of horses in the distance. Lucy lifted on tiptoes to whisper loudly in Alessandra's ear. "He wuvs horses, Awess. You should go see them."

Everything in Aless wanted to follow the young leader, but all the adults had daily jobs and their day had only begun. Maura was busy with Mrs. Ransbottom in the kitchen. Other adults had scattered to their various morning chores. Alessandra was expected to take charge of the children's schoolwork.

She seated them in age groups and handed out books and paper. When they were settled and working on assignments, she looked toward the front door. Grabbing an apple and biting off a chunk, she chewed thoughtfully. She could go out. Only for a little while. She placed the bowl of apples beside Marcella, who was conjugating Latin verbs. "Watch the little ones for a minute? I'll be right back."

Sunlight had almost cleared the highest ridge in the distance. Morning air was sharp against her cheeks. Aless relished the moment. Green leaves were tipped with gold and rust and the aspen had already shifted into golden hues. Nocturnal animals had returned to burrows and red squirrels chattered at each other as they leaped from branch to branch. A woodpecker rattled a large pine that towered high, its canopy reaching up to the sunlight.

She smelled her approach to the stables before she saw them. She'd have to muck out the stalls later that afternoon. Louis and Marcella would help after their studies. Now, though, the manure and hay and saddles merged into a warm scent that drew her like home.

Other than the waterfall, the stables were her favorite place. She and Aiden gathered wild mustangs every year from the open plains, and she loved every minute of the chase. Aiden had taught her how to train the new arrivals in gentle ways tailored for each one. Her own mare, Orion, was in a smaller stable below the meadow. She'd fill a bucket of oats for her and see how the men were doing.

Tareq, Aiden and Rory gathered on one side of the corral. Deep in conversation, Tareq stood beside his own horse as Aiden studied its hoof. Tareq turned his head to Aiden with a crease in his brow.

Rory stood by with arms crossed over his chest. Aless knew that look. He was in his protector stance, poised to leap into action. Aiden had taught them to be on the alert in a place where a rogue cougar could lurk, or a grizzly might scrounge for food. Rory's eyes weren't on the forest around them, though. They were keyed on Tareq.

Was he jealous? She'd never seen him act like this. It was true that from all appearances Tareq's men were confirmed barbarians. Their leader, however, carried himself with genteel ease and was certainly no threat.

Heydar was the first to see her approach. He spoke a guttural word to Akeem and sniggered as he mounted his stallion. Aless blushed and looked away. She hurried into the stables where a sack of oats rested against one wall. Filling her bucket, she carried it into the corral where Aiden and Tareq still examined the pale stallion.

Tareq bowed slightly when she placed her bucket on the ground. She brushed the animal's neck gently, and shushed a low, "Easy now." Ignoring Rory's frown, her fingers combed through its silken mane, and she admired pale lashes that framed its blue eyes. "He's magnificent. I've never seen a horse like him."

Tareq stroked the animal's nose as it nuzzled him. "His name is Ghost. He's never failed me."

In one step, Rory positioned himself beside Aless. He snorted in uncharacteristic derision. "How could a horse fall short?"

"He's carried me through storms, rugged terrain," Tareq continued, ignoring Rory. "Even on battlefronts. I purchased him from traders who traveled many leagues north of us." He pulled the stallion's mane away to stroke a muscle that stretched along its upper back. "Strong and brave, as well as beautiful."

Akeem's stallion was a dappled gray, while Basir and Heydar both rode Arabians, one black, the other chestnut. The three warriors moved in formations with their animals in the corral, over and over. At their terse commands, each mount moved in sync, first sideways, then backing up and coming to a stop.

"What are they doing?"

"Practicing. They must be ready for whatever we face on our journey, even if its battle." Tareq pointed to Akeem's chestnut horse. "Watch. The rider leads his horse into each position by shifting his weight in the saddle."

Akeem carried a one-handed sword that rested over his lap and hung over the opposite side.

"He carries his sword like that so he can stab from every side," Rory said, keeping his focus on Tareq. "When he slashes the weapon down from the opposite side, it's called a murder stroke, for that's what it does."

Alessandra knew a taunt when she heard one. She wanted to somehow intervene, but had no idea how, as

Tareq and Rory squared off, eyes intent on each other, looking as if each waited for the other to pounce.

"Look straight on at a horse, and he'll see you as a predator," Tareq said, holding Rory's gaze and then turning his attention to Alessandra. "Although they're trained for war, there's a strong bond between rider and horse. One of absolute trust."

"War. Bonds of trust. Interesting. Is it war that draws you now?" Rory asked, with a stern voice.

"No," Tareq answered firmly, as if he'd countered a chess move. "I'm on my way to Sanctuary for business."

"Warriors on their way to a commercial venture?" Rory wasn't letting this go.

Tareq never lost his composure. He watched as Basir took his horse through the maneuvers, explaining each one to Alessandra.

Basir held a single-handed sword against his lap, tapped the horse on the back of the neck, then let it brush its back and ears.

"He's making sure the horse isn't skittish with movement around its head," Tareq said.

The fierce Basir was tender with his horse, which was as peculiar as she, Tareq and Rory standing together with tension crackling around them.

"Aiden!" Maura's voice shouted from the chateau. Strident, it broke at the end into an almost wail. This was no ordinary voice, calling them for a mid-morning break. Something was wrong. Terribly wrong.

Chapter 3

Aiden made it inside the chateau before her and Rory. He knelt on the floor by the long plank table beside a little form dressed in brown muslin. It was Lucy.

The other children crowded around the little circle, either wailing or silent, frozen in fear.

Aless pushed everyone in her path aside and knelt by the little girl. The edges of Lucy's mouth were blue, and her body was limp. This was her fault. She'd left the children with young Marcella.

Aiden grabbed Lucy from behind and pulled up on her belly again and again. Finally, a chunk of apple spewed out on the floor. Lucy took a deep breath, hiccupped, and then yowled.

Maura rushed to gather her into her arms, and Lucy buried her face into her mother's chest.

"Breathe now, breathe," Aiden said, his arms around Maura's shaking shoulders. Each of the children had melted into a soggy mob of tears.

Mrs. Ransbottom was there, clucking, trying to comfort them.

Aless backed away in horror when Rory tried to wrap her into his arms. "What if he hadn't been able...I'm so sorry. I thought..." Shame flooded over her.

Marcella sobbed on her knees at Maura's lap. "I couldn't. I tried."

Maura sat, rocking Lucy back and forth. The woman's breathing hiccupped once and then sputtered in short whiffs. She didn't respond to Marcella, or to anyone.

It was Aiden who gathered Marcella into her arms and comforted her. "It's all right now."

Aless held two of the smallest children in each arm. A wave of sweaty, mourning little bodies pressed against her, threatening to knock her over. They wailed in fear. "We thought Lucy were dead," cried one. That brought another loud howl, releasing flood gates to more tears.

Alessandra's own heart splintered as she patted cheeks and hugged one child, then another. "I'm sorry. So sorry," she said, as she apologized to each one. Even though it would never be enough. Her words released another wave in the children, until their mingled tears became a small lake.

Rory clapped his hands until every eye was on him. "Avast, ye young buckos," he barked in his pirate's voice. "No more shivering timbers and shaking eyelids. Join me in the galley for lemonade."

The children perked up and dried tears as he and Mrs. Ransbottom herded the children into a line, smallest ones to oldest at the end and headed to the kitchen. "Tis drink for all!"

Aless watched the entire company of children follow Rory without question. With only one command, Rory shifted the children out of calamity and into the security of daily life.

Lucy wriggled out of her mother's grasp and ran to the front of the line. She jabbed her hand into Aiden's and strutted forward as if nothing had happened.

Aiden turned to Maura, then to Aless. "Hey, it's

okay. She's fine now."

Alessandra's voice rose like a shout instead of a response. "This was my fault. Don't try to make me feel better. I could've…"

Maura still knelt on the hard stone floor, her face blotchy with tears and hand to her chest. She kept her eyes to the ground as if Lucy still lay there, choking.

It was all Aless could do to gather herself upright and scurry upstairs, longing for a hidden place. She stumbled on a stray toy in the hallway she hadn't noticed through her tears. When she finally made it into her room, she closed the door and fell on the bed.

There was no shelter there, either. What was wrong with her? Leave Lucy and the children to see a man she barely knew? She pounded the pillow in frustration. A knock sounded at her door.

Rory opened it and ducked his head inside. "Lucy is fine. Come join us downstairs."

"Leave me," she spewed out in rage. "Alone. Stop hovering over me."

Rory backed away, hands up as if to protect himself from the barrage. "Okay, okay. Come and get me if you need to talk." He turned and left. In the next moment, the room felt empty.

A gentle knock on the door sounded. "What?" she asked, in a snarl.

Maura, instead of Rory, came in and sat on the bed beside Aless. The bodice of her simple brown frock was streaked with tears, her own mingled with the children's.

When she placed a slender hand on her shoulder, Aless jerked away as if she'd been hit. "I didn't think." Aless refused to look at Maura. "She could've…"

It'd be easier to face Maura if she was angry.

Instead, her beautiful cousin was silent.

Horses whinnied outside and Aiden's voice sounded in calm, even tones, back to helping Tareq and the men. When she finally peered up at Maura, she noticed finely etched lines across the woman's forehead. When had they appeared? Maura had aged before her eyes, and she'd never noticed.

"Enough." Maura words were quiet, but firm. Her cousin touched Alessandra's shoulder, then dropped her hand. She was quiet for another long moment.

Aless struggled to figure out which emotions rolled around her belly in a relentless heap. She tried say something, anything. No words came out of her mouth that usually had plenty to say.

When Maura spoke, it was a simple statement. "I've seen them before."

Startled, Aless looked up with a question. "What? Who?"

"Our guests. I saw them in a dream. A long time ago. My first night in Sanctuary."

Aless knew about Maura's gift as a seer, which included dreams. Not that she put much stock in them. Maura did, though.

Her cousin turned from the window and sat beside Aless, this time a little closer. "I know it doesn't make sense. The dream was a warning then. Perhaps it speaks for today." She combed her fingers through Aless's hair. "I understand. He *is* handsome."

Aless bristled, and her cheeks flushed. "That had nothing…"

Maura held up her hand in protest. "I'm trying to understand why my heart is unsettled at their presence."

"Only because they're different." An image came to

her mind of Heydar and his glittering black eyes trained on her bodice.

"I don't think so." Maura studied Alessandra's face. "Sanctuary had its share of unusual people. Aiden, Hildegard, Tobias. All mysteries in their own way."

Aless remembered stories about Sanctuary when Maura'd been on trial for the death of a child. It was another reminder that there were big holes in her past. Questions that Aiden and Maura had tried to answer. Especially about her mother.

All her life she'd had to rely on other people's memories of a woman she should have known but didn't. That ignorance was the biggest hole of all. It had shaped her wonderings for as long as she could remember. She gazed at the picture Maura had painted for her years ago. A woman with flowing black hair, ivory skin, and regal stance stood with a graceful hand on a little girl's shoulder, looking down at her with a smile that lit her face.

"Did my mother love me like that?"

Maura's eyes crinkled into sadness. "I have a seer's eyes. Remember? I paint what isn't always seen on earth."

"Yes. But did she love me?"

"I know she did."

"How could you know that?"

Maura and Aiden had kissed her hurts, corrected her bad behavior, and prayed over her at night. She should be grateful. But sometimes it was all she could do to feel that she really belonged here, in a family that was wonderful, but not her own.

Maura kept her eyes on the painting. "Although it's hard to understand, your mother protected you by sending you away. She entrusted you to us before she left this earth. One of our best gifts, by the way."

"Will I…" How could she speak the unspeakable? She was her mother's daughter, and that meant something. She wasn't sure what. Every time she exploded in anger; she'd wonder. Was her mother hot-tempered, too?

And now with Lucy. She'd left this morning because she wanted to see Tareq. Something more exciting than the children had beckoned her away. Maybe that's why she'd been taken to the boarding school when she was so young. Her mother had found a better life than one with her daughter.

"I work so hard to be careful." She combed fingers through tangled hair. "Responsible. Rational. It never works for long. I'm still impulsive. And when I'm terrified, I get mad. Am I like her that way?"

Aless peered into the sweet face of the woman who'd been a better mother than she deserved.

Maura leaned forward. "You're like her in the right ways," Maura said, simply. "Remember the prophecy? *Though an enemy builds its shelters on high and sets its nests among the stars, she who carries the light of stars will find and bring them down.*"

"Of course. It has nothing to do with me, though."

"Those words were spoken over your grandmother, over your mother and me." Maura answered in a low voice. "It's a prophecy that defines our lineage. You're a part of it, whether you understand or receive it."

"An enemy that builds shelters on high? One that settles its nests among the stars. All I know is a chateau filled with children, a place where every day is the same. I don't carry light of the stars. Only bowls of oatmeal and arms of laundry. And I don't do that very well."

Maura looked thoughtfully into the sky outside the window. Sparrows ducked in and out of eaves. "My life felt small when I took care of Nicolaus. That changed in one night."

Aless sighed. She'd heard this story many times.

"Yes," Maura answered. She'd always been able to read the tiniest shift in Alessandra's heart. Loving, although usually inconvenient. "You heard what happened. The words of this prophecy carry layer after layer of meaning, even from generation to generation. They, like the stars, never stop speaking." Maura took Alessandra's hands into her own. She studied them, as if seeking an answer.

"Destiny will command these hands at unexpected times, in unusual ways. When the weight of your gifting becomes heavy, we'll be here to help." Maura lightly kissed her forehead. She stood and exited the room, closing the door with a quiet thud.

Chapter 4

The next morning, Alessandra watched Suzette's copper-hued curls bent over Tareq's stallion. Her petite hand reached out to tenderly pet Ghost's mane. The stallion bent his head to nuzzle the pint-sized healer as she applied an ointment of pressed herbs and flowers to the infected hoof. Reaching up on tiptoes she whispered a familiar blessing. "God of the universe. Heal your beloved."

That was it. She planted a resounding kiss on the horse's neck, turned and meandered back to the chateau, stopping to pick a ragged bouquet of weeds.

Suzette knew about healing. Know was too mental a word, though. Her gift was more like instinct, as ingrained as the birds' flight south in early fall. Her presence calmed the injured animal — or person. When she extended her small hands, they shivered, then remained as a lingering touch. She'd been attending to a wounded rabbit in the woods behind the chateau when Lucy choked. Otherwise, she'd have been with her little sister.

Tareq motioned Alessandra over. "Look."

The hoof that had been inflamed and oozing was pink and healthy. The warriors muttered surprised expletives as they leaned over to examine the animal.

Aless tried to smile, but disappointment flooded her thoughts. Tareq's horse was no longer lame and there was no reason for him to stay. She wasn't sure why she cared. He was handsome, of course. But there was something else she couldn't name that beckoned her. Was it adventure outside this mountain life?

She'd never ventured far from home. Not that she hadn't loved the pursuit of wild horses with Aiden, or the wonder of a forest awakening after a night's sleep. The children filled her heart as surely as the waterfall that called her at the end of the day. Still, she was seventeen now. She yearned to see a world broader than the one that greeted her every morning.

Aless returned to finish chores in the house. When she was done, she slipped back outside. Rufus was busy entertaining children in the sprawling library upstairs. This time she was grateful to be alone. Gusts in the autumn air ruffled fallen leaves and sent them spiraling into vibrant funnels. She sprinted through the meadow, into the woods, and up the steep incline to her refuge. Her breathing slowed at the sight of ridges that fell into sunlit valleys and rose onto snow-capped peaks.

The chateau was barely visible, tucked away and surrounded by trees far below. Her body trembled when she remembered the sight of Lucy's limp form.

She considered Maura's sober warning about Tareq and his men. It was unlike her cousin to be guarded and visitors were usually warmly welcomed. Since Tareq and his men arrived, Maura had stood in the background casting furtive glances in their direction. Supposedly, these strangers had appeared in her dream years ago.

Tareq was anything but dangerous, though. His eyes looked into hers with open promise. Not that it mattered. He'd be gone in the morning.

"Hello, my friend."

37

Startled, Alessandra lifted her head from her knees and brushed hair out of her face to see Tareq standing beside her. Rufus hadn't been there to warn of his approach. Or to scare him away.

"Your heart has found a place of rest?" Tareq sat on a grassy patch and peered over the waterfall.

Aless studied his profile, with aquiline nose and chiseled jawline. Black hair escaped the turban in long strands that brushed his shoulders. His arms were exposed in the sunlight, bronze and muscular. He smelled like sandalwood and layers of fragrances she couldn't name. She'd never seen a man who carried authority with such a calm demeanor. He was royalty of some kind, regardless of his unembellished tunic. Taking a deep breath, she looked away. Anything to break whatever drew her to this man whose eyes lit up as if she were a newly discovered treasure.

"Something about this waterfall," Aless said, staring into its spray.

"Adventure. A world without boundaries calls."

Aless glanced at him, then back to the vista. Tareq had spoken what she'd always felt overlooking the water's turbulent descent. "My world has velvet cords that connect me to nineteen children. Children who need my care every day. I love them, though."

Tareq stared into the distance. "My father sent me away to school as a young boy. I lived in a strange city with walls that towered around me, obscuring the sky I'd awakened and gone to sleep beneath every day of my life." He took a deep breath and glanced at her. "Instead of my family, I endured strict teachers who demanded long hours of study. I couldn't play outside. Or be a child."

"Why couldn't you stay home?"

"My father believed I needed the training it offered. For whom I was to become."

"And that was…"

Tareq shrugged. "I'm called to discover uncharted territories. And to plumb their riches."

"I heard your command the first time we met, but don't recognize your language. It's not Spanish. Or Portuguese."

Tareq seemed to perk up at the mention of his language. "Vostede e' fermoso."

"Translation?"

"You're a beautiful woman."

Alessandra willed her face not to react to his compliment. "I was sent away as a child, also. Aiden and Maura adopted me after my mother died and brought me to the chateau. It's hard to remember a life outside this one. These mountains, the stars overhead, the people. They're all home for me."

"And your dreams for the future?"

Aless lifted her head and searched the sky, still brilliant blue and warm against her face. "To see the world. To ride my mare, Orion, hour after hour with no one calling my name. Not having to run away for a moment's quiet."

Rory's voice called from below.

"Speaking of being called…" Tareq tried to suppress a grin but didn't succeed.

Aless stifled her disappointment. Rory knew where to find her, of course.

Her friend appeared, huffing for breath as he maneuvered through the brush. Steadying himself against a tree, he grimaced when he saw Tareq. "Oh. I thought you were alone."

Tareq looked amused.

Aless gathered her skirt and stood, trying to hide her irritation. "We were talking."

Rory looked once at Tareq, then to Alessandra. His cheeks flared red, and his brows crinkled. "Lucy was looking for you. That's all." He turned and walked away, his familiar loping gait turned to an uncertain lurch.

Afternoon sunlight pushed through the giant pines when Aless and Tareq returned to the chateau. Tareq joined his men at the stables while Aless hurried, hoping to check on Lucy before she went to bed.

When the front door creaked open, Lucy dashed outside and into Alessandra's arms. "I been watchin' for you, Awess. To tell you I'm okay. See?" Lucy took a deep breath and blew it out in a spray of spit. She lifted her arms and twirled until she plopped on the ground in a tumble.

Maura looked at the little one who'd tried her patience and won her heart since she'd wailed in her arms as a baby. "I can see you're better than okay. The best, really. My very favorite treasure."

Lucy giggled and held her belly. "Like a pirate's chest?"

"Exactly. Full of rubies and gold."

"Silly Awess. I'm your sister."

"Indeed, you are. Head inside. I'll be there soon." Aless waited a minute longer to gather her thoughts before facing the crowd of children and grown-ups. Guilt clung to her like an unwelcome guest. She didn't have words for it and couldn't explain it away.

Two men approached through the aspen. One of them rode a mottled gray stallion, the other swayed on the back of a dogged mule. She was about to let Aiden know they had more visitors when he appeared from the stables and ran to greet them.

"Clarion!" Aiden whooped in joy. He embraced a tall, angular man with finely cut features who dismounted his horse. Golden hair fell in long waves down the man's back, and a cygnet engraved with ivy circled his head. A scent of evergreen filled the air. That was good because the man who stood beside him looked like he needed a bath.

"What brings you here?" Aiden asked, draping his arm over Clarion's shoulders. "Join us inside." He nodded to the other man. "You're both welcome." He led them to the front door and shouted. "Maura," he called. "We have company."

Maura appeared from the dining room. She lifted her arms and practically skipped at the sight of the men. "Clarion! You've come to see us. Aiden, set up chairs in the library. It's quieter there," she laughed, gesturing at the children around them. "Aless and I will bring tea and join you."

As Aiden led the two men into the library, Maura led the way into the kitchen. "Tea and biscuits, dear."

Alessandra filled the kettle with water and put it on the fire as she prepared tea and pulled biscuits out of the pantry. Maura reached into a top cabinet for the ancient silver tea service. A sure sign these were special visitors. By the time they carried trays into the library Aiden had pulled chairs into a half-circle and motioned everyone to sit. The only adult missing, besides Mrs. Ransbottom, was Rory. He was probably working with the children.

"We have plenty of room at the chateau. Please stay," he said, chattering a river of words for the usually quiet man. "You and your friend are most welcome." He nodded in direction of Clarion's travel companion.

"This is Brocagni," Clarion replied with a wry grin. "His name means badger, as his countenance suggests. Broc, these people are friends of mine." His words sounded more like a warning than introduction.

"Come. Sit," Aiden said.

The stodgy man looked as if he preferred war council to polite company. While Clarion stood, slender and graceful, his companion skulked beside him like an ancient, gnarled pine. Two swathes of white hair burst forth from his temples over frizzy black hair that spewed over a worn velvet collar embroidered with vines. He glared in Alessandra's direction, then took a seat on the end, as if he joined the party unwillingly.

Clarion took a seat beside Broc and studied Alessandra.

Aless held the ornate tea pot in one hand, unsure of what to do with the rest of her body. Was she like a schoolgirl called in for bad behavior? Not that being in trouble was out of the ordinary, even after she'd graduated from student to teacher. Her heart always led her outside to the mountain air, where she could run unhindered, like the wild horses she loved. Aiden understood, but Maura, not so much.

Aiden noticed the focus of Clarion's gaze. "You can trust her. She's our daughter."

"Daughter?" Brocagni growled.

Alessandra suddenly felt small in the large room.

Aiden walked to her side and placed his hand on her shoulder. "Our daughter in every way, except by blood."

Clarion looked her over, then turned to Aiden. "Very well, then. Our news is grave. We've come to warn you of an attack. An army approaches from the east and is heading this way."

"How did you find out?"

"From the trees. The enemy has been decimating forests, cutting down our aged friends and burning what remains. We heard their cry. Creatures of the forest are on the alert as well. They recognize an old enemy advancing."

Aiden had never hidden his lineage as a Magi arborist. He and Aless often walked through the forest together, where he'd introduced her to each tree by name. He reminded her that an unseen network connected them, carrying nutrients, and supporting the young saplings. "See this forest, Alessandra? We're like that for you — as your family."

When she'd looked into his eyes, she'd believed him. Now, as Broc, the gnarly arborist scowled at her, she'd never been more certain she didn't belong.

Maura came alongside Aiden. They stood behind Aless, their reflections like silhouettes against the latticed windows.

"Who are they? What fuels their hate?" Aiden asked.

"They gather under the banner of Gad El Glas." Broc's words were growly and gruff. Spittle ran down his mustache and dribbled down his beard. Part of his last meal still clung to his whiskers.

Maura clutched hands to her chest and turned pale. "That can't be. I saw the end of that evil."

Clarion's towering frame trembled. "Another people have embraced its banner. And its hatred. We've seen it before." He paused and waited as if for a silent command. "You've known it first-hand, Aiden."

"No," Aiden said, muttering the word like a protest.

Brocagni snorted. "Aye. T'were a show of its power to destroy. Men. Women. Children. In one night."

"Stop. Now." Aiden held his hand up. Maura stood frozen in place.

Brocagni was unmoved. "What? The girl don't know about her mother?"

"What about her?" Aless swung around to face Aiden and a spray of hot water from the tea pot trailed around her.

Aiden began to speak, then stopped. Finally, he stuttered. "It…We couldn't…"

As if they'd become a painting on the wall, each person seemed attached to a scene they couldn't escape. No one moved, except Brocagni who snorted and appeared unaware of friction all around him.

Alessandra slammed the pot onto the cart and stalked to the center of the room. "I'm seventeen. I want to know."

Aiden started to move toward her but stopped and addressed the two arborists. "Maura and I need to talk to her in private. Not here. Not now."

"Why are you talking to everyone except me?" Aless shouted and pounded one fist into her thigh. "Tell me."

Aiden's face turned crimson as he studied the patterned carpet. "There was a massacre. Many years ago. At the chateau."

Maura bowed, hands over her face.

"What do you mean?" Alessandra asked. "The chateau was deserted when we arrived. I helped…" She remembered blacked stones of the chateau, half-buried timbers, and vegetation sprouting from ash that had become part of topsoil.

"All slaughtered," growled Brocagni. "At the command of the witch, Lilith Gunter herself."

Chapter 5

The only sound in the room was a loud belch from Brocagni. Clarion shifted in his seat and looked away from his sullen friend. Everyone else stood, silent.

Until Alessandra faced Maura, her voice trembling. "My mother? Why haven't you told me?"

"We needed a new beginning." Maura scowled at Brocagni, leveling her tone on purpose. When she turned to Alessandra, it was with a plea. "Your mother asked for forgiveness. She was free of that evil tyrant when she left this earth. How could you possibly benefit from knowing what your mother did when she was controlled by a demon?"

"I'm not a child. How could you keep this from me?" Aless spun around, as if answers hid in one of the people who sat around the room. First horror, then anger rolled in one terrible knot in her belly. "Magi blood spilled here? By my own mother. And you never told me."

Maura reached for her, but Aless backed away.

Aiden stepped in, this time with a decided stance. His face was stricken, yet beneath it she saw tenderness that had won her heart as a child. He spoke to Alessandra as though there was no one else in the room. "You're our daughter. Nothing less. We didn't tell you because we wanted your memories to remain unstained. You had so little of her."

At that, Aless took a deep breath and shuddered. Questions about her mother had shouted for her attention for years. One memory lingered, probably fabricated from a little girl's longing. Dark hair brushed her cheeks, and the scent of jasmine caressed her senses. That was it. A tiny image Aless embraced at night when wolves howled from the woods. In countless ways her mother would always be a stranger. Now she understood it was better that way.

Aiden's voice, which sounded strangled, interrupted her thoughts. "What could Gad El Glas want in Sanctuary?"

Broc's face glowered even more if that was possible.

When Clarion spoke, his words gathered substance and hung in the air around them. "They seek Alessandra."

"No!" Maura cried out. She and Aiden wrapped their arms around Alessandra's shoulders as if to protect her from attack.

Aless longed to disappear as they hovered, crooning over her as if she were a child.

Broc sneered and looked around the room for somewhere to spit.

Clarion cleared his throat and stood tall and regal.

"Why Alessandra?" Maura asked, wild alarm in her starburst eyes.

Clarion spoke simply. "It seeks the power Lilith held, hoping to find it multiplied in her daughter. You know the kingdom aligned with this plot, Aiden."

Brocagni snorted. "The Nayeli."

Aiden's body swayed as if a gust of wind blew through the closed windows. He and Clarion faced each other silently.

What pain was so deep it had no words?

Clarion's voice was subdued. "They have the Stones of Promise hidden in a Nayeli stronghold. Now, they seek the one who must carry them." He studied branches that swished against the window in the darkness outside. "They've scoured every inch of conquered territory for that person—the only one able to unlock their power. Somehow Lilith Gunter's daughter is linked to that discovery."

"How can we protect Aless?" Aiden asked.

Warmth flooded Alessandra and softened the tearing pain in her chest. Maura had explained that losing the Stones and their wisdom was an incalculable blow to the Magi. Yet, in all this catastrophe, Aiden's attention was on her safety.

"Keep her here, with you," said Clarion. "Your family is her true sanctuary. We'll place an extra guard around the chateau. We're gathering Magi forces even now from all over the region."

Aiden paced back and forth in front of a bookcase that lined one wall. Aless knew this walk when his mind was as active as his legs, pulling ideas like thread into a plan. Except this time, he plopped into the nearest chair and peered up at Clarion. "What can we do?"

Clarion bowed to Aiden and Maura first, then to Alessandra. "You're part of us. And that includes Alessandra. You're not alone."

A knock sounded at the door followed by Marcella's voice. "Dinner is ready."

Aiden addressed them all. "You should know we have other guests. A young man and his companions arrived the other night with an injured horse. They leave for Sanctuary in the morning. We'll meet here after they leave and discuss how to respond. Together." He stood, as if to issue a command. "One last warning. Guard your words and your faces. Nothing can be said until we have time to prepare the children." Aiden opened the door and led the way out of the library and into the dining room.

The atmosphere shifted as unexpectedly as a snowstorm in late summer. Brocagni stopped at the arched entrance that faced the dining room table, where Tareq and his men were seated.

Until they saw Broc and Clarion. The bench seat wobbled and threatened to overturn when they stood as one, even with the small bottoms of the children still perched there.

Brocagni, planted like a sawn-off tree trunk, trained his eyes on Heydar, then Basir and Akeem. "Oi. Barbarians, are ye?"

Clarion placed his hand on Broc, but he shrugged it off.

Akeem held his hand over the dagger hidden in his waistband. Heydar's hands clenched and unclenched, ready to pounce. Basir watched, as if waiting for a command.

Maura looked terrified at what looked like an imminent battle in front of the children.

Only Tareq seemed unabashed by the ferocity that suddenly overtook the room. He stood his ground and bowed slightly. "We'll go." He turned to Aiden, then Maura. "Thank you for your hospitality. There's nothing to delay our journey to Sanctuary. We'll leave at first light."

Heydar took one look behind and found Alessandra, his mouth stretched over missing teeth, and smirked. The next moment they were gone.

Chaos overtook the dining room. The kids clamored Clarion and Broc with question after question, even as they stood at the doorway. Lucy ran to Clarion and touched his hand. "Why does you have weaves in your hair?"

"They're leaves, not weaves," Suzette argued.

Lucy ignored her and turned to Broc. "Are you's a skunk? Can I ride your mule?"

The children seemed unaware of tension that remained even after Tareq and his men left. Their curiosity was undeterred by Broc's gruff answers and Clarion's aloof dignity.

Aless searched the large dining room. For the first time, she noticed faint black smudges here and there along the benches and scattered along edges of the table that extended from one end of the room to the other. Soot stains and burns that had been sanded away.

It had been plucked from a fire. She peered around, looking for other evidence. Blackened grout lined tile at the entrance and its stain that always resisted cleaning. Another shadow of devastation.

Maura extended her hands to Alessandra. "Don't be angry. We always hoped our love would be enough."

"Enough to erase what my mother did? I walked those hallways day after day, never knowing they were stained with Magi blood." Alessandra's voice came out in a loud hiss. "You knew. All this time."

Lucy stopped chasing one of the children and stared at her.

Aiden took Maura's hand, as if in a united front. "We…Nothing has changed. We're your family, and this is still your home." He turned to interrupt the chaos. "Children. Now. Dinner table."

Alessandra watched, as the children scurried to their seats. She couldn't think, couldn't remember how she'd fit into this family for so long. Everything she'd known and trusted had overturned.

Maura came as close as she could before Aless backed away. "Go. Take some time to think. We'll talk later."

Aiden escorted Clarion and Broc to the table. He looked back to Aless, then to Maura.

Aless hurried to the bottom of the staircase, listening to the familiar commotion before a meal. She knew when everyone quieted that Aiden had held his hand up. Suddenly, she couldn't leave, couldn't face the silence of her room alone. She took a seat by Lucy, where Mrs. Ransbottom offered a plate of food.

"We have guests for dinner tonight," Aiden said, his voice wavering only once as his calm demeanor shifted what had been chaos moments earlier. He shook his head in Lucy's direction.

Her fingers were poised, as if waiting, over her plate. "We's wants to use our hands," Lucy said, in a whine.

"Not tonight." He nodded to Rory. "Will you pray?"

Rory bent his head and paused for a minute, as if to gather his thoughts.

He hadn't been there. Had no idea how her world had shattered with what she'd learned in the library.

Rory cleared his throat. "We invite You, God. No matter where, no matter what, no matter how. Amen."

Aless felt every eye was upon her. Without a word, she fled outside, hearing Lucy protest to her mother. "How come Awess gets to leave?"

The sun sank low over the western ridge of

mountains as she ran to the shelter of hawthorn trees at the entrance of the sprawling lawn. As she looked back, the soft light of candles wavered through the towering front windows of the chateau. A horse neighed inside the stables.

She searched the corral, but Tareq and his men were nowhere in sight. Neither were their stallions. No voices bantered in the unfamiliar language. Maybe they'd left, though she hadn't heard an exit.

The events of the day whirled around in her mind, twisting, and turning. She sat on the ground and covered her head in her arms. A rustle sounded in the leaves, and she looked up.

It was Rory, standing uncertain, his sunny face twisted into a worried look. "What's wrong?"

Such a simple question. One truth had rattled her once secure foundation like a thundering earthquake. She couldn't tell Rory yet. Couldn't explain what felt like a mortal wound.

Rory sat beside her on the damp grass. He crossed his legs and nodded toward the chateau. "That was a strange confrontation at the dinner table. Are you okay?"

Again, she couldn't find words. Even with her best friend.

Rory didn't wait for a response. "Who are the two men who came for dinner? They sure stirred things up."

"Arborists." Her voice didn't sound like her own. It was as if an Alessandra she'd never met peeked out of ashy ruins. "Friends of Aiden and Maura." She shifted to find a comfortable spot on the damp ground, then gave up.

"They despised Tareq and his men," he said. "A mutual feeling, judging from our equestrian visitors' quick exit."

Aless cast a side glance his way. "You don't like them, either. Why?" Her voice came out hostile, accusing. Is that what she wanted?

Rory brushed away a tiny caterpillar and stretched out long legs. "There's something about them I can't figure out."

"It's not like you to let some vague suspicion take over your judgement. I asked you once, but you never answered. Are you jealous?" She turned away, suddenly embarrassed.

There was a hint of that dimple in his cheek. "Maybe. I just think there's more than we see in them."

"You don't trust them."

"Exactly."

Aless crossed her arms and turned to face him. "Based on nothing except an odd foreboding."

Rory gazed at her with those wild, golden-flecked blue eyes. Just like Maura's.

"I'm assuming you're playing the seer card," she said, trying to sound flippant, but failing. "What do you supposedly see that I don't?"

"Are you angry?"

"I'm not. I only want to know." She *was* mad, though.

Rory took a deep breath and blew it out. "There's something dangerous about them. I can't explain how I know, but I do."

"Not Tareq," she said, her voice harsh. She leaned back for a moment, unsure why she defended a man she barely knew. Her gut stirred with a heat that didn't make sense. "His men are fierce, but that's because they're warriors. Not teachers."

"There's more," Rory said, the teacher in him refusing to respond to her barb. "What is it?"

Aless folded her arms tight around her chest. She couldn't repeat what she'd heard from the arborists. It was too terrifying. Shame threatened to rise and spill out in tears. She wasn't sure when the weeping would end. Especially with Rory standing there, reminding her of the times she'd shared her heart with him.

"I heard something about my mother. From the arborists."

Rory tightened. "What did they say?" He shifted his gaze to a mountain peak in the distance. There was something he knew. Something he wasn't telling her.

"I've known you all these years. You're hiding something. What is it?" Her words came out in a croak.

"I don't know what you're talking about."

"Yes. You do." She struggled to keep her voice calm and measured. But couldn't. "You've never lied to me."

Rory's face flushed to a deep red.

Her voice was stony, cold. "Tell me."

Rory spoke to the ground at his feet. "I saw your mother. Once." He stopped, as if hoping that was enough. He leaned forward and clasped his hand around his knees. His hair fell over his face as he fiddled with a blade of grass.

"You saw my mother? She was gone by the time you and Nona arrived at the chateau. How could you have met her?"

Rory separated a pebble from the dirt and tossed it. Then another.

"Tell me."

"I can't."

"You aren't any different than Aiden and Maura.

What was she like? Where did you meet her?"

He hunched forward like he'd been punched in the gut. "I saw her in an arena. In Sanctuary."

"What were you doing there? You were so little." Her questions tumbled out in a hurried heap of fear and hope.

"I was five. My parents were already gone. Nona had taken me in."

A vague foreboding shrouded Alessandra. "So, you were with Nona when you met her?"

"No. At least not at first."

Why was Rory being so evasive? He'd always been direct when they talked about what mattered. "Look, I just found out something more terrible than I ever imagined about Lilith Gunter. Tell me."

His body shuddered, then he straightened and looked into her eyes. "I was summoned as a sacrifice, offered to Gad El Glas."

Aless held her chest. What was it like to have a heart attack? Her heart was under siege, and she wasn't sure it would survive. She sucked in the brisk evening air. Shock, disgust and finally anger rose like a giant. "You never told me."

"I couldn't. Wouldn't."

"You lied to me." She stood and jabbed her finger at him. "You acted like I was your friend. All along you knew."

Rory held up one hand, as if to stop the progress of her words. "Aless. Don't. Not now."

"When did you plan to tell me? I'm the daughter of a woman so evil she intended to kill a child — my friend," she said, choking on the last words.

When Rory moved closer, she pushed him away.

He almost fell backward. Then lowered his head for a minute. When he looked up, his face was ashen. "This isn't what I came to talk to you about. I know… This is horrible timing. I have to say something, though. Now."

His hand reached for hers, but Aless jerked her own away. How could he stand to touch her, knowing what he did about her mother?

"Alessandra," he said, measuring his words. "This…all this doesn't change you and me. Walk forward with me. Not to a time we had no control over, but to what has always been true. I love you."

Aless stiffened. What could she say? That she already knew? That she loved him, too. None of that mattered now. "You've never known me."

"That's crazy."

She wanted to run, but there was nowhere to go. "I'll tell you what doesn't make sense. The fact that everyone around me has lied. They've only pretended to…" She couldn't finish the sentence. Rory, Aiden, Maura. They'd only tolerated her presence. They'd known the unthinkable and let her live as family with them, totally unaware.

"No one has pretended anything. I'm not here to defend Aiden and Maura. Or me. I'm here for you. I sense trouble."

"How insightful. A warning because I'm the daughter of a witch who murdered our people."

"No. That's not it."

"A bigger threat than knowing you kept a secret from me all these years?" She was afraid in a way she'd never known. Because she knew. She carried something evil from her mother. Something that could hurt Rory. And the others. "Go. Now."

"I'm not leaving." Rory shook his head, stunned. The gold around his blue eyes flashed. "Love for you allows me to see a trap ahead. And it isn't about your mother. It's about you."

"Me? So, it's my fault now?"

"Please." Rory looked crestfallen. Finally, he shook his head.

Aless turned away so Rory couldn't see her tears. "Leave me alone. I know when I'm only pitied." She sprinted away, refusing to turn back, even as Rory's words echoed through the night.

"Love is all around you, Aless. Whether you recognize it or not."

Chapter 6

It was late. Tree frogs and crickets vied for attention in the night air. A hoot owl sounded in a tree by her window. She'd waited for Rory. Hours earlier, even as she'd tucked Lucy and the little girls into bed, she'd tried to understand a day that had made no sense.

By the time the children were asleep, she was sure Rory would appear at her door. They'd talk. Everything would be like it had always been. He'd never come, though. And nothing would ever be the same. She'd trusted in the love of those who'd never shared an awful secret. Hurt and betrayal shouted over every kindness she'd felt in this home. She'd forever stand outside this fold.

A violent wind had swooped down on her life, destroying all in its wake. She'd always known that she was a tree without roots. What kind of justice kept Aless from a mother she'd never known and then revealed why she'd never want to? Years of peace with a loving, adoptive family had blown up with one horrible reality.

That fact, though, revealed the true enemy. It didn't matter that Lilith Gunter was in the grave. She still ruled, dead or not. Aless steeled her heart. No more hoping, longing for a reason to believe Lilith was a woman she'd longed to know. She swallowed an almost sob and wiped away what she decided would be the last tear she'd ever shed over a woman called her mother.

One thing was certain. She couldn't hide in the protective covering of the chateau any longer. No one was safe with an army in search of her. It wouldn't take an artful spy to discover her presence on the mountain. There were no guards, no barred gates. The children were totally unafraid. How would they tell the little ones it was no longer safe to play tag in the meadow or climb trees, dangling like small monkeys from the branches? She wouldn't let that happen.

Her mother had ruled in Sanctuary. If she could get there, she'd gather evidence to prove her own innocence. And Lilith Gunter's guilt. She'd go to the city and find whatever platform she could to justify herself and condemn the evil woman.

The evil woman. Those words stirred an ache that had always seemed right below the surface of her being. They also confirmed why she'd never left the mountain. Aiden and Maura had protected her from what she might learn if she ever left the confines of their refuge.

Rory's grandmother lived in Sanctuary, although Aless had never gone even for a visit. She only knew Nona from holiday celebrations at the chateau. What would a trip there look like? According to Aiden, the ride to Sanctuary took two days in the best of circumstances. This time of year, a snowstorm could blow in without warning. Grizzlies were ravenous as they prepared for hibernation. There was no way she and Orion could go alone.

Tareq and his men were headed there in the morning. Maybe she and Orion could follow behind their troop unnoticed. Or at least try. That plan had lots of holes in it. Tareq and his men were seasoned warriors and would know if someone trailed them.

Aless peered into a night sky that was a long way from morning and then around the darkened room. An ancient chiffarobe tottered in one corner of the room. She dug around at its base until she found a woven bag and stuffed it with extra clothes. Her riding clothes hung in a corner all their own, ready for journeys with Aiden.

The aspen were a soft green and the air had smelled like freedom the last time she'd worn the brown split skirt and riding boots. As she dressed for an uncertain journey, she noticed Hildegard's shawl nestled in the middle of a pile of sweaters on the top shelf. She reached for it and remembered when it had first become hers.

It had been her sixteenth birthday, her own kind of debutante party. Only she was surrounded with kids who put fingers in the cake and gave her sticky hugs. Rory had led them in a rousing birthday song of his own creation. Maura handed her a package wrapped in a muslin sheet. Aless unwrapped it to find a shawl embroidered with ivy and crimson roses intertwined with rich hues of purple and gold. The tree of life came alive in streams of sunlight through the trees on the front lawn.

Maura's cheeks had been rosy with pride. "In case you ever need a safe place and we're not around. Hildegard would be happy to know you have it."

Aless shook her head to clear it of memories. Winter approached with cold nights and frosty mornings. She'd need the shawl for her journey. Journey. A trek that led away from the only home she'd known. What would that look like? Uninvited tears washed over her face. Aiden and Maura would be frantic in the morning when they couldn't find her. The children wouldn't understand why she'd left without a good-bye. Neither would Rory.

They'd try to stop her, though. And would never

agree with her plan. Standing in her room, wrapped in the shawl, fear stabbed through her consciousness. What if she carried something terrible from Lilith Gunter?

No. She'd prove that. Somehow. With another look back into the room she'd known for twelve years, she turned and left.

She crept downstairs and into the kitchen, careful not to awaken Mrs. Ransbottom. A basket of apples rested on one counter, and several loaves of freshly baked bread waited for breakfast. Aless stuffed several apples and one of the loaves into her bag. Slipping out the back door, she gazed into the night sky. Aquarius, the Water-Bearer, was overhead, pouring water into the mouth of Pisces, the Southern Fish. Adjusting Hildegard's shawl against the chill, she traced a path in the light of a full moon to the lower stables. She half-expected Rufus to come running to her side, but he was probably sound asleep in Lucy's bed. Orion snorted, and steam rose from her muzzle when Aless entered the stable. Leaning her head against the silken mane, she whispered. "Will you go with me, my friend? So that I'm not alone?"

The mare nuzzled her chin. Alessandra gave Orion an apple and placed a blanket on her back. She adjusted the saddle and tightened the cinch, wishing she could erase a rising dread in her belly. She'd never put her horse at risk with unknown conditions along the way, except she couldn't keep up with Tareq and his men without her. Waiting in the darkness, she murmured softly to Orion and peered up at streaks of slate that coursed across an ebony sky.

Within minutes, Tareq sounded a quiet command, and the men rode in single file through the trees. Bright fabrics of their tunics flashed in the moonlight. Wispy clouds drifted over the cool moonlit sky.

Alessandra waited until the last stallion disappeared. She glanced back at the dim outline of the chateau that shimmered through the trees. Wrapping Hildegard's shawl tightly around her shoulders, she promised herself she'd be back. Then, clicked her tongue to Orion, and off they went, picking through the underbrush as they left home behind.

Orion knew these woods by heart, but Aless was glad a full moon lit the way in its pale glow. A small animal skittered across the path and a rustle sounded in the bushes nearby. Was it a growl she heard? Tree branches cast wavering shadows in a gentle breeze and the hush of the woods wasn't much of a hush. There was lots of life all around her. She just couldn't see it.

On and on, she and Orion picked their way through the forest, keeping to well-trodden paths when they could. Her eyes were scratchy and an indistinct ache in her body reminded her of a night without sleep. She tore off a piece of bread and munched it, hoping it kept her awake when everything in her body longed for slumber.

Finally, the sky became a faint blue instead of gray. She and Orion navigated a narrow precipice that signaled they were almost at the bottom of the mountain. Rolling grasslands beckoned in the distance at the base. She'd worry about how she'd keep up with the horsemen later.

The sun shone full in blue skies flecked with puffs of billowy clouds when the men reached the foothills. With the mountain towering behind, they raced forward into the flat lands.

Aless finished the descent with Orion and kept her eyes on the horsemen as she rode alongside a forested area. Orion picked up her pace to a gallop. Tareq and his men rode without any detours, as if they knew where they're going and how to get there.

She regretted her impetuous late-night decision. Then anger reappeared and affirmed her quest. She had to go to Sanctuary. No more secrets. No more Lilith Gunter rising from the dead to yank Alessandra into her terrible web.

Orion slowed to a trot at the base of the mountain and pulled toward a stand of trees. Her mustang was as exhausted as she was. Leading her to a creek that gurgled nearby, Alessandra dismounted and stretched stiff legs and sore muscles. Scanning the plains ahead, she searched for a glimpse of Tareq. The men and their stallions were nowhere in sight. Full morning sunlight warmed her back. Peeling off the shawl, she knelt upstream to splash her face and arms with cool water as Orion nibbled on grassy patches along the bank.

A throaty chur, chur sounded from a branch overhead, and a crow swooped through the trees with its coarse kaw, kaw. The chatter of squirrels scolded. Many hours in the forest had made Alessandra alert to its changes. She peered at the shawl on the ground and saw that it had transformed into colors of the forest with green leaves and rich browns. Maura had told her stories of how its colors changed and became like camouflage when she'd needed a hiding place. Did she need that now? Aless retrieved the shawl despite the warm day and put it over her shoulders as she crouched behind the trunk of a mighty oak.

Orion pawed the ground nervously. Something or someone had entered the grove. A flock of birds broke cover and took flight. A flash of bright red appeared through the trees. It was Tareq's men. Aless looked around in panic. She couldn't escape on Orion. They were both too tired. The men jeered in their language, no longer worried about sneaking up on her. The metallic sound of swords clanked. She smelled rotting flesh as they cursed and slashed through underbrush, drawing closer to her hidden form. Pulling further back against the tree, she prayed for help.

"Soltar!" Tareq's voice sounded from the clearing.

Alessandra ran out from the cover of the tree and let the shawl drop around her arms. "It's me. Alessandra. From the chateau."

Tareq strode over to her, and a shadow clouded his eyes for an instant. Then his gaze turned to open concern. "What are you doing? Why are you here — alone? If we'd known, it was you behind…"

One of the men came into the clearing and shook his head. Tareq nodded and turned back to Alessandra.

Her voice came out in a squawk. "I-I have to go to Sanctuary."

Chapter 7

Basir growled and spewed angry words in their language. His hands were stained and dirty. Mud splattered the base of his tunic and around the sleeves.

Tareq peered at her thoughtfully, his face placid and eyes unreadable.

"I'll only ride as far as the city," she said, making the appeal she'd practiced over and over. "I'll stay there when you and your men leave."

The men had bowed their heads, glancing at their leader from time to time. Tareq scanned the perimeter of the grove. Finally, he turned to Aless and gestured to Orion. "You're a brave woman. Accompany us the rest of the way."

A glint of anticipation flashed in Heydar's eyes. Akeem spit in disdain. Both dropped their gazes and stepped back when Tareq scowled at them. "There are still hours of travel left in this day." He walked Aless to Orion and waited as she mounted. "Follow me." With a wave of his hand, he mounted and signaled their departure.

Without a word, the three other men led the way as they re-entered the open plains.

Aless trembled on the warm morning with the memory of the three warriors hacking the brush and bellowing in triumph as they searched the grove, certain that she was trapped there. She'd have to stay close to

Tareq. He'd make sure she made it safely into Sanctuary, she comforted herself. Then she'd be rid of the other men.

Tareq stayed behind with her as Orion struggled to keep up with the stallions. He pulled his stallion closer and leaned in as he spoke. "What made you do this? In the middle of the night. Weren't you afraid?"

Aless looked down, abashed. "I guess I'm known for that. Quick decisions. Not much forethought."

Tareq kept his attention on her as they fell behind the other horses. "Nothing more than a rash journey on horseback to reach a city you could've visited with your family?" His eyes searched hers. Even after hours of riding, his carriage was lithe and upright.

What could she say? He was right. She'd have to explain or look like a fool. He deserved to know why she'd followed him without invitation. She took a deep breath and blew it out. "Yes, there's more. I'm going to Sanctuary to…find out about my mother."

"A long ride for such information. What made you leave suddenly?"

His face appeared etched by a skilled artisan in light mahogany. She couldn't tell him about the army yet, but she'd trust him with as much truth as she could. "I wasn't raised with my mother. I've always wondered who she was…and why she left me as a child." Aless paused to get a grasp on emotions that buzzed through her exhausted mind. "Anyway. I need to know…what she was like."

"You left in the darkness, alone."

Aless shifted, embarrassed. Tareq was direct and asked for honesty. She'd offer it. "I'm pressed for information I can only find in Sanctuary. Circumstances are tangled, and I don't know where to begin. My mother ruled in that city. People knew her there. Such mystery surrounds her. I need answers."

"Your mother ruled in Sanctuary? Gunter. Lilith Gunter?" Tareq reached out and touched her hand. He studied it for a moment, then grazed her chin as he searched her face. "No wonder I recognized you. My father was a trader here years ago. I traveled with him and met your mother."

Alessandra cheeks flushed at his gentle touch. "You knew her?"

"I was only ten years old at the time. My father did, though. I'm going to Sanctuary to conduct business for him."

The scent of sandalwood and a note of cinnamon brushed her senses. "I know many things about your mother. Good things. I wonder why you were never told."

Alessandra looked at him in surprise. He was sadly misinformed. Still, she needed his escort to Sanctuary.

Akeem and Basir were no longer far ahead. They'd turned and cantered back to Tareq who pulled away to speak with his men. Akeem muttered a guttural word and Tareq lifted his hand. The sun had dipped into the western horizon and the wind was even colder.

Tareq sounded a command and led their small company into a dense forest. Canopies of towering pines stretched high, hiding sunlight that lingered in the west.

Aless's legs ached. Neither she nor Orion had ridden so long. Orion slowed her pace and followed the other horses into a clearing with a narrow river that meandered through the trees on one side.

Basir prepared a fire while Akeem and Heydar

finished tethering the horses near the river.

Aless waited for them to finish, then did the same for Orion. She glanced around the boundaries of their campsite with a nervous gaze. She and Aiden had occasionally camped on their journeys in search of the wild mustangs. Aiden kept a fire burning throughout the night and had taught her to store their foodstuffs high in the trees. Those cautions were for wild animals. Tareq's men presented danger, too. The kind she had no way of anticipating. The young prince's vow of shelter faded in the reality that she was spending the night with three men who hunted her down earlier that morning. Her mind and body were in full alert as she searched out every possible exit.

As the men gathered their own provisions around a fire, Aless sat as closely as she could to Tareq. She watched where he placed a small pallet at the base of one of towering conifers and positioned herself there when she was done eating.

The men lay on the ground, swords at one side. In the next moment they snorted in ragged breaths, sound asleep. Their snoring was a noisy relief. The equestrians would be no threat tonight. At least she hoped not. She tossed against the hard ground and wondered how she'd find shelter to relieve herself the next morning.

Tareq dragged his pallet close to the patch of grass where Aless had settled. He nodded at the fire. "You'll be safe here. Sleep. You need it."

Aless settled on her own pallet with the shawl wrapped around her, feeling exposed in the open air. Twitters of nocturnal animals and insects sounded around her. She recognized most of them. It was the ones she couldn't hear that nagged her. Would one of the men awaken in the night? She curled herself into a ball under Hildegard's shawl, finally too exhausted to stay on guard. In what felt like only minutes later, dawn signaled yet another ride.

Aless ate several chunks of bread and refilled a skin of water that Tareq had given her. She was still hungry. Icy wind still blew from the north as they prepared the horses for another day of riding.

"How are you, my friend?" Tareq seemed composed and unruffled considering a night of sleep outside.

Unlike her. "Longing for a cup of tea." She pulled her hair behind one ear, wondering how she looked after rolling off the ground and little sleep. It had been embarrassing to hide behind a stand of trees as far from camp as possible to relieve herself. Then drag herself back up a small incline to saddle Orion. What had she expected from this journey? Nothing, really. Practical details hadn't crossed her mind when she'd rushed forward with her plan.

The three warriors were mounted and riding ahead as she and Tareq led their horses out of the forest and back onto the road. Or at least the flatlands that extended for miles ahead, surrounded on both sides by woods. Birds that had sung joyously only the day before were silent. How much longer would the trip take?

Tareq and his stallion rode beside her and Orion. He lifted an imaginary cup to his lips and smiled. "And this tea must be a custom in your morning."

"Yes. A comforting one."

"We have tea at my home, also. It's brewed with spices I don't know in your language. Cardamom, I think. I miss it when I'm traveling."

"Do you travel often?" The north wind blew against

her chest and Aless wrapped Hildegard's shawl tighter with one hand.

"Our city is remote, and its commerce depends on trading," Tareq answered. "Journeys are often rugged. Like today. Still, our destination will be in sight before long."

"You speak English well. Did you learn it at school?"

"Yes, although, it isn't the only language I speak. Many travels, many tongues. Part of the adventure."

This equestrian sounded like he'd been to finishing school, adept in languages and cultures. Compared to the three men who followed him, he was an enigma, indeed. "You said your home is isolated. What's it like?"

"I live in a city named Akkad. My father is there, also."

"Your mother?"

A flash of sadness crossed his eyes. "She died. When I was a boy." Tareq glanced up at a stray nightingale that sounded from a tree ahead. "I understand wanting to know your mother," he said. "Even now, I miss my own *nai* waiting at the city gates when I arrive home."

Aless felt a pang of loss. She took a breath and blew it out. It was time to focus on Tareq. Anything other than on her own sorrow. "What's your city like?"

"Very different than your home. Mine is built among the cliffs in a desert region. All seems brown and sandy there, compared to your mountains. The sky is our wonder. Rose, orange, and shades of blue paint our early mornings. They're new every day."

"Homes among the cliffs. I've read about them, but never seen anything but the mountains I grew up in. At least until now."

Tareq looked at Alessandra in wonder. "Never traveled? Miles and miles of countries outside our own have filled my life, as early as I remember." The young prince paused to search her face with a grin. "Perhaps someday you will see my city for yourself." He pointed to something in the distance. "Look. There's Sanctuary."

A burnished dome shone through the gloom, rising over other structures in a city she'd never seen, only heard about. Aiden had described the magnificent Hall of Justice, center of the city's government.

Tareq rode ahead to speak to his men who circled him with their horses and leaned in, as if to hear new orders. Moments later he was back at her side. "Where do you need to go in Sanctuary? I'll escort you there."

"To the Hall of Justice." She did her best to speak confidently, despite knowing she was only making a stab in a plan that had no guarantees. She'd seek out old records, and interview officials. She'd find people who had known Lilith Gunter and gather all the information she could to prove she had nothing in common with the woman. With a shudder, she knew there was one more place she'd have to see. The arena.

Tareq interrupted her thoughts. "Do you have a place to stay?"

Aless groaned inside. She didn't have money. Such a simple reminder of a life never lived outside its borders. "I can stay with my friend, Nona. I'll be fine." She bowed her head to hide a flush that rose from her neck and covered her face. This would be their parting. Suddenly, she was shy and uncertain. "Thank you for…your kind patience. I'm grateful to have had your protection — and your company."

"And I, you, Alessandra Gunter." A smile lit his face. "I hope to see you again. Before I return home."

Home. She'd wondered what that meant for her new friend and guide. She remembered that he'd face those city gates without his mother to welcome him back.

"That would be…lovely." Tears rushed to her eyes, and she had no idea why. Breaking away from his warm gaze, she patted Orion and nudged her forward.

Tareq's expression shifted from her to the city, as if he noticed something he hadn't seen before. He prodded his stallion into a canter and joined the other men, shouting a command.

"What's wrong?" she asked when he returned to her side.

"There are soldiers guarding the entrance."

Aless took in a sharp breath. The army. They were already in Sanctuary, looking for her. As they rode closer, she saw company after company of crimson-garbed soldiers filling the streets. Then remembered that Aiden had once worn the same uniform when he'd been employed by the Hall of Justice. "These men are military from Sanctuary. I don't understand why they're in full force at the entrance of the city, though."

A battalion of soldiers aligned themselves against a broad gate as they approached. Tareq joined his men, speaking in insistent tones. They nodded and murmured in response. Aless rode closer, hoping to hear their conversation. Abruptly, the warriors stopped talking and looked away.

Tareq signaled his men to stop. He dismounted and approached the soldiers. "My name is Tareq Kaurem," he said. "My men and I are here for business with the Minister of Trade and Commerce. My young companion is here to visit family." He pulled out papers from his saddle bag and handed them to the soldier who perused them.

"What kind of business?" The golden buttons strained at the man's belly and gray tinged his hair. He looked like someone's grandfather instead of a soldier.

"My father, Dhamar Ghalib, and I have a long-time trade alliance with the Hall of Justice. We'll finish our business no later than tomorrow and return to our homes."

The guard scrutinized them up and down, then glanced at Alessandra, who was still wrapped in Hildegard's shawl for warmth. He returned Tareq's papers. "Go, then. Be aware that you must produce proof of entry at checkpoints throughout the city."

Tareq bowed again. "May I ask why security is so tight in a city that has always opened its gates to us?"

The soldier growled a bit. "That I cannot say. Go, now. Unless you'd rather return without your business accomplished."

Akeem placed his hand on his belt, the dagger visible through its bands. Basir and Heydar looked at each other, then toward the guard. Both appeared ready to pounce until Tareq shot a piercing glare their way. They waited for their leader to mount, then led the way into the city.

Icy mist dripped from bare branches of cherry trees that lined the entrance of a park and signaled their entrance into Sanctuary. Alessandra longed for clean clothes and a warm bath. A thin layer of frost covered stone benches scattered under what were shade trees in the summer. Now, all was barren. A river gurgled over rugged stones on one side of the park, where tiny white crosses had replaced makeshift ones of branches and twigs. There were no gatherings of neighbors chatting outside their homes. Each door was closed, and shutters were drawn. The soldiers, many who looked very young, squinted nervously about the area as they patrolled.

Chapter 8

Tareq reined in his stallion and rode alongside Alessandra. "This city is expecting war," he whispered, keeping his eyes on soldiers who stood at attention at the intersection ahead. "They're guarding the borders from a fearsome adversary."

Alessandra trembled. Clarion had warned of an army who sought her. Was it the same one?

Tareq touched her arm, as if in concern. "It's not safe to travel in this city."

"I'll go to my friend's house first." Not that she had any idea how to do that.

"Good. I'll complete my transaction and take stock of the business district. If it appears secure, I'll come and escort you there."

She bowed her head, overtaken by Tareq's compassion. "Again. Thank you. More than I can say."

Tareq reached over and kissed her hand lightly. "I don't know you well, Alessandra Gunter, though I would like to. In the meantime, my responsibility is to make sure you're protected."

Aless longed to follow him, but he was right. It was best to find Nona's house, even if she wasn't sure how to get there. Rory had described the stone cottage where he'd lived with his grandmother. He'd told story after story about her love for children. She'd witnessed that at the chateau. Her games and freshly baked cookies were

75

in constant demand during the holidays. She was also a master gardener, with a special fondness for roses.

White latticework that lined the base of a home drew her eye. Vine after vine of roses in vibrant hues, wound together in fragrant tangles that lingered along a trellis. Next door, a white-washed building sprawled in a long rectangle. It had large windows and a grassy area in the back. There weren't any children to be seen, but there was no doubt it was a school. Rory had inherited his grandmother's pied piper heart that gathered children of all sizes and shapes. Except for now. Where were the little ones? Was Nona even going to be home?

For a moment, Aless panicked. What if this was the wrong house? Or perhaps Nona had moved. She'd be lost in a city she'd never visited with no one to guide her. Except Tareq. And he was gone. Searching the streets, she noticed a contingent of uniformed men marching several blocks away.

Aless led Orion to the corral between the cottage and school. She tethered her mare near a stash of loose hay and a trough of water. She'd barely reached the front door when Nona opened it and pulled her inside.

The woman's strong arms wrapped around her in a sudden embrace. As Nona held her, a long cry rose out of Alessandra, overtaking her like a spring river raging with snow melt. She quaked, fear and relief both pouring out on the woman's broad shoulder. With a shuddering breath, Aless pulled away.

Nona dabbed Aless's cheeks with a handkerchief. Tears reappeared as Aless felt the refuge of Rory's presence in his grandmother's eyes.

"Oi. It be good to see ye. Sit, while I make tea," Nona said, interrupting the moment. She led Aless to a bench pulled close to an oaken plank. As she sat with an exhausted plop onto the bench, Alessandra suddenly felt like one of the many children, herded inside after skinning a knee. A fire crackled inside a hearth in the center of the large room. A kettle dangled over it. Hot tea. What she'd longed for since the early morning she'd left the chateau.

Aless had almost forgotten the gnawing in her belly with a snatched piece of flatbread for breakfast. Nona prepared the tea, then sliced warm bread and set a bowl of butter on the table. Finally, she stoked the fireplace and added more wood until the fire blazed and warmth filled the room.

Alessandra longed to curl up on the floor and sleep. In the peace of this home, a universe of its own, maybe she'd wake up to find she'd been dreaming. She rested as Nona's unadorned hands, etched with bulging veins, poured hot tea into porcelain cups.

Years ago, Nona had lived at the chateau with Rory, going back and forth to Sanctuary to fulfill her responsibilities as Minister of Education. Finally, Aiden had needed Rory's help in the stables and like Nona, he was a natural with children. One day he stayed on the mountain when she returned home. Since then, he'd never left.

"All this." Nona gestured sturdy arms toward the window, then took a seat across from Alessandra. "Tis about your mother. And the Magi." The words in her powerful brogue inserted the unexpected just as suddenly as her embrace.

"My mother? This couldn't be about her. She's been dead for many years." Besides, wasn't she the one riding day and night with four strange equestrian warriors because of an army that pursued her?

"The soldiers. Did they stop ye?"

"Yes, but I didn't know why. What's going on?"

"I just came from the Hall and heard strange reports." Nona leaned back and peered at her quizzically. "Why have ye come? I be happy to see ye. I would've made things ready, though."

"I'm sorry, Nona. I was going to the Hall of Justice. The military presence was so strong I came to you first."

"Why the Hall?"

"I've been…I need to know about my mother."

A crinkle appeared on Nona's brow. "Rory didn't come with ye? Who are the men I saw?"

So many questions. Aless sighed and pressed back against the chair, exhausted. "They're equestrians who visited the chateau. Rory doesn't know I came. Not yet."

"Ye left without telling him?" Nona pursed her lips as if she couldn't imagine that. She knew as well as anyone at the chateau that Aless and Rory had been inseparable since they were little. "What about Aiden and Maura?"

Aless shook her head and looked away.

"Something happened to make you flee the chateau without telling the ones who love you." Nona's gaze was intent, unwilling to let her questions go unanswered.

Aless sighed. "I don't know where to begin." She swallowed a hiccup and straightened tired shoulders. "Two arborists visited the chateau. They delivered a strange message. An army is looking for me." She blurted out the last sentence in a hurried jumble. If only it was another proof of her over-active imagination. Fingering a knot in the smooth oaken table, she glanced at Nona. "Something from my dead mother draws them.

Something they believe lives in me."

She thought Nona would be shocked, but she wasn't. "You aren't surprised."

"No, beloved. Sadly."

"Maura said that you knew Lilith. What can you tell me about her?"

"I worked fer a time in her home." Nona slathered butter on a slice of fresh bread, placed it on a small plate and handed it to Aless. "She was a powerful woman. Feared, obeyed. Leaving me post to check on Rory after his accident gave her a reason enuf to fire me."

"What was she like?"

"She had a goal, Alessandra. To rule without question. And she did. Her greatest mercy was in sending ye away. In doing so, she protected ye."

Aless tried to stifle a bitter laugh. "Abandoning me to a place where I was raised by strangers was not protection. Or kindness."

"It didn't look like love. But it was." Nona leaned in and placed her hand on Maura's arm. "This ye must know. Lilith Gunter bowed her knee to a terrible demon," she said, her voice low. "She renounced her Magi lineage. Or at least she tried. Bitterness fed the demon's power. And raged against the Magi."

"I know about the massacre. And Rory in the arena." Aless felt the last bit of strength leech out of her being.

Tears filled Nona's eyes. "I be sorry. Truly."

"No one told me. It wasn't right. Now that I know, I'm here to do something about it."

"And what would that be, exactly?"

"I'm here to expose who she really was."

"How will that be helpin'?" Nona reached for Alessandra's hand, warming her cold fingers with her grasp. "Aiden and Maura gave ye the best life they had, ever since ye were a wee one."

"They should've told me. It was wrong to let me believe…" Aless didn't want to finish that sentence. It had been cruel to let her believe the illusion that she'd ever had a mother who loved her. That the one who had birthed her had any virtue to cherish. When, instead, she'd only been a fiend.

Nona spoke in a firm tone, as if to remove any question. "Ye had a right to grow up free — loved and secure, without the burden of yer mother's deeds."

Alessandra pulled away from Nona's touch. "I was raised by Magi. I lived in their home and loved their children. And yet, I carry my mother's past." Her voice rose. It took more strength than she had to lower it. "It isn't fair. I was lied to — at least by omission. No matter how noble everyone's intentions."

"And Aiden and Maura? What did they say?"

"They were sorry I heard about the massacre from someone else. Maura talked about the prophecy. As if that changed anything. Something about an enemy building a shelter on high and one who carries the light of stars. Whatever that means. She hoped that somehow the prophecy would connect us. I've never understood how."

"I know the words. Prophecy tis' a pattern — as enduring as the stars. Tis' a picture of what can be, what will be — as long as we believe. Far stronger than yer mother's pain."

"She had no right to feel pain. She was the purveyor of it. Not the victim."

"We don't know why her heart chose a lie." Nona glanced at the nearest window and then back to Aless.

"Tis that force arising once more. Make no mistake — this attack is against the Magi. Again." She stood to peer outside, then turned to Alessandra. "Tell me about the men you followed to the city. I've never heard of them."

"They stayed at the chateau to rest and let an injured horse heal. They're from a tribe far from here, although their leader said he'd done business in Sanctuary."

"Why are ye with them?" Nona's eyes searched hers.

Aless lowered her head to her cup, suddenly cautious. She watched the tea swirl, then lifted it to her lips and sipped its warmth. "They were coming here. I...couldn't travel alone. If I'd told Rory, or Aiden and Maura, they would've stopped me. I had to come for myself. To put things right."

Nona walked to an aged walnut cabinet and searched a drawer until she pulled out a silk pouch. "This is Rory's. He wanted me to keep it for him until...Anyways, he'd want ye to have it."

"Rory wouldn't want me to have anything." She'd seen his eyes the last time they'd talked outside the chateau. He'd never come back that night.

"Nonsense." Nona pulled a small chain of gold from the pouch. At the end of the chain hung a pendant the size of a small coin. Its delicate multi-colored beads spun in a circular pattern around a small opal. "Ye'll need this — to see the unseen on your journey."

"How could I see the invisible with a necklace? What journey are you talking about?"

Nona gently fastened the necklace at the back of Alessandra's neck. She paused for a moment as she took her seat at the table. "I see ye have Hildegard's shawl. Tis a mystery, also, and one you'll need. Rumor sez an army marching under the banner of Gad El Glas is close and will overtake the city as early as tomorrow. The soldiers roaming the streets be our own. Looking for ye."

"Why would they want me?"

Nona studied her hands and twisted them into a knot. "Many remember yer mother in this city. Many recall her tyranny. They believe yer dead body will keep an army far greater than their own from attacking Sanctuary."

A boiling mass of confusion and outrage rose in Alessandra's belly. The peace she'd felt in this home vanished. "No. I never knew her. I…" Her mind raced. She picked up her shawl and went to the door. "I have to tell them."

Nona rose with such strength, Aless froze. The woman strode to the front door and positioned her body against it like a human shield.

"You're wrong," Aless protested, her words beginning strong. "They have nothing to fear in me." Then ending weakly. "They'll believe me. They must."

Nona's words were unyielding as the granite walls of the chateau. "They won't."

It was a stand-off. Only for a moment. Nona held out her arms and Aless fell into their shelter. "They don't even know me. How could she? How could she do this to me."

Nona patted her back and whispered low shushing sounds.

Why should she suffer for her mother's sins? She stiffened and stepped away from Nona. "I'll make her pay for this. Somehow."

Nona brushed a lock of Aless's hair from her eyes. "Tis Magi protection ye need."

"No," Aless said, resolute. She wouldn't let Lilith Gunter rule her from the grave. She was more than the daughter of a murderess. She didn't know in what way exactly, but that didn't matter now. She'd find a way to deal with this. Then again, she couldn't stay at Nona's. And couldn't go back to the chateau. She was stuck.

She remembered Tareq's offer to escort her to the Hall of Justice. "Tareq will take me where I need to go. I'll return to Sanctuary as soon as things settle down." She was making things up as she went. All the city bristled, anticipating an enemy army that sought Alessandra as their prize. Surely, Tareq would take her back home.

Soldiers shouted on the street outside Nona's door.

"One thing ye must know." Nona placed her hand on Aless's. "Your gift is more than who you are as Lilith Gunter's child."

"I refuse any claim the woman had to me by blood or in any other way."

Nona shook her head as she cleared her throat and dashed away a tear. "This I know. Sometimes life forces us to begin anew. Our Aiden, he did. And Rory were only a wee one when his parents died." Nona drew close to Aless, smelling of lavender and comfort. "Ye aren't bound to your mother's choices."

Aless braced her arms against her chest. "Not true. The army that pursues me and the city that wants to execute me are proof I'm captive to what she did. I *will* be set free from her. No matter what it takes."

"These things are best solved with the ones who love ye. Let me friends take ye back to the chateau."

Hooves clattered outside the window. Aless rose from the table and cracked open the shutters to see Tareq reining in his stallion as he searched the area around Nona's home. "You're in danger if I stay. Tareq and his men will help me get back to the chateau."

Nona snapped the wooden slats closed. "Return to the mountain quickly as ye can. Aiden and Maura'll be worrying their selves sick. As any good parents would."

Aless couldn't keep the heat from rising to her cheeks. "They aren't my mother and father."

Nona's voice quietly implored. "They call ye daughter."

"Only because they're caring people." Tears streamed down her face. Aless turned away from Nona so fast she bumped the table and tea spilled out in rivulets on the oak. She had to leave before she gave in to the love she felt in Rory's grandmother. She no longer belonged to any of the people she'd known as family.

Nona shook her head as she deftly mopped up the tea. Aless opened the shutter again and saw Tareq beckoning to her. She closed the blind firmly, then turned and gave Nona a short, fierce hug. "I have to go."

"Wait." Nona wrapped the loaf of bread in a towel and tucked it under her arm. She took Alessandra's hands into her own, held them to her lips and kissed them. "Go then, dear one. Unlock the gates that stand before ye."

Boots stomped on the wooden porch. Someone pounded on the door and commanded, "Open now, by the authority of the Hall of Justice."

Nona pulled her away from the door. "Quickly. Go out the back." Opening a drawer, she pulled out a pair of Rory's pants, a shirt, and jacket. "Wait. Put these on."

The pounding continued until Aless feared they'd break down Nona's door. Nona grabbed a wide-brimmed hat from a hook on the wall as Aless changed into the clothes. She bundled up Alessandra's curls and smashed the hat over them.

"Don't forget the shawl," Nona murmured.

Aless rushed back to the chair where she'd let the shawl drop from her shoulders. She wrapped it around her waist and put Rory's jacket over it as Nona gathered the evidence of their tea and placed the cups and saucers inside a cabinet. A loud crack sounded in the heavy timber of the front door. Nona ran with her to the back of the house, peeked out the small window, and shoved Aless out the door. "Go."

Chapter 9

Aless pulled the hat over her head and held the jacket tighter in the sudden chill as she stood, wondering what to do. She heard Nona open the front door.

"Oi. Why ye be pounding on me door? Ye'll be payin' fer the damage, of that ye can be sure. Come inside, ye pack of hyenas. Maybe a cuppa will improve yer disposition."

As Nona invited the soldiers in, Aless crept to the front of the house, placed the bread in her pack, and untethered Orion. She reassured her horse, whispering, "Easy, girl." She jumped when Tareq appeared at her side.

He stood tall and commanding. What had happened to his business at the Hall? He pointed to a line of timbered buildings with empty tables that looked like a deserted open-air market. His stallion was tethered at an empty blacksmith's stall. "Meet me there," he said, then sprinted across the road.

Aless had mounted Orion when a commotion drew her attention to a group of soldiers gathered in a small clump around a man with black tufted hair. It was Heydar. Catching her gaze, the warrior bent over to one of the red-uniformed soldiers and pointed in her direction.

"There she is. By Nona Grisham's," yelled one of the men. Others picked up his cry and rushed toward her, some mounted, and others on foot. Soldiers trampled Nona's porch as they exited her house and ran to steeds tethered nearby. Heydar, the leering one, had sold her out. He looked back at Alessandra with an evil grin.

Alessandra bent low over Orion. "Fly, my girl. Fly." She and her mare charged toward the only open space between soldiers. They had to make it to the entrance of the city and worry about bursting through its defenses later.

"It's her. Stop her." Dust rose from hooves that pounded dirt streets. An arrow pierced the fabric of one sleeve. It dangled from her forearm, then dropped to the ground. The wheezing snort of a horse signaled its rider was closing the gap between them. Aless lowered herself over Orion's neck and leaned forward. She and her mare were still ahead, although soldiers raced in to surround her on both sides.

Without warning, a blaze engulfed a white framed building to her right. Soon, buildings on both sides were on fire. Dense smoke filled the air, obscuring her vision and descending like a thick cloud around her pursuers. Aless grasped Orion tighter. Her mare's heart pounded and sweat that flowed from her muscular neck soaked Alessandra's sleeves. Her beloved friend hadn't asked to be taken into battle. Still, she fought to stay ahead, as if she knew Aless needed her. Nona had been right. These men didn't care about the truth. It didn't matter that her mother's villainy hadn't been her own. Aless screamed, "I'm not the one. I'm not the one you want."

Akeem, Basir and Tareq charged through the half-circle of Hall soldiers that had been closing in. The equestrians advanced with precision, like a saber slashing through opposition. Aless looked around, at first in relief. Hall soldiers were falling back. Then she saw why. Blood sprayed the air and splattered the haunches of the soldier's steeds. One after another, red uniforms fell to the ground as their horses sprinted away in confusion.

These equestrians weren't part-time soldiers. They were relentless, experienced warriors. Their weapons cut obstacles of armor and human flesh with brutal force as they broke through the lines of offense. Akeem thrust a curved knife into a soldier's body, then withdrew it. Aless looked on in horror as the man's intestines spilled outside his belly and he tumbled to the ground.

Heydar rushed in through billowing smoke. Her betrayer. What did that mean for battle? The warrior slowed his stallion and positioned his sword on the opposite side of the hand that grasped it. In a moment, Aless recognized the hold. It was the murder blow. Heydar's hand lifted and the sword swept down on a young man whose ruddy cheeks and blonde curls escaped a brazen helmet. He fell, only to be trampled by his fellow horsemen.

Basir and Akeem held their swords out with Tareq and Alessandra behind them, advancing to the borders of the city. Orion wavered. Her mare was at the end of her strength. They were almost free when a group of crimson-coated soldiers charged from a flank position. Akeem, Basir, and Heydar formed a tight circle around Tareq and Alessandra. They raced on, outdistancing the approaching soldiers.

The last soldiers formed a line across the road on the outskirts of the city. After motioning to Aless to stay back, Tareq rode to the front to join his men. They formed their own offense, with heads down and swords extended. Basir stabbed a young soldier through his armor and into his belly. Akeem threw a dagger with skillful aim into the exposed throat of another. The soldier toppled off his horse, his life soaking the ground in a crimson flow. Life that belonged to a young man, determined to defend the city — against her.

Tareq gave a loud command, and they galloped away. He circled around and rode on one side of Alessandra as they left the city. Aless looked back to see a lanky man in homespun brown standing in the road behind them, surrounded by smoke. It was her imagination, longing for her friend. After all, Rory didn't know she was here.

As they left behind the bloody combat amid plumes of smoke, countless questions filled her mind. Who had started the fires and why? Soldiers who were protecting the city had no reason to do so. Was Nona safe?

On and on they rode until mountains appeared on one side. She remembered Aiden's words. "Look to the sun, Alessandra. You'll find your way, even when you're lost."

The rise and fall of the ridges towered to the north as they rode east. Aless searched familiar pathways to the chateau. Crimson cloaks of Justice soldiers stood at every entrance like bright plumage, blocking any return. Without time to think or decide, she and Orion kept riding, with Tareq and his stallion beside them.

They rode without speaking until the mountains looked like cloud formations against the horizon. Foothills turned into a grassy plain and finally, all sight of home was gone. Wild, unreasoning terror that had coursed through her body left her limp with exhaustion. Finally, when Aless was sure she'd fall off Orion,

Akeem led the way through a stand of trees with grass and a brook nearby.

Tareq helped her dismount and steadied her in his arms when she tottered. "Don't be afraid, Alessandra." He spoke her name like a caress.

"How can you say that?"

Tareq's touch on her shoulder traveled lightly down her arm. He reached for her hand. "Come to my home. I'll protect you."

"Why would I do that? I need to get back to the chateau."

"Your home is dangerous right now."

Tareq understood what she hadn't. Hall of Justice soldiers not only pursued her out of Sanctuary, but also waited at the base of her mountain. What did that mean for her family at the chateau? They'd be safe — if she wasn't there. Home was no longer her refuge.

She was so weary. Grief stirred in her belly, although she only had strength to let it out in a sigh. She'd imagined traveling to foreign lands, discovering worlds beyond the chateau. Only not with images of carnage as they'd battled their way out of Sanctuary. She wanted to tell Tareq that Heydar had betrayed her to the soldiers, but the hateful man was only steps away. Now wasn't the time.

Her mind spun in confusion. Everything she'd known and trusted had become a trap. "I have no idea what to do." Her voice quivered. "I need to find a way back to the chateau."

"You want to know more about your mother. Did you know she lived for a time in my country?"

Aless shook her head. "Are you sure? *My* mother?"

"Yes. Father remembers much more than I do. He

can answer your questions about her."

Aless peered into the sky, as if it hid answers that evaded her on earth.

"I'll escort you. And take you home when this warfare is over." Tareq placed a hand over his heart.

Aless looked into the young prince's eyes. He was tired, also. None of this was his fault. He'd risked his life to battle their way through Sanctuary. She wiped sudden tears with one hand. "Only until I'm sure my family will be safe when I return." With a deep sigh, she let go of what she'd planned that night in her bedroom at the chateau and chose to receive what stood before her. "Thank you, Tareq."

Tareq bowed slightly. "It is my pleasure, Alessandra Gunter."

When he turned to answer one of the men, Aless led Orion to a stream for a much-needed drink. She pulled a handful of oats out of her pack. "You, my friend, are a champion." Aless pressed her face into Orion's black mane, overwhelmed by the courage of her mare that had refused to quit. She'd driven herself beyond her ability to carry Alessandra to safety.

She pulled out the bread Nona had sent out of her pack, remembering the peace in her cottage right before the ravages of battle. Nona hadn't wanted her to leave. Staying with that kind-hearted woman had seemed impossible at the time. Now, she wasn't sure. Gruesome pictures of young men dead on the ground as they'd fled Sanctuary dogged her thoughts and drained her heart of courage.

When Tareq sounded the command to ride again Aless hoisted herself back onto Orion's back. This time, their ride settled into a relaxed gait. Tareq and his men were quiet, as if the aftermath of the morning's battle lingered even over seasoned warriors. Exhausted, Aless struggled to stay on her horse, much less try to talk.

The sun was setting when they made camp in a clearing surrounded by towering pines. Alessandra tethered Orion in a grassy area near a pool of water. She planned to make a bed beside her horse and go to sleep at once. Instead, Tareq called her to the fire for dinner. After a meal of flatbread and long strips of salted meat, she settled against a rock, grateful for the fire that gradually eased her aching body and took away the evening cold. Her head bobbed with fatigue.

Every time she looked toward the men, she caught Heydar leering, sending an ominous cloud over her heart. Ribbons, strands of hair, and delicate necklaces that had been woven together dangled from his grimy neck, an amulet hanging from it.

The barbarian warriors respected their leader, though. Even as they threw dice by a roaring fire, they kept their voices low. Tareq settled near the men without sharing a skin of drink that made Akeem, Basir and Heydar belch and weave as they sat cross-legged around the fire. Alessandra couldn't stand their company or keep her eyes open any longer. Finding the base of a tree outside their circle, she leaned against its trunk and fell sound asleep.

Hours later, she woke up shivering. She patted around on the ground, looking for the warmth of Hildegard's shawl. Then groaned when she remembered she'd left it in her pack. Rippling water sounded from a stream nearby and a patchy layer of clouds drifted over a crescent moon. Aless felt the pendant on her collarbone and grasped the tiny reminder of Rory. Nona hadn't understood how she'd left her dearest friend that night at the chateau. Even now, longing stirred in her aching body. If only his arms were around her now.

A random memory visited as she rested against the tree. She and Rory had gotten lost in the woods when they were eight years old. A monarch butterfly had landed on a laurel branch, then flitted away. Aless followed, determined not to lose sight of its graceful flight. Rory had yelled to her. "Come back!"

Of course, she'd ignored him. Until they were hopelessly lost in brush and undergrowth. Aless spun in circles in a grove of sycamores, then plopped to the ground in tears. Only to find that Rory had marked their trail along the way.

Aless was deep in the memory when she heard a deep *huff, huff* in the darkness. Her entire body leaped awake as leaves crackled and a branch snapped. Without Hildegard's shawl, she had nowhere to hide and no weapon to defend herself. Clouds shifted over the moon, making it an unreliable torch. She couldn't see where Tareq slept since the once blazing fire now smoldered.

An overpowering musky stink grew stronger. Large, pale eyes gleamed ahead. Alessandra backed into the tree. Its rough bark scraped against her spine. Her heart caught in her throat, and she rose from the ground. An enormous cat padded toward her in slivered light. She tried to scream, but only a muffled cry eeked out. She couldn't climb the tree or outrun whatever predator it was. There was nowhere to go, no help in sight.

As quickly as it appeared, the cat was gone. She peered around in the darkness. How was that possible? She got on her hands and knees, determined to crawl until she found Orion. Damp ground soaked Rory's pants that she'd slipped into at Nona's house, just before their escape from Sanctuary. Her fingers sank into wet ground and fallen leaves. She'd only moved a few feet when a dangling tree limb smacked her head. She fell backwards, dazed. Halfway embarrassed, she rubbed her forehead and tried to get her bearings.

A giant cat had been about ready to kill her. Then it had disappeared. Had it gone after the horses, instead? Cloud cover was thick, and it was impossible to see anything except shadows waving in the steady breeze.

Movement stirred behind her. As she turned to face whatever it was, muscular hands jammed a wad of dank cloth into her mouth and slammed her to the ground. Surface roots smashed across her backbone as rancid breath pressed against her face. Rough, groping fingers burst open the buttons of her shirt, then yanked at her trousers. A hard object slapped her skin.

Survival morphed into a mindless fight. Alessandra jabbed her fingers into flesh, determined to find the attacker's eyes. She heard a muffled, *ahh*, and stabbed again. When the assailant lurched, she rolled away.

A violent blow wrenched Alessandra's curls and slammed her head onto cold earth. She grabbed a handful of greasy hair that had whipped against her face and yanked.

Another slap hurtled her head to the other side. The man's body pressed her deeper and deeper until she couldn't breathe. Grunting rasped in Alessandra's ear as hands tore at her body.

Still, she fought, kicking, punching until the hands stopped groping and pummeled her again and again. A flame erupted in the darkness as something cold, metallic whizzed past her ear.

With a shrill, rattling "Ayyye," the light of the torch wavered, and the man's weight lifted from her chest.

Aless sucked in a long breath of air and sat up, pulling together her tattered clothing. The thud of a dull impact, then a low groan sounded. Then another. Torchlight shone in erratic gashes in the darkness.

Aless pulled a long string of fabric from her mouth, gagging on its gritty strands. She gathered her torn shirt in one hand and rose with a wild leap. With no sense of time or place, she sprinted, tripping on undergrowth. Steadying herself, she ran again reaching her arms out to fend off whatever stood in her way.

Pebbles rushed and twigs snapped as footsteps crunched behind her. Heavy breathing sounded. Something large was being dragged through the underbrush. Leaves rustled and branches broke as another set of footsteps ran toward her. Someone was coming.

Aless whirled around. She fell to her knees, scouring the ground for a rock or branch to bludgeon her foe. Light bobbed in the hands of a shadowy form running toward her, ghoulish face lit by wavering flames.

"Alessandra. It's me." Tareq spoke urgently and extended his arms. Silken fabric brushed her face as he held her for a moment, then half-carried her to the smoldering ashes of the campsite. Laying her gently on the ground, he stoked the fire until it blazed, then returned and cradled her like a small child.

"I saw a panther," Aless whispered, pulling on his shirt. "It has to be somewhere." Her breathing rushed in shallow puffs. She had to warn him that somewhere, another predator lurked.

Tareq's voice was low and gentle. He held her

closer. "Hush, now. There is no panther."

Aless could only utter one word. "Who?"

Tareq hesitated. "Heydar. He won't hurt you again. Sleep, if you can. I'll be here." He held her as warmth from the fire and his arms finally lulled her into a fitful sleep.

Chapter 10

The eastern horizon was deep purple when Alessandra opened her eyes. A blanket covered her, and another had been placed under her head. Her body cried out in pain as she shifted on the ground. For a moment she didn't know where she was. Ashes of the campfire smoldered nearby. The sleeping form of someone on the ground shifted. Then she remembered. Terror sped over her being, as real as it had been that night.

Alessandra jumped to her feet, ready to flee. Even in the semi-darkness, she could see Rory's shirt askew, dangling over her chest by one button. The pants she'd shrugged on at Nona's house straggled over her hips. Exposed and ashamed, she crumpled into a ball on the ground and shook.

Only the thought of finding Orion made her rise and look around. No one stirred. She searched dark shapes of sleeping men but couldn't tell which one was Tareq. It didn't matter. She was leaving. Wrapping the blanket over her torn shirt, Aless sprinted to Orion. There, only yards away, was Heydar's horse, untethered and munching grass. The man been planning to run away.

She was halfway through saddling her mare when dry leaves crunched on the ground.

"Alessandra. What are you doing?"

Aless jerked around to see Tareq approach, then turned back to her mare. "I'm going home." Pulling out a handful of the oats she'd kept her in pocket, she offered them to Orion's wet nuzzle.

Tareq touched her arm and she jumped. He stepped away and bowed slightly. "Forgive me. I should've…It was my job to protect you."

"It wasn't your fault." She shuddered, feeling her gut tighten and soreness around her belly and groin. She buried her face into Orion's strong neck, willing her legs to keep standing. How could she flee when her body refused to obey?

Two of the men tended three horses and gathered packs silently. The base of the tree where she'd been attacked was stained in a deep brown circle. A splattered trail led out of the clearing and into a wooded area. Her hands covered her mouth with a gasp. "Who? Who killed him?"

"We had no choice."

A brutal attack with an equally brutal response. Aless looked at Tareq, then toward the other men. Who had dealt the death blow? "I'm leaving."

Tareq lowered his head for a moment before he spoke. "I've fought many enemies within and without. And made hard choices." He paused, as if searching for words. "You don't know me. Our cultures are different. I understand."

A mourning dove sounded in the pinion pine overhead. Aless tightened the cinch around Orion's middle. "I can't stay."

"I would take you back if I could. I must return to Akkad."

"I'll find my way."

Tareq took a step closer. "I can't bear to think of you traveling alone. One thing before you go?"

Tareq was so close, Aless felt the warmth of his body and remembered how he'd navigated the way to Sanctuary. He'd done his best to guard her. Now blood of another man soaked the ground.

Heydar had been a predator as surely as the panther she'd thought she'd seen. She remembered Nona's description of Rory's necklace, that it would help her see the unseen. Had the giant cat been real? Or only the foreshadowing of another beast just as deadly.

Tareq waited, quiet as she smoothed Orion's mane. "My father knew your mother," he said. "She lived in Akkad at one time. It's possible that destiny has led you in this way." He cleared his throat and brushed a strand of hair from his eyes. "I believe it has. And vow to protect you."

Aless turned to him and shook her head. "You can't be with me all the time."

"I can while we're on our journey. And have many people who do my bidding in Akkad. You'll be safe. I stake my life on that promise."

Aless looked up at Tareq. She wished she could discern the unseen in his heart as clearly as she'd seen the panther that night. "I'm afraid, Tareq."

"As Crown Prince of Akkad, I invite you as my guest. Stay by my side. The men understand the price of touching you."

There was no way she could continue this path. No matter how powerful Tareq was in Akkad, he couldn't guarantee her safety. No one could.

Why had she come in the first place? Really, she hadn't made that decision. She'd been chased out of Sanctuary, and every road back home had been blocked. Even now, she couldn't say she really had a choice. It was dangerous to travel alone, though no more than following Tareq. Heydar's attack had proven that.

The decision wasn't about which was more hazardous. It was about what she'd begun the journey to accomplish. Gather evidence against Lilith Gunter. Disavow her evil deeds. Maybe it was true that fate had led her in this way.

She searched Tareq for the tiniest shift in his eyes or any reason not to trust him. Surely, he had no reason to lie about her mother having lived in Akkad. She hadn't been able to research the Hall of Justice for evidence, much less, vindicate herself. His city could become a valuable resource.

Tareq stood close by as she offered Orion another handful of oats and didn't speak.

She looked down at her torn shirt and saw her breasts, chaffed, and bruised. Yanking the blanket tighter, she turned away from the young prince. He'd seen the attack, if only by torch light. She was aware of her chest, the curve of her neck, even her bare legs. Morning had only shed light when she longed to hide. She turned away to hide the rush of fear, and the filth Heydar's groping hands had left behind.

A low cooing sounded now, back, and forth from the trees. Tareq had kept his stance at her side. Her stomach quivered, no matter how many deep breaths she took. Her brain was muddled, and her emotions were a tangled knot. Even if she could make it home, would her presence still endanger her family? She couldn't know the unknown.

"Will I be able to go home when I'm ready?"

"I'll take you, myself."

Tears filled her eyes. She'd never been alone before.

Rory, Maura, Aiden — the ones she'd always counted on, were miles away. It was time to decide and hope she was right. "I'll come with you. Only because I need to know about my mother."

Tareq nodded and handed her a flatbread and a skin of water. "I'll honor your quest. Whatever that means." He pointed to the bottom of a grassy knoll where a stream gurgled around a pebbled beach. "I'll stand guard. Take your time."

Tareq's concern was like a healing salve. He understood that she needed to feel clean, if only on the outside. She sipped the water and chewed on a piece of the flatbread, then pulled a fresh riding skirt and muslin top out of her pack. Wrapping herself in Hildegard's shawl, she steadied herself against Orion and walked down the hill toward the running water.

Aless took off her shoes on the pebbled shore and splashed water on her face that was so cold it felt like a blow. She lifted the front of her shirt to wipe away the icy streams. When she pulled the fabric away, a rusty stain bled into another, then another. Heydar's blood.

Leaning over the water, Aless heaved until her stomach ached, and bile burned her throat. She vomited until she only had strength to kneel on the shore, its gravel pressing on her hands and knees. She couldn't go on. Couldn't stay.

In a quivering lurch, she stood. Bracing herself against the frigid waters, she slogged her way through a gentle current to a small pool ahead. Taking a breath, she dipped into the water and went under. The current flowed through her hair, over her body. She ducked lower and sat on the sandy creek bottom, totally immersed.

Sunlight filtered through mottled branches as the

stream gurgled around her, until her limbs grew numb. Still, she ducked up and down in the cleansing baptism. Water stroked her body, washing over the bruises, the shame, and the horror. Finally, shaking with cold and grateful for its distraction, she crawled to the bank where she'd left the clean clothes.

She wrapped Hildegard's shawl around herself and used Orion as a shield from the sight of the men. She stripped Rory's clothing off and tucked it under a large rock. Then dressed in clean riding clothes. Something metallic glinted near a mound of freshly packed dirt. A familiar strand of hair, ribbons, and thin chains of gold lay beside it. It was Heydar's amulet.

Touching her cheek, she remembered the object that whipped against her face when his body slammed against hers. Her stomach churned again, sick at the memory of his fetid odor of days without bathing, spilled blood, and decaying food. That, and a deep, woody scent of something she couldn't identify. She knelt, waiting for strength to stand again.

Tareq had mounted his stallion at the top of the incline, and sat, facing the road ahead. Akeem held the lead of a lone steed without its rider. Basir reined in his Arabian, who pranced with what looked like nervous energy. Heydar, the leering one who'd laughed in contempt as he'd stripped her with his eyes had been killed by one of their hands. Which friend had dealt the death blow?

She had no energy to leave but couldn't stay. Taking hold of the saddle horn with both hands, Alessandra willed first her legs, then her body onto her horse. She quivered with an emptiness that had swallowed her whole. Leaning against Orion's strong neck, she whispered. "Help me, my friend."

As if by silent assent, Orion trotted up the hill and followed the equestrians out of the clearing and onto the dusty plains. Peering ahead to a sunrise faded by heavy cloud cover, she wondered where her decision led. Who were Tareq's people? If they were anything like his men, she was a fool, indeed.

Tareq fell behind and rode near Alessandra, his eyes troubled as he glanced at her from time to time. Morning sun was full now and they continued traveling east.

When Tareq held out another piece of flatbread, she knew she had to eat. The first bite rumbled in her belly and finally settled. As she ate and sipped water from the skin at her side, she was strong enough to stay on Orion's back as she rode.

Aless was too tired to think of pleasantries. She knew nothing about the prince. It was too late to mince words. "Tell me about Heydar. He…betrayed me in Sanctuary," she said. "He told the soldiers where I was. He knew they were looking for me."

Tareq continued riding in silence until Aless wasn't sure he would answer. Finally, he shifted in the saddle and turned to her. He shook his head. "I don't know why. Heydar has been one of my trusted men for many years. He knew he'd never escape my hand if he touched you."

"His horse was saddled and ready for flight."

"True. Although he knew I wouldn't rest until you were avenged. Nothing about his attack makes sense."

Warmth flooded her heart with his words. He was a powerful man. And a man of honor. Did he truly care for her? His words and his actions seemed to prove that he did. It was a struggle to sort out anything that made sense, though. "I've never done anything to him, I never…"

"He had no reason to hate you. He rode with me as a faithful warrior. My men would never treat you with anything but respect."

She'd felt far more disdain than respect from Tareq's men. Akeem's mouth had twisted in a nasty smile when a scorpion almost stung her leg. He looked away as Tareq smashed it into the ground.

Tareq searched the horizon. "You're foreign to the men. They understand you're under my care, though. Heydar's actions were wrong. He knew to expect swift vengeance.

Aless cringed, remembering hands that had invaded her body, a stubbled face that rubbed her face raw. She struggled with the urge to bolt, to ride in the other direction as fast as she could. "What kind of city am I riding into?"

Tareq reined in his stallion to keep pace with her. "One on the brink of change."

She studied the sinews of Tareq's arms as he nudged his horse lightly, communicating with an animal that responded in a moment with his shifts and commands. Did people obey him in the same way?

Days stretched out, one after the other until the terrain changed from grassy plains to jutted mesas of sand and red stone. Mountains appeared on the horizon, though not like any she'd ever seen. Instead of being laden with pines, aspen, and green in every shade imaginable, the peaks ahead were brown domes of dirt and stone. The horses picked their way through patches of stony ground before they reached flat lands.

Orion was suffering, unused to long hours and many days of riding. She leaned over and murmured to her.

"Strength, my friend. This will be over soon." At least she hoped.

Tareq pulled beside her. "It won't be long now. I promise." He hesitated for a moment. "We're going to our capital city. My father has ruled Akkad since he was a young man. When I was old enough, my mother brought me to his side during tribal councils. That is, after our early morning rides — just the two of us. There were no words for the beauty that lit the sky. We raced the open plains, breathing in fresh desert air, free from protocols that demanded my compliance, even as a child. She let me win. Most of the time." Tareq grinned ruefully.

"You loved her. So much."

Tareq gripped the reins and looked away. "I did."

"Can I ask what happened?"

Tareq pulled his hand through silken black hair. He straightened his shoulders and took a breath before he spoke. "She died of a broken heart."

A gust of wind chilled Aless even in the arid heat of yet another day in the desert. She'd fallen into private ground of the heart she had no right to tread. Unless invited. "I wouldn't have believed that was possible until recently." News of the massacre had killed whatever hope she'd had for the future. So unlike Tareq's grief. What would it have been like to cherish a mother? She'd never know.

She wondered if Tareq's quiet authority had come from his mother. Even with his men, he spoke a command and they obeyed as quickly as his horse, in seamless movement. Even now, Akeem and Basir appeared to be on the lookout, paving the way for their leader. They prepared the fire each night, as well as the simple meal they ate around the campsite.

The next morning a deep *thump, thump* vibrated the earth beneath her head. Tareq motioned to her. Aless ran to him, and together, they crouched against the base of a tree. She wrapped Hildegard's shawl around her shoulders as the pounding came closer and dust rose in the distance.

A rider appeared over a rise in the flat lands, garbed in mottled gray and greens. He scanned the perimeter as if taking note of every detail. He glanced at the grove of trees and kept riding. The scout had probably seen them. Why hadn't he stopped?

Another contingent of men came on his heels, dressed in swathes of black. Black turbans and feathered headdresses bobbed in perfect sync with their horses and each other. They were intent on an unseen, but certain target. Another troop followed wearing colorful turbans and silken robes that billowed out like plumaged birds behind them. They, too, rode forward as if nothing would stop them. On and on, troop after troop of equestrians swarmed the flatlands like brightly colored locusts. Curved swords clanked against their scabbards. A few warriors glanced in their direction, then looked away as if what they saw didn't matter.

Aless looked around in confusion. "Are they your warriors?"

Tareq stood and helped Aless to her feet. "Yes. They're off to explore unknown lands."

"So many?"

Tareq grinned. "Many to you, brave woman, who ventured out alone. They're highly skilled equestrians. You'll see many of them in Akkad, either in training or riding out."

The sun had risen warm and dry when the final contingent disappeared. Tareq lifted one hand, and his men saddled horses without a word.

That afternoon, Alessandra struggled to stay on Orion. She drifted off to sleep, then jerked back to attention over and over. It was the full alert that she'd felt since this journey had begun. After Heydar's attack, sleeping, even for a moment, scared her beyond reason. Her eyes were scratchy, and her mind struggled to put thoughts together. Tareq continued to ride beside her, only leaving long enough to speak with his men and then return. "What else do I need to know about your kingdom before I arrive?"

Tareq studied her, and then the landscape ahead. "We are equestrian traders. Some would say our culture is a monarchy, led by the chieftain, Dhamar Ghalib. It is more like a theocracy. Our worship and our lives are inseparably linked. That, perhaps, will be what intrigues you most. And what presents the greatest mystery."

That was odd. What did that really mean? "How will I address your father? Is he fearsome?" She had in mind swords and swash-buckling pirates.

Tareq smiled, as if he read her thoughts. "A barbarian? In some ways. He values courage. Don't be intimidated or reluctant to ask about your mother."

They kept riding east, in the opposite direction of the army that had passed them. Smoke wafted through spaces in what looked like an intricate beehive built into a mountain. As they wound around the base on a narrow dirt path, she spied dwellings built into the mountainside.

"Is that your city?" Questions bombarded her tired mind. Where would she stay? Tareq promised to guard her, but she missed home. Rory, most of all. It was late afternoon, and the adults would be gathered in the kitchen, dodging Mrs. Ransbottom's wrath as they teased the aged kitchen monarch. Grief found its way to more tears as she looked ahead into the maze of rocks called a city.

She stilled her heart with the reminder of Tareq's words. He'd take her back to the chateau as soon as she found out what she needed to know about Lilith Gunter. Orion huffed an exhausted puff of air. Her mare needed water and rest. "I've never heard of your people." She pointed toward the cliffs.

"Ah, little mountain-dweller," Tareq answered with a smile. "You've never left your nest before."

Aless studied his face, puzzled, as words of the prophecy came to her mind. According to its warning, an enemy set its nest among the stars. This was no nest. A dark series of spires like jagged knives rose from what looked like a temple towering from the mesa above the city. Easements circled its crown, as if builders were determined to reach even higher into the desert sky. A golden dome, much like the one she'd seen in Sanctuary gleamed across from it.

The sun had become a fiery sphere in the western sky as they approached the cliff dwellings built into the mountain. Water cascaded down the mountain and fed a river at the bottom, where a wide bridge forded its muddy flow. An enormous iron gate outside the mountain's base was the only entrance into the city that she could see. Fields stretched for miles in front of them.

Men, women, and children dressed in simple brown tunics stooped over crops of grains, corn, and other crops Alessandra didn't recognize. She'd stretched up for a closer look when a gong sounded, then another and another. In unison, the workers bowed to the ground. Mothers herded little ones under their bodies and an eerie silence followed. Not a child whimpered. There were no sounds of greeting. No excited smiles like there would've been at the chateau. Instead of the welcome of a beloved leader, the atmosphere felt like terrified submission.

She turned to Tareq, whose posture had become ramrod straight. "They look afraid."

Chapter 11

"They bow in reverence." Tareq's attention was on a trail that wound up the mountain, instead of the people around him. He dismounted and a slave hurried to take his horse, while another took Orion. Lines and lines of stables stood as far as Aless could see. Acres of green pasture stretched behind the stables, where Arabian stallions, mares, and other horses of every variety grazed. A vast sand-covered arena spread out in front of the stables.

A young stable hand stumbled when he took Akeem's horse, and the warrior backhanded the boy, who fell to the ground with blood on his lips.

"Akeem struck that child." She wasn't going to stand by and do nothing, no matter how new she was to this city. Stalking over the warrior who towered over her, she planted her feet in front of him. "Stop. Now."

The boy trembled violently and glanced at Akeem.

Akeem's face became stone-like. He looked toward Tareq who gestured with one hand. Controlled rage seemed to fill the brutal warrior, but he bowed to Alessandra, turned, and walked to the stables.

"I'll deal with this," said Tareq. He held his arm out and Aless took it. Together, they walked toward the massive gate of black iron she'd seen earlier at the base of the mountain. At the center of rugged iron latticework, flames curled around a brazen serpent with gaping mouth and fangs extended. Its eyes stared, adorned in what appeared to be diamonds. The trace of a memory stirred an uneasiness inside. The gate loomed in front of a path that began wide and then narrowed as it wound up the mountainside. Aless scanned the perimeter of the cliffs but found no other entrance.

Tareq walked over the bridge to the ornate gate. He spoke a low command, so indistinct Aless couldn't tell which language he used. A low hum sounded and reverberated through the iron frame. Aless put her fingers in her ears to stop its relentless drone until finally, a giant lock unlatched, and the hum ended as the doors opened in a slow, certain swing. They stopped when fully open, as if waiting for their company to enter.

She and Tareq stood at the base of the trail. It was impossible to find words for how she felt. Was it anticipation? Or dread. She couldn't tell. When she looked at Tareq, his face twisted into a grimace, only for an instant. When he turned to her, he smiled. "Welcome to Akkad. I'm happy to have you at my side."

A rush of heat flooded Alessandra's cheeks. "Are you glad to be home?"

His face became unreadable, and he took the lead, navigating the narrow path that snaked from the bottom of the cliffs to a plateau that appeared in snatches and then disappeared as they scaled the mountain.

At first, Aless was fascinated with the dwellings carved into the red stone and a higher vista from the top of each switchback. Soon, her legs ached, and sweat poured down her back. She already missed Orion. They scaled the cliffs higher and higher until they overlooked emptiness at each sharp turn.

The temple rose overhead like an omen, darkening

the sky over the city. Aless kept her eyes on the trail as Tareq trudged on ahead of her. It was strange to be following him, instead of being at his side. Laundry hung and fire pits signaled small dwellings at various turns. Women peeked out of doorways and pulled curious children inside.

The ascent grew steeper long after Alessandra was worn out. The air was thin, and her lungs ached. She pulled Hildegard's shawl over her head, to protect herself from desert sun. The shawl that had become a reddish brown breathed in cool puffs that kept her from fainting with the heat.

A watercourse curved nearby, perhaps fed by a spring or even several throughout this maze of buildings carved into the mountain. It would be impossible for anyone to find her here, or anyone else, for that matter. Where were all the people? Every dwelling place appeared deserted as they continued to climb the mountainous path.

A blaring horn sounded from above. Then drums. Boom, boom, boom through the clear desert air. Indistinct chanting with the drumbeats became louder and louder. They reached a broad pavilion at the top of a mesa. The temple stood on one end of the expanse. It faced a magnificent, sprawling palace on the other side of the plateau. In contrast to the dark temple, rays of sunshine reflected on the pale stone walls of the palace, making them appear golden. Palm trees lined a broad veranda of variegated stone, leading to a pearl-like marble arch that curved over its main entrance. A smaller version of the massive palace was attached on one side in a curling half-circle. There were individual entrances, as if each presented another lavish room.

A dark-haired little girl ducked outside from one of the doorways. She was dressed in a simple white gown and peered over at Aless. Before Aless could wave, someone grabbed the child and pulled her out of sight.

Aless wiped a damp strand of hair from her face and a trickle of sweat rolled down her neck. She was dirty and unprepared for the extravagant beauty around her.

Tareq stood beside her. His body seemed to tense, and his normally tranquil face was forbidding.

The temple seemed only more ominous. She had to crane her neck to see the top of its spires. A procession of white-robed priests appeared from its massive entrance. They moved in a serpentine line toward her and Tareq.

Warriors emerged on the tiled entrance of the glittering palace. Feathered headdresses bobbed over faces painted like leopards, bears, and lions. They stalked forward with thick spears at their sides. Women swayed to finger cymbals and strings of bells stretched over their bellies as they followed the warriors.

Tareq held out his hand to Aless. "They're here to welcome us." He didn't look impressed. Or, for that matter, excited to be greeted.

Alessandra scanned her sweat-stained clothing. She wiped her hand on one leg and tried to smooth back her hair. It was hopeless. She hadn't had a bath for days. There was no way to look presentable at this point.

Priests with towering white turbans and pristine robes bowed low to Tareq as they waved smoking censors and chanted in a deep, sonorous chorus. The warriors approached from the other direction, banging spears on the ground in a rhythmic cadence. Two of the men, as big as trees, strode forward with arms raised.

Wings of colorful feathers extended from their arms, and they bellowed in unison, "Dhamar Ghalib."

"Follow my lead," Tareq whispered. He bowed deeply.

Alessandra drew in a deep breath as the warriors parted and a man strode toward them. At least she thought it was a man. He looked like a man-sized peacock ready for war. Vibrant feathers stood up in a headdress lined with precious, rectangular stones that loomed over his face. His armor was leather, studded in turquoise. Gauntlets covered muscular arms. His feet were bare, his ankles encircled with spiked metal bands.

Aless bowed beside Tareq, grateful that she didn't have to figure out how to actually address this fierce ruler.

In a whoosh of fabric and feathers, everyone around the tribal chieftain fell to the ground, except her and Tareq. Surely, they were honoring Tareq, although a thin scowl dashed across his implacable gaze. He embraced his father. When he turned back to Alessandra, he extended his hand. "This is my friend, honored Dhamar Ghalib. Alessandra…Gunter."

"A pleasure to meet you, Alessandra Gunter." The warrior sounded like a European gentleman, refined, and educated despite his war-like appearance. He breathed heavily, as if the activity all around him used up too much oxygen. "I knew your mother," he said, taking in shallow puffs and scanning her up and down. "I can see that you are her daughter. Her beauty was unparalleled. As is yours."

He knew her mother. Alessandra took in a gulp of air, then remembered to curtsey. Or was it bow? The old chieftain's eyes were trained on her and somehow, she couldn't break the power of his gaze. The colors, movements, and pageantry around his presence were intoxicating. Two women approached and stopped at a distance behind her and the prince.

Tareq barely acknowledged their presence, and spoke to Alessandra, instead. "These women will care for you. We'll share a meal with my father tonight. I'll come for you."

She looked down at her tattered, stinky clothes. "I'm a mess."

"You'll find our provisions more than adequate." Tareq seemed oddly formal, and unaware of the old woman on her face in the dirt. The young woman lifted her head as she knelt.

The horns sounded again. The priests resumed their chanting and returned to the temple. War shouts and spears jabbed into the sky as the strange animal-clad warriors followed the Crown Prince and his father into the palace.

Aless looked around in confusion. What happened now? Tareq said she was their guest. What that meant, she wasn't sure. The older woman's striped robe shifted, and her black scarf bobbed over her head as she rose from the ground. The younger one glanced at Aless with open, brown eyes.

Aless wished she knew the women's names, but neither of them spoke. The elderly woman charged forward as if she led the way into battle. Alessandra followed obediently with the young slave behind her. They approached the smaller version of the lavish palace. A broad opening covered only by sheer fabrics billowed in a gentle breeze.

Entering through the gauzy fabric, cool

temperatures shifted the mesa's intense heat. Sunlight filtered in long rectangles through a lattice-work ceiling and windows opened on three sides. Alessandra hugged her tired, hot body in delight. At the center of the large room, a pool of water swirled against ornately patterned tiles. Fountains flowed at each end. Stone benches covered with soft cushions were positioned on each side. Scents of almond oil, cinnamon, and other fragrances she didn't recognize filled the room. Female voices murmured, even though Aless couldn't see anyone.

Lingering by the pool, she admired Doric columns, and flowering plants that filled graceful urns. Who came here? Maybe it was a pool to cool off in the desert heat. It seemed very feminine, though. She couldn't imagine the hairy Dhamar Ghalib taking a dip in the pool that extended almost to the end of the room.

Aless was lost in the wonder of it all when she noticed the older woman had stopped and was glaring at her. Aless picked up her pace as they walked down a long corridor with rooms on each side. There were no doors, only flowing fabrics that concealed what looked like individual apartments. Blue sky beckoned from outside through the last doorway, separated from the others. An apartment carved out of stone overlooked the valley below. Aless ventured to a broad ledge outside the room and held out her arms in pleasure. It was like sitting near the waterfall at home, basking in the expanse of sky and mountains around her. A pathway offered outside access to the mesa above and to a winding trail below.

She stepped back into the lavish room and took in a deep breath in the still coolness. Torches burned in each corner. A silken coverlet in purple, blue and crimson spread over what looked like a low bed made from cushions and draped in canopy of golden fabric.

The young servant tripped as her sandal caught uneven stone and bumped into the old woman's broad rear end. She straightened herself, and bowed to the aged woman, who drew herself up in an indignant huff. A gnarly hand curled into a fist, then unraveled into a harsh slap. The young one staggered, regained her stance and held one hand over the welt on her face. When the woman's arm extended again, Aless rushed to catch it. "No more."

The woman's rheumy brown eyes crinkled in scorn, and she yanked her hand out of Aless's grasp with unexpected strength.

Aless helped the young slave to her feet. She wasn't sure she had the authority to intercede for the young woman, but it was time to find out. "My name is Alessandra." She turned to the other and pointed her finger at the open doorway. "Leave us."

The woman stood, immovable, her face twisted in contempt. She pursed her lips. Brown spittle spewed out of her mouth, just missing the young slave positioned at Aless's side.

Aless jabbed her finger in her direction. "I said. Go. Now."

The woman sneered. Traces of tobacco dribbled down sagging chin. She shot a venomous look at the young woman, turned, and left.

"What is your name?" Aless asked.

"Shema." Her voice was strong for such a tiny, almost elfin girl with a heart-shaped face and round eyes. It was hard to tell how old she was. Nor could Aless read those tranquil eyes, which seemed filled with knowledge beyond her years. Shema's skin was the color of dark honey, like everyone she'd met so far. She was more than a slave, even though she hurried to wipe the old woman's spittle off the floor with a nearby cloth. Something about the way she carried herself spoke of a regal lineage.

Shema gathered clothing that had been laid on a chair and led her back to the pool. She placed a long sheet of fabric on a bench, pointed at the water, and turned to prepare an assortment of porcelain vessels on a marble table.

Grateful for privacy, Aless slipped out of her riding clothes. She dipped under water that greeted her skin and washed over her hair. Grime and exhaustion from the journey disappeared as she ducked back under again. When she came to the surface, light filtered from the ceiling, dancing on mosaic tiles that lined the pool.

Shema appeared overhead and waved. Aless rested a moment longer, then grabbed the towel and covered herself as she exited the water.

High-pitched female voices stirred from a hallway on one side of the atrium. Alessandra hadn't seen anyone since the wild procession that had greeted them at the pavilion. She wasn't sure who to expect. A woman dressed in a rich brocade of purples and gold entered the room and stood with the air of a self-ordained empress. Jabbing one hand onto her hip, she pointed a long, manicured finger at Shema, then Alessandra.

"Foya!"

Shema quickly gathered the vessels in one hand and hurried out the door. When Alessandra lingered, the woman charged her, spewing rage she didn't have to interpret. Aless kept her eyes on the pompous, overbearing woman as she backed out of the room. As she was leaving, a company of girls dressed in simple white gowns arrived.

The girls looked like they ranged in ages between ten and fourteen. They were a study in contrasts. One had blonde curls that extended over her shoulders and fair skin that certainly wasn't made to survive desert sun. A willowy, dark-skinned young woman with round black eyes carefully attended to her task of placing ornate vials from a basket on one of the marble benches. Another with almond eyes and delicate features placed a stack of white towels on a bench near the perimeter of the pool. Aless looked for the little girl with dark curls she'd seen only moments before who reminded her of Lucy.

A raven-haired woman followed the women. She stood, imperious, chin lifted and crimson gown falling off ivory shoulders. In effortless motion, the gown drifted to the floor. Aless was embarrassed but couldn't turn her eyes from the woman's perfect body marked only by the tattoo of a serpent etched from the top of one thigh and extending to her ankle. The snake almost appeared to slither up the woman's leg. The woman glided into the pool, her presence barely shifting the surface.

As Aless watched, fascinated, the woman's onyx-colored eyes suddenly met hers a malevolent stare. Aless struggled to break away until Shema's strong arm yanked her out of the room.

Chapter 12

Shema's calm demeanor turned to anger. "Come. Now."

"Who is that woman? Why are the girls serving her?" Aless asked.

Shema shook her head, and hurried back to the apartment, where a platter of figs, goat cheese, and flatbread were arranged on a table. Aless looked at the food with longing. She hadn't eaten since their campsite that morning. Forgetting her manners, she devoured a fig in two bites, then slathered the flatbread with cheese. Its creamy deliciousness made her groan with pleasure. A goblet of cold water stood nearby. She drank, filled the goblet again, and finished it. Her once parched, hungry body sank into the cushions, refreshed.

She watched Shema who pulled oval jars of cut glass from her bag. The young woman retrieved an ornate golden incense burner from a nearby shelf. "What are you doing?"

Shema motioned her to sit like herself, with legs crossed on a cushion at the center of a patterned carpet.

"It's a process. One used for centuries. Be still."

Shema brushed a musky scented lotion on Alessandra's arms, shoulders, and legs. Then applied a tiny dab of a pungent ointment to the back of her hand and index finger.

"It smells like the mountains where I live," Aless

said, with a pang of homesickness. The fragrance reminded her of climbs through fallen trees that hung over a noisy stream of spring melt. The same dank woodland scent filled the air when she struggled to keep up with Rory on afternoon hikes.

"It's found in evergreens. Very rare." Shema gently touched Aless's wrists and pulse points with the ointment. When Aless stood to leave, Shema held up her hand. "Wait. I'm not done."

Shema lit a charcoal disc at the base of the ornate incense burner, adding scented wood chips and resins. As smoke rose from the burner, a veil of exquisite scents descended over Alessandra, saturating the pores of her body.

Finally, when Alessandra's hair and clothing and body were infused with their layers, Shema lightly spritzed what smelled like jasmine with a hint of orange. A memory came to life in its fragrance. It was the scent of her mother when she'd bent to hug her. "Could I remember this aroma? My mother lived here for a time."

"Indeed. If you lose a sense of smell, you lose memories. Cherished and otherwise."

Otherwise? What kind of memories had defined Shema? Hildegard's shawl had been folded and placed with her traveling clothes on a table by a bed. Shema towel-dried her hair, then brushed it into long curls that fell onto her shoulders. She helped her step into silken trousers. A lush robe the color of midnight was cinched by a jeweled belt. Shema finished by placing a V-shaped, curtain necklace of precious stones around Alessandra's neck. The fabrics were cool and moved freely. There were no mirrors to show her reflection, but Aless felt as if she'd stepped into another universe. For the first time in many days, she felt beautiful.

Crimson lined the sky, and black clouds filled the horizon miles away when Tareq arrived with Akeem and Basir at his side. Aless felt a catch in her belly when she saw the young prince.

Far from the traveling clothes she'd seen him wear for days, he was dressed in swathes of rich fabrics with bands of gold that circled his neck and arms. Bronze highlighted his cheekbones, and slender lines of black outlined dark eyes. Tiny scarlet feathers adorned a robe with a high collar of precious stones that draped over baggy silken trousers. A golden medallion embossed with the image of a dragon hung around his neck and settled over his bare chest. He, too, had been anointed, but Aless couldn't identify each of the layers of aroma he carried. What kind of memory did fragrance carry for him?

Tareq smiled and winked.

Aless sighed in relief. It was still her friend under all that finery.

They walked arm in arm over semi-precious stones that outlined marble tiles in an enormous circle at the center of the mesa. Palm branches waved in a cool evening breeze as they approached the entrance of the palace. The breath of air was its own welcome considering her arrival hours before. She peered up at granite walls that towered on each side. An army of strong backs and skilled craftsmen had labored not only to bring the massive stones to the top of this mesa, but also to craft them in exquisite beauty.

A broad canopy of purple fabrics stretched over an atrium just inside the palace entrance. Men dressed in simple cotton tunics played stringed instruments and drums she'd never heard. The whole atmosphere sounded with noisy, chaotic celebration.

"What instruments are they playing?" she asked Tareq.

"The one that looks like a guitar is an oud. The long slender stringed instrument is a sitar. You recognize the tambourines." He pointed to women who held them in their hands as they wove through the crowds in bare waists and sensuous flowing trousers. Without a word, each of the musicians, as well as the dancers, fell prostrate to the ground as she and Tareq passed by.

Beyond the canopy, Tareq led Aless to an inner pavilion with columns draped in sheer fabrics and torches that jutted from the walls. Polished marble arches glistened with flecks of gold. Fabric-covered benches were scattered throughout the room, ready to receive honored guests. Music grew louder and morphed into a strange cacophony of sound and rhythm. Wave after wave of this exotic world threatened to topple her senses.

Two warriors met her and Tareq as they walked through the pavilion. Dressed as ferocious panthers, the men wore headdresses of black feathers and fearsome paint on their faces. Alessandra jumped when one of the scowling warriors stalked to her side and the other one positioned himself next to Tareq. They led the way to yet another area filled with sumptuous couches and Persian rugs. Women stood demurely around the chieftain who was seated at a U-shaped table at the back of the room.

Once again, as if by silent alarm, every onlooker in this interior room bowed to the ground. Embarrassed, Aless gazed over the heads to the women who surrounded the chieftain. A tall Nordic beauty with blonde curls and blue eyes knelt at his side, holding a bowl of fruit in one hand. Another young woman with green eyes and cascading auburn waves looked up for a moment, before dipping her head.

Each woman, despite the ways they differed from what appeared to be native dark skin and black hair, was dressed like this culture. Their flowing pants were gauzy and exposed bellies ornamented with dangling jewels. Every shade of hair dangled over blousy tops, and rich, silken robes. Were they slaves taken from family in native lands and hauled here to serve Dhamar Ghalib? Their expressions bore no resistance, though. Or did they?

The auburn-haired woman's glance was so fleeting, Aless couldn't be sure that it meant anything. The woman had already averted her eyes to a dish laden with meat and cheese on a table filled with food. None of the other women looked up from the chieftain, though each one acknowledged Tareq's presence by bowing.

The Dhamar Ghalib was dressed in royal robes and looked just as savage as when she'd met him that afternoon. The old man stood from a nest of plush cushions and held out his arms to them. Aless followed Tareq's lead and bowed low seven times. "My son. Alessandra. Sit," the man commanded. Alessandra took a seat beside Tareq on a rich animal skin and tried not to squirm.

The chieftain lowered himself back into the elaborate throne of pillows. He breathed heavily with the exertion and received a drink from one of the hovering young women. He was dressed in an embroidered scarlet robe without headdress or any of the ceremonial garb she'd seen earlier that day. Something about the set of his shoulders and his eyes looked weary. Aless peered around at the grandeur of the room. A brazen etching of the sun covered a wall at one side. A dragon glowered over a tapestry behind the chieftain's couch. Serpents etched in golden columns circled the perimeter of the room, as if to caution all who entered.

With a nod from their leader, people stood and continued their work. Women served her and Tareq, offering platters of lamb, bowls of yogurt, soft cheese, and flatbread. Aless reached for a round of the same bread Shema had served in her apartment. She layered it with a generous dollop of cheese and took a bite with another grateful sigh. Their journey hadn't presented many options in the way of food. Her mouth was full when the chieftain suddenly addressed her.

"You want to know about your mother."

Aless startled. No preliminaries, the man evidently preferred getting to the point. She chewed and swallowed with a gulp. "Yes. Sir. Your majesty."

The old man nodded in her direction, a bald patch showing on the crown of his head. What kind of business had he done in Sanctuary as a tribal chieftain? What could he have bought or sold in Sanctuary?

"Your mother was a mighty queen," he said. "My brother trained her in what became destiny — ruler of nations." The old man puffed in short breaths before continuing his lofty rhetoric, as if Alessandra needed convincing. "It was here that she was trained as high priestess in our temple. Her gifting was strong. We knew she'd rule over many. And she did. Her dominion extended over a vast territory from her throne in the city of Sanctuary."

Aiden always said simple truth was best expressed in simple words. The chieftain, on the other hand, drew up his chest as if prepared to continue his spiel. He droned on, scanning the crowd, and landing on Alessandra from time to time. "Her memory is prized in this city. Her imprint indelible. We honor you, Alessandra Gunter, as her daughter and heir."

Heir? What was the old man talking about? She wanted nothing of her mother's inheritance. Noticing the rapt attention of the crowd, she decided to wait for a better time to question the tribal chieftain. "Tareq said that you met her in Sanctuary many times."

"We were allies."

"I told her that you were traders," Tareq said.

"Ah, yes. That, too." The man leaned heavily against the pillows. His eyes shifted as a noise sounded from the entrance of the pavilion.

The woman Aless had seen at the pool earlier that day entered the room. Her black eyes, lined with kohl, focused on Tareq. Hues of black, gold and brown swathed her body. Her hips swayed to a hypnotic melody played an unseen flute.

The woman, Laila, didn't have dark skin. Her raven hair and porcelain skin were a stark contrast to everyone around her. She was beautiful, though cold, and as intent as a viper preparing to strike.

It was a solo dance, clearly performed for Tareq alone. He glanced at her, then away, as she made her way closer to him. Was it a hiss that came out of her mouth? The woman tapped finger cymbals in a languid cadence and angled toward him like a cobra. Lust filled the room like a heavy perfume.

"Who is she?" Aless whispered to Tareq. Every part of her body tensed, half-expecting to see the woman's tongue slide in and out as her body twisted and writhed in a provocative call.

He murmured, "Laila. One of my father's concubines."

"She's dancing for you."

Tareq cleared his throat and coughed. "Merely a ceremony for our entertainment."

"One with you in mind."

Tareq glanced at Aless, amused. "And you care?"

Aless blushed, despite herself.

He leaned over, his breath upon her cheek, and whispered. "*You're* the focus of my eyes. And have been since I saw you at the waterfall."

Still, the dance continued. Aless didn't know where to look. She'd invaded an intimacy that belonged only to Tareq and the sensuous woman. Suddenly, the chieftain rose, and the woman fell to the ground, her arms extended as if in a plea.

Tareq stood and bowed to his father. "Father, we take our leave with your permission."

The Dhamar Ghalib nodded. Tareq lifted Aless to her feet. Laila had risen to her knees and watched Tareq, her eyes bright and hungry as he and Alessandra walked toward the entrance. Laila touched Tareq's arm as they passed. His body quivered for a second. He quickly covered his reaction, though not fast enough.

Tareq led Aless out of the pavilion and into the darkness with Akeem and Basir carrying torches behind them.

"Leave us." The prince commanded his men as they neared her apartment. He took one of the torches and placed it inside a crevasse in the rock wall as his guards strode away.

Together, they stood on the ledge that overlooked

shadowy mountain ranges. The city beneath them twinkled with firelight in the darkness. Tareq seemed to compose himself. He took a deep breath. "Welcome to Akkad. A beautiful city, yes?"

The clouds Aless had seen hours before approached like a black wall against the night. A storm was on the way. Taking a deep breath, she smelled rain in the air. "A majestic one. I'm used to living surrounded by mountains and stone. The air is different here, though, and sound carries. I never expected to visit a city carved into a mountain side."

Tareq brushed a lock of her hair away from her face, his hand lingering on her cheek. "It took many years to build our city. My father, grandfather and great-grandfather led the way. Stories of its construction are engraved on the walls of our temple." He pointed up to it. "I'll show you tomorrow if you'd like."

Their arms brushed together. Aless was equally thrilled and terrified at the electricity in his touch, somehow intensified in the flickering torchlight.

"I have much to share about our kingdom," he said, in a gentle tone. "And much more I want to know about you." Before turning to leave, Tareq brushed her hand with his lips. "Es moi especial. I'll send a guard for you tomorrow morning. There's something in the temple I want to show you."

Aless entered her room after he left, trying to ignore the same flurry inside she'd felt when she first met the Crown Prince. His regal ways were so tender with her. And yet had been equally decisive and brutal with Heydar. She peered around the darkness lit only by a flickering torch. Suddenly the lavish room felt like a tomb. She had to get outside to think.

Perching on the open ledge, she recalled events of the day in a world so far from her own. A stone toppled and skipped down the rocky wall. Maybe a nocturnal desert animal.

Maura had spoken of unforeseen change. Although Aless hadn't believed her, her cousin had been right. Aless had plummeted into a culture beyond anything she dreamed, miles away from what she'd known and loved. As she stood in lingering moonlight, the outline of the temple extended into the sky like the jagged blade of a sword.

Thunder rumbled in the distance and the scent of rainfall grew stronger. Large watery plops sizzled against the heat of the desert stone. Minutes later, sheets and torrents of a thunderstorm rushed in. Alessandra raced into the shelter of her room as wind whipped across the ledge. She huddled against the pillows of the bed until the tempest finally retreated and she fell into a spent, dreamless sleep.

Chapter 13

Hues of peach and crimson streaked a rain-washed sky. Shema's petite form scaled a long footpath from below. She waved as she finished the last ascent up sandstone steps.

"You're not even out of breath." Aless remembered how she'd huffed and puffed on her first climb, struggling to breathe in the thin air. "Have you lived here many years?"

"Enough to be accustomed to uphill climbs. And unexpected obstacles."

"You mean like the twists and turns of that desert trail?"

"Yes. As well as other dangers that lurk." Shema busied herself around the room, preparing breakfast and laying out another assortment of vessels, some carved in ivory and others glass-cut.

"Like snakes?" There weren't many rattlesnakes on her mountain, but she knew enough to back away from the distinctive sound of their warning.

Shema didn't answer. She lifted Hildegard's shawl from a chair with a delicate touch. She fingered its vibrant threads as she folded, then placed it on a small table. "The tree of life."

"Yes. How did you know?"

"My mother had a shawl much like this one." Shema paused, as if she were unwilling to let the fabric go.

"Does your mother live here, also?"

Shema shook her head and turned away. "No. She...doesn't." Picking up a long cotton towel, she motioned to Aless to follow her. "Time to get ready."

Shema led the way back to the enclosed pool, where she handed Alessandra the towel. "I'll be back."

Aless took off the clothes she'd fallen asleep in and went under the water. She half-expected to see the menacing woman peer down at her when she came to the surface. The murmur of voices was so faint, she couldn't be sure she'd heard anything.

Back in her room, Shema oiled her skin as she had the night before, then toweled her hair until it was almost dry and brushed it smooth. She separated strands of hair and braided each one into plaits that dangled around Aless's shoulders. When she was done, she wrapped and fastened each braid to the top of her head.

Aless looked up at her with a question as Shema pulled out a white gown. A small dread tingled in her gut. She had no idea what to expect of her visit to the temple with Tareq.

Shema held the dress over Aless's head. Soft, buttery fabric cascaded as the gown flowed to the ground. She laced on a delicate pair of calf-skin sandals as Shema prepared cosmetics. Then tried to hold still as the tiny woman lined her eyes with kohl and smudged a dab of clay-like cream high on each cheekbone.

Shema positioned a wreath of laurel leaves on the crown of Alessandra's head and fastened a gold medallion with an opal at its center around her neck. She backed away as if to admire her work.

"Should I take off the other necklace?" Aless asked, touching the beaded pendant at her throat. How could she remove the only reminder of Rory? The necklace had warned her of the attack that night as they traveled. She didn't care if it matched her outfit. She needed it.

"Keep it." Shema held out her arm to direct Aless outside. Sure enough, Akeem and Basir approached on the trail ahead, fully armed. Evidently, their show of power was necessary even to escort their master on a social call. She refused to look at either of them, ignoring their filtered contempt. They bowed low and made way for Tareq, who came from behind his guards.

Tareq stood before her, his almond-shaped eyes trained on hers. Was he yet another shapeshifter, only this time as the Greek god, Adonis?

Heat that crept from her chest and up her neck proved he was very much flesh and blood. Dressed in a white tunic, pants, and turban, Tareq didn't look like a warrior anymore. His eyes were outlined with kohl, and he wore a single medallion of gold with an opal center, like hers. Even her gown complemented his priestly robe.

The message was clear. In some way, they were connected. She wasn't sure if she was excited or alarmed. What did this mean for a visit to a temple that lurked over the city like a bad omen? The edifice seemed likely to offer a clue about her mother's wickedness. Although, what if she was expected to do something, to know something?

Aless shivered with fear that washed over her. Then straightened her shoulders and lifted her chin. It was time for secrets to be made known. That's why she'd come.

Tareq reached for her hand. She took it, determined to remember she had a mission. Even if the prince smiled as though he'd been waiting to see her.

"Shall we go?" he asked, as if they were alone.

Akeem and Basir led the way to the other side of the plateau where the temple jutted out on the southern edge. Morning light reflected on the glossy black stone where hieroglyphics shifted and changed as the sun climbed in the eastern sky.

"What do the symbols mean?" she asked.

"A new message appears as the sun ascends. Each one represents an aspect of our god." Spires reached from obelisks at each corner that pierced blue sky. "It must touch the heavens," Tareq said. "It must grow higher, even as we must grow as worshippers."

"Who do you worship?"

"The stars, the sun, the moon, the earth. For they are ours to govern. We're rulers, dominion carriers, shapers of the world around us."

"We worship Yahweh, Creator of heaven and earth."

"Perhaps very similar. With a different name."

Aless shook her head. "I don't think so. Our worship is a simple celebration. Usually outside, where we feel the sun on our faces, touch the grass, smell the pines. And know that they are not our own creation, but a work of His hands."

Tareq turned and commanded Akeem and Basir. "Wait here."

Frigid air slammed Aless when she entered the temple doors, dispelling desert heat instantly. A metallic scent of lightning brushed her senses. Glittering prisms of crystals dangled from a towering ceiling, and lights shivered at the base in each of the five corners. A primitive fire pit filled the center of the room. Frayed ropes dangled from its circular rim.

Unreasoning panic came as suddenly as she entered the immense room. If it hadn't been for Tareq, she would've run back out the door. The Crown Prince walked toward a gleaming silver throne that stood behind a simple altar. Aless planted her feet, determined to steady herself. What kind of god presided over this cold majesty? In front of her, two nondescript stones sat, unadorned on the altar. "What are those two rocks?"

"A treasure. One kept here, but not understood. They're called *Light of the Stars*."

"They don't fit into all this splendor." Alessandra lightly stroked them, wondering what kind of riches they concealed. As she touched them, the stones glowed with a dim, wavering blue light.

Tareq stepped back, almost losing his balance.

"What's happening?" Alessandra asked. Instead of moving away in fear, she welcomed their warmth. Their light increased as her fingers remained on them.

"I've never seen their light. Only heard of it." Tareq peered at the stones and then back to her. "Perhaps they know you."

As if by unseen hand, a fine script appeared on first one, then both the stones.

Aless studied the writing as Tareq backed farther away. "What do they say?"

He didn't answer for a moment. When he did speak, his voice was uncertain. "I don't know. I don't recognize the language."

Strangely, two ordinary rocks beckoned like unexpected refuge. "Where did they come from?"

"Legend says that they're pieces of a constellation. The Archer, I believe. They've been a powerful enigma for many years." He returned to Alessandra's side. "Your mother worshiped in this temple. Her body vibrated with the power she looked for and found in this place. Everyone bowed in reverence as it flowed out of her fingers."

Aless lowered her head and placed the stones back on the altar, missing their warmth at once. Her mother had served a demon. How convenient. Something or someone else to blame for murdering her family and defenseless children. Hatred for Lilith Gunter surged, along with the unwelcome grief that always whispered behind it. She shook her head, determined to shut down what felt like a raging river inside.

"What is it?"

"My mother." Aless cleared her throat and tried to speak lightly. Even with her best efforts, her voice sounded shrill in the quiet around them. "While other children were rocked to sleep at night, mine plotted a massacre against people I love." She shouldn't reveal this. Tareq might use this information against her in some way. She couldn't stop the emotions that swelled like a ferocious tide with the hated truth, though. It didn't matter who stood before her. Or how sympathetic his gaze.

"I have to know," she said. "So that I can cut any ties that tether me to her. I'm here…to prove that there is nothing of Lilith Gunter in me." The words burst out with such force that her body quaked.

Tareq extended his hand, almost, but not quite touching her arm, as if to steady her. He was probably careful about being contaminated with that bitter spewing. "Are you sure what you've heard is true?" he asked.

"People I trust, family who knew and loved her

attest to her deeds."

"Ah. So, you, my friend, are on a mission. To disavow what your mother carried."

"That's what brought me here."

Tareq sighed, then looked away.

"You had a loving mother who adored you. You couldn't understand."

"Not in a way you'd think. My mother was here, in this temple when she died." Tareq's eyes darted to the ground and stayed.

"What happened?"

Tareq shook his head. "Gad El Glas is a god we serve, if not willingly, at least out of fear."

"Your god isn't good?"

"Our god is just, requiring payment for misdeeds no matter how small the infraction."

A shudder went through Alessandra's body. Lilith had been here. Perhaps she'd stood at this very place. She wondered what kind of ceremony the unyielding god required. And how it had marked her mother. "What does payment look like?"

Tareq gazed at the massive fire pit, surrounded by rows of stone benches. "Some mysteries are best unraveled when we're old enough to understand."

"Was that true for you?"

Tareq pivoted away from Aless. His body became rigid, and one hand curled into a fist at his side.

Aless's cheeks burned with confusion. Tareq was a strong man. Surely her words weren't powerful enough to hurt him. "Forgive me," she said.

When he turned to face her, Tareq's eyes seemed even blacker, although that didn't seem possible. Someone had murdered Heydar. Tareq had either commanded his death or been the one who carried out the vengeance. Did she know him, at all? She took a breath and stepped away.

His composure returned, though his face remained stern. "I'm successor to a throne. Heir to a culture."

Aless stood, silent as she watched the man retreat without going anywhere. Tareq was like an exquisite vase that hid its contents. Maybe it was loneliness that still ached from when he'd been sent away as a child. Or something much worse. "I'm leaving. Now." She turned back to look at the Stones one more time.

They continued to glow in soft, blue light. What about them drew her? Nothing else in the temple did, though. She forced herself to walk, not run out the door. Tareq had led the way throughout this journey. This time, he was the one who followed.

Aless took a deep breath of relief in the warm morning air as they exited the temple. Fear retreated the farther they walked away, until finally, it lingered only as a threatening shadow. They stood side by side on the marble tiles at the center of the mesa.

Tareq gestured in a wide circle across the mesa. He attempted a smile. "I grew up here. At least until I was sent away. What I learned about the temple came when I was older. And able to understand." Tareq kept his back to the temple's soaring walls. Even Akeem and Basir faced away, toward the palace.

Aless weighed the decision to tell him everything. "I never told you why I journeyed to Sanctuary. And why I came alone. Do you remember the two men who came to visit? The arborists said an army approached Sanctuary. Its warriors sought me, hoping to find something of my mother. I'm here to discover what that is." She choked. "And see if it's true." She blushed furiously. She hadn't planned to bare so much of her heart to Tareq.

He pulled her into his arms and held her until she stopped shaking. His lips pressed her forehead. "It was no accident that we met in the forest that evening. You aren't alone any longer. Together we'll discover what an army desires in you, Alessandra Gunter." His touch was soft against her waist, caressing, and then bringing her face to his. His lips brushed hers lightly. Her first kiss. She'd thought it would be with Rory. Would it have been sweet?

She was suddenly aware of Akeem and Basir. Were they looking on and smirking, or remembering their comrade, Heydar? Aless pulled away from Tareq's embrace and turned to the sound of rushing water. She'd been so preoccupied when they'd entered the building, she'd only been vaguely aware of it. This wasn't a brook meandering in the distance. "There's a waterfall nearby."

"I'll show you." Tareq took her hand and led her to a broad area behind the temple that overlooked not one, but three waterfalls spilling over the edge of a cliff. Cascading water plummeted hundreds of feet over what looked like a bottomless gorge, full of jagged rocks and outcroppings of red stone. Hope flooded her as she took a deep breath of fresh mountain air. Until she looked further into the gorge below. Vultures. Fifteen, twenty, more than she'd ever seen, circled, and swooped over some unknown death.

Chapter 14

Other than the storm her first night, every day had been marked by a cloudless expanse of blue, broken only by jagged red rocks of the mountain. A rim of gold appeared on the horizon, breaking indigo into dawn. Alessandra peered over the ledge outside her room and watched as another battalion of equestrian horsemen rode in the darkness. Swords flashed as brightly colored tunics and feathered turbans bobbed by torchlight. Tareq had said they were off to explore new lands. Instead, like all the others, they looked ready for warfare.

Since she'd arrived in Akkad, she'd endured night after night of fanfare. The feasts were an extravaganza with festive music and low tables sagging with foods she'd come to recognize. The beautiful woman, Laila, hadn't reappeared since their first night. Now, on the beginning of a new day, Aless was still tired after a night's sleep on the lavish cushions.

She changed into a pair of baggy pants and loose-fitting tunic, relieved not to have to go through perfuming first thing in the morning. Stuffing a couple of purple figs in one pocket, she headed outside.

The temple's opaque walls reflected the sunrise. She'd seen Tareq's face when he talked about his mother. A god that required payment for misdeeds. A terrible place where terrible things had happened. Some perhaps by the hands of Lilith Gunter.

She shuddered with an awful reminder. Her mother would've known the Stones. She may have been able to read their messages. Although it was likely she'd manipulated their words to serve her own wickedness. As much as Alessandra despised the temple's cold terror, the Stones themselves drew her back. For whatever reason, their light shone in her presence.

Tareq had grown up in Akkad and been in the temple often. Still, he seemed shocked to see their light, as well as the writing that appeared.

There was no one to tell her why two nondescript rocks released their mystery in her hands. But they had. Those long winter days at the chateau when snow piled so high they couldn't go outside, had mattered after all. She and Rory quizzed each other in one language after another. She'd longed to see the countries they represented. Rory was the one who picked up each sentence structure and sang little songs to teach the children. If she could connect the words she'd seen on the Stones to a language she knew, maybe they'd speak to her about Lilith Gunter. It was time to find out.

Alessandra made her way across the mesa when a small brown figure dashed in front of her and leaped onto an area of sparse desert vegetation. A little girl weaved between rocks, dodged into crevasses, then dangled, fearless, from a precipice. She was intent on catching something faster than herself, which narrowed the targets.

A petite young woman sped after her. It was Shema, zigzagging past narrow turns, with one focus in her pursuit. The child. Why didn't she just call her? And why wouldn't she let her play? Shema hurried, sometimes on the winding path downhill, and other times plowing past yucca plants and cactus. She got close, then lost the child as she ducked into a narrow gap in the stone below the mesa. Finally, she stood at its entrance, her arms out and legs planted as if to prevent an escape.

Sunlight rose over an eastern ridge of mountains as the little girl crawled out with something in her hand, holding it out to the woman triumphantly. She bent down to admire the prize and held her hand, palm up to the child. She used her other hand to make a sign. The child nodded, then noticed Alessandra. She placed two fingers on her forehead and pointed at Aless.

Instead of bringing her to Aless, Shema took the girl by the hand and hurried up the path to an open area outside one of the homes. Skirting a firepit and ducking under laundry hung outside, she disappeared with the child inside. When Shema reappeared, she was alone.

Aless paused, unsure. Maybe she should just wave and go on her way. Except something about the child drew her, as surely as Shema's quiet wisdom. She hadn't seen inside any of the homes on the trail beneath the mesa. No one had invited her in. Strangely, anyone she met on the trail bowed to the ground and stayed there, face in the dust. There were no greetings, much less conversation. Children were whisked inside before she could smile and introduce herself. She felt like one of the intimidating walls of the temple.

Shema waved to her. "Come. Join us for breakfast."

Going to the temple could wait. Aless angled down the winding path until she arrived at the home set into desert stone where Shema and the little girl stood just inside the door.

The little girl stretched out her clenched fist to Alessandra where a lizard's tail wagged furiously back and forth. She offered a crooked smile with several teeth missing. Her black hair sprouted every which way, as if she'd sprung out of bed for just this reason.

Aless pulled one of the figs out of her pocket. She squatted on the ground and held out both hands, curled into fists.

The child knew the game at once. She studied Alessandra's hands until she saw part of the fig peeking out. Pointing to that hand, she jumped up and down and chuckled in an odd little strangled voice. Aless handed her the fig, and she stuffed it in her mouth in one bite, keeping the lizard captured in her other hand. The little girl smiled broadly until, suddenly, the lizard wriggled away. In the next moment, she was off on another chase.

Shema watched her speed down the winding trail. "My daughter, Amira." She wrinkled her brow as the child leaped over a gap in the rocks and kept running. "She's deaf. She can read your lips, though. If she stands still long enough."

"Ah," Aless said. "She reminds me of a little friend from…home."

"She has to run, so I let her. At least in the early mornings." Shema led the way into large, open room lit by torches. Two beds were tucked into one corner. An elaborately carved table stood on the other side.

Aless recognized the rich walnut Aiden often used to craft furniture for the chateau.

She pointed to one of the legs that seemed etched from the forest, with vines and feathery leaves that stretched from the floor and attached to the table. "Beautiful. My…a dear man from my home is a craftsman, also."

"Ah. And where is your home?" Shema glanced up

from a wooden cabinet stacked with pottery and several finely painted teacups.

"A mountain. Not like this one. Our home…" Alessandra stopped, stuffing down another rush of homesickness. "Our mountain is green in more shades than you can imagine. And white with snow in the winter. It's magnificent, though often dangerous. Mountain lions, hungry grizzlies, exposure if you get lost."

Shema nodded. "This city, like your mountain, has its own perils."

Aless studied the young woman. Shema didn't offer information freely. Instead, she measured her words as carefully as she meted out the aromatic oils she'd layered on Alessandra's skin. "Is Akkad dangerous?"

"It is. Though not in a way you'd expect.

"What do you mean?" Aless wasn't sure what would draw her out, so she kept talking. "I came because I needed to find out about my mother. She used to live here. Her name was Lilith Gunter." Aless stood back and watched for her reaction.

Shema pulled a large circular bread from under a fabric cover and gathered a bowl of figs in the other. She brought two plates, poured water from a pitcher and motioned Aless to sit down at the hewn table. She hadn't answered Alessandra's question. "Would you like to meet my grandmother?"

Had Shema been listening to her at all?

Shema sat across from Alessandra. She dipped her head for a moment, then took a bite of the bread. "Her name is Bethiah. She may remember your mother," she continued as if knowing Alessandra's mother was nothing out of the ordinary. "She's almost blind. And hard of hearing, for that matter. She loves visitors, though. Her house is next to ours. You're welcome to stop by."

Tears clouded her eyes at Shema's offer. Embarrassed, she wiped them with one hand. Tareq and his father, Dhamar Ghalib were the only ones she'd met who'd known her mother. How would the old woman's memory be different? By the time they finished the simple meal, courage breezed in as surely as Shema had arrived that first day in Akkad. "I'd like to meet your grandmother. Could I visit later this morning?"

Shema stood to clear the table and then turned to leave. "Her house is the small one with vented roof next to ours. If she's at work, the fragrance will show you the way. Just tell her who you are. She'll look forward to meeting you. I have to find Amira."

By the time Aless walked outside to see a rosy, purple dawn, Shema was half-way down the trail, waving her hands at a small figure dashing in and out of curves and crevasses. She turned once and pointed to the tiny dwelling next to her own.

Aless waved back, acknowledging the grandmother's home. She wondered about Shema's words, that she *had* to find Amira. She'd watched other women in Akkad pull children back inside when she'd approached on the trail. It was an odd gesture in a warm climate that encouraged children to play outside. She and Rory let the children loose after breakfast and before their studies to run off first light energy.

Shema had said Akkad was a dangerous place, although she never explained why. Aless trembled in a stiff breeze. She didn't know the city, couldn't foreshadow the potential threats like she had at the chateau. Still, she had to go back to the temple. She needed to study the Stones undisturbed.

Hiking up the trail from Shema's home, Aless took a deep breath before scaling the last steps to the mesa. A few villagers kneaded lumps of dough and stirred embers of fire in clay ovens. Otherwise, all was hushed. There were no guards outside the temple and the light wasn't strong enough to illumine its strange symbols.

She stood before it's enormous doors and wondered if she was trespassing. Surely, it was open to everyone, although she couldn't imagine why anyone would want to enter freely. The door slid open when she pulled on a long, narrow bar. She peered around, but no one she could see had followed her.

Inside, the temple was dark, except for diffused light outside its windows. A soft glow appeared on the altar as she stepped over the threshold. It was the Stones, drawing her back into this cold edifice. Gathering her courage, she searched the interior for anyone who might already be inside.

No one.

She glanced from side to side and approached the Stones. Her courage rose as their light grew brighter. No reason to be afraid. Was she hoping someone followed her? Or praying they didn't. She wasn't sure. As she stood by the Stones, their light illuminated the entire temple. Aless stood in wonder only for a moment, determined not to get distracted. The Stones were why she'd come. Once again, they'd responded to her presence.

The Stones were warm, even comforting at her touch. Aless clutched them as she would on a winter day, hovering over the kitchen hearth to warm her chilled fingers. As she held them, a picture rose in her mind.

The children from the chateau. The ones she loved and missed, were gathered around the large plank dining table, bent over their studies. Rory peered over each small shoulder, pointing out an answer, encouraging another. When he reached Lucy, she took his hand from her shoulder and planted a kiss on it. Rory tousled her curls and bent to kiss her head.

Rage washed over her. She hated Lilith Gunter for countless tiny moments she'd stolen from her daughter. Shadowy images of a cold room, its darkness broken only by a large window, were all she could remember before Aiden and Maura had arrived to take her to their mountain home. She couldn't recall her childhood before the chateau except in snippets of loneliness that arose in the most unpredictable times.

Unlike that trip when Maura's warmth surrounded her like Hildegard's shawl, the journey to Akkad had been far from the adventure she'd longed for. She'd come on this quest, not drawn by a loving memory, but by a vow to separate herself forever. Day after day had passed in the red sandstone cliffs of Tareq's city. It hadn't mattered how heartfelt her decision had been. Regardless of time, distance or place, an unseen cord bound her to a person she despised. No matter how hard she tried to deny it.

As quickly as the vision appeared, it was gone.

Writing etched from an invisible hand on first one stone, then the other. *He sets his stars in place, calling them all by name.*

Wrath trailed away as astonishment replaced it. She could read the Stones.

Not that she understood their message.

Maura was the one who loved the constellations. A stately telescope stood on the top floor of the chateau, where windows, instead of ceiling, opened their view of the night skies. On warm summer nights, Maura helped each child press a face against the telescope. She'd point out the constellation Sagittarius, the Archer, in the Milky Way.

Rory pretended to be the mighty centaur. He galloped, roaring, through the room, threatening each with his imaginary bow and arrow. The children ran screaming until Alessandra stood against the half-bull, half-man and demanded his weapons. Then, she and the children pummeled Rory to the ground, rolling like puppies as they conquered their foe. Finally, little heads nodded, and the adults carried one after the other to bed.

Who set the stars in place? She'd always been a skeptic at heart, though it was hard to deny a divine hand in the heavens. The design had gone vastly wrong with Lilith Gunter.

Movement in one of the corners of the temple caught her eye. A dark shadow moved against the floor. A black snake with yellow markings on its spine curled like a rope unfurling.

A snake in the desert wasn't uncommon. It didn't look like a rattler, native to this desert climate. Still, fear gripped her heart, and she held the Stones to her chest.

Suddenly, light flooded even the darkest corners. The walls, once dark as a smoke-filled sky, became as transparent as glass. Inside them, like a gruesome terrarium, snakes of all shapes, colors and sizes writhed. Elliptical cat-eye pupils glimmered on broad, triangular heads and colorful patterns slithered over and under each other in tangled masses. Fangs bared, warning that these were no garden variety serpent. They were venomous. And they'd been there all along. Greater light had only exposed them.

Aless couldn't breathe, couldn't move. The snakes were encased in the wall as a warning. What was their purpose, except to captivate by terror? What wicked force released them? Mesmerized by the walls that had come to life, she stood, frozen.

Finally, she laid first one, then the other stone back on the altar. Their light dimmed as she backed away.

Another snake slipped out and crawled along the base of the wall. Then another.

She rushed back and grabbed the two rocks again.

Each snake retreated into the wall.

It was a bizarre stand-off between light versus darkness. And one that seemed to depend on an invisible partnership between she and two rocks that appeared ordinary in every way. She couldn't stand here forever, holding them in each hand, hoping that the snakes were never released. In a single move, Alessandra dropped the two stones on the altar, turned and ran.

Chapter 15

Alessandra raced across the mesa, almost mowing down a burly guard whose legs stood like tree stumps. She looked up at his tattooed face and feathered headdress with a start. Where was she? And how fast could she get home.

Ducking through the entrance of her room, she leaned against its stone wall, breathless and panting. Everything about the lavish surroundings — its torchlight, the silken cushions, even the table of aromatic oils—filled her with longing for her family. No one said she had to stay. She'd seen enough. It was time to go home.

Tareq had said he'd escort her whenever she was ready. She was never sure where he was during the day, only that he appeared every evening to escort her to the festive meal. She had no idea how to find him in the palace, other than asking one of the fierce guards. She'd go to the stables first and find Orion. She could send a message to Tareq from there.

Aless stuffed her own riding clothes into her pack, adding figs, naan, and a circle of goat cheese. She searched the room, wondering what else to bring when Shema entered quietly.

Aless startled, as if she'd been caught in a crime. She reminded herself that she never had been a captive. Tareq would prove that. Shema had been an ally and deserved to know her plans.

"I was wrong to come," she started, then finished in a rush. "Rory…the children. They need me. I don't belong here." She rattled off her words in short gasps. Then noticed Shema wasn't speaking.

Shema picked up one of the vials from the table, studied it and then added it to Alessandra's pack. "You'll need this one to disguise your scent."

"What? I won't need anything like that." She remembered Nona's necklace and how it foreshadowed Heydar's attack. That evil man was gone. "I'm free to go. As soon as Tareq prepares himself, we'll leave."

"Perhaps. Still, it won't hurt to have an extra defense along the way." Shema placed a jar of ointment into her pack. "This is the one that reminds you of home. It will comfort your heart as you travel." Shema paused and studied Alessandra's eyes. "I'll miss you, Alessandra."

Aless caught Shema into a hug. "You've been a faithful friend. I don't know what I would've done without you."

Shema pulled away and peered into Alessandra's eyes, as if she was a child needing instruction before planning another escapade. "The gate. You'll need Amira's help to open it."

"Amira? I've never seen anyone except Tareq open it."

Shema gathered several more figs and naan. "Don't let her linger there. Not for any reason."

"Amira can open the locked gate?"

"Yes. But it's dangerous for her to be seen. We must act quickly. Are you ready?"

Shema didn't even question her decision. Didn't tell her she was crazy for coming to this strangely beguiling,

Stones of Promise

yet dreadful place. She had already headed out the door before Aless placed the pack on one shoulder and followed her. They wound down the path until they came to Shema's home where Amira came out, her mouth full of bread.

Shema held her daughter's chin in her hand and waited until her gaze settled on her mother's. "Amira. Take Alessandra to the gate."

Amira looked up at her mother with sober eyes. Without a word, she took Alessandra's hand and together, they walked down the steep descent.

The child held Alessandra's hand tightly as they navigated every curve in the pathway down the mountain. It was the same one that Tareq had led her on when they first arrived. They didn't speak, although Aless wondered what was going on in the little girl's mind.

Suddenly, Amira turned her body against Aless, blocking her way.

"What is it?"

A rattle sounded yards ahead. Amira threw a rock into the corner of an overhanging ledge. A large diamond-back rattlesnake slithered across the trail, zigzagged along the sand, and disappeared beneath a large yucca.

Alessandra squeezed Amira's shoulder in thanks.

The little girl offered a crooked smile, then grabbed Aless's hand for the next descent down the mountain. The immense bronze gate stood like an admonition with the brazen snake, its diamond eyes glittering in full sunlight. By the time they arrived, Aless was sweating, and her calves ached with muscles that tightened at every turn and patch of loose gravel.

Not Amira, though. She approached the gate, humming in a peculiar, rhythmic cadence. Taking Alessandra's hand, she placed it over the serpent etched on the center of the doors. Amira's low voice became a brooding melody, like one droned by monks in hidden sanctuaries. It released a vibration that Aless felt through her fingertips and into her thin sandals.

In moments, the impenetrable gate swung open.

Aless was confounded. Her hands had opened the gate. How had that happened? She bent down to face the child as she'd seen her mother do. Amira's face was much like Shema's — wide-eyed and serious. Her eyes were jade green, unlike Shema who had the dark eyes of almost everyone in Akkad. And a glimmer of joy that fueled a bounce in every step. "Thank you, Amira. Again."

Amira hugged Alessandra's legs, then turned and ran back up the trail.

People were already at work in the fields. Only a few glanced up at her as she walked by guards who held whips under one arm. What kind of culture required labor overseen by men with weapons? She stopped and glared at one of the guards, who held his lash over a young woman who'd stumbled on a clod of dirt. He lowered his head to Alessandra, keeping his eyes to the ground as she moved on.

The stables were just beyond the giant arena. Grooms had already prepared horses for the day and handed their leads to warriors. Akeem appeared to be overseeing the arena where warriors approached, bowed, then received their horses. Basir led each group of warriors in drills, like the ones she'd seen them practice at the chateau.

Aless straightened her shoulders and walked toward the stables. Akeem stepped in front of her. He bowed deeply, standing in her way. The familiar bulge in the bands of fabric around his waist revealed the dagger. Was it the one he'd used to kill Heydar? She retreated two steps, then stopped. She had Tareq's protection. She didn't need to fear this man. "I need to see my horse."

Akeem stared at her with expressionless black eyes. A vein down the side of one temple throbbed. Still, he didn't move.

"I said. I need to see my horse. The Crown Prince and I will be leaving soon."

Akeem stood, silent. This time, Basir, with plaited locks flapping in a sturdy breeze joined him. They positioned themselves side by side as an unyielding wall.

What was she going to do? They weren't defying her with nasty guffaws, although their eyes darted back and forth from her to each other, communicating an alert of some kind.

A man appeared from one of the stalls, carrying a curry brush in one hand and bucket in the other. He looked like a specter from the mountains. Aiden had told her about men who lived secluded from the eyes of civilization. Men who knew the mountains as familiar friends and lived by their bounty.

The man paused outside one of the stables, appraising the situation. His shoulders stooped, as if accustomed to working on something that required him to bend his long frame. When he approached, he straightened, and an air of authority overtook what had appeared as a humble stance. He ignored the two warriors and addressed Alessandra. "Hullo, lass. Ye be in the wrong neck of the woods, so to speak."

Akeem shot a vicious look his way, then with a silent nod, he and Basir strode away.

The aged man sounded like Nona. "I need my horse," she said, voice trembling.

"Ah, be sure that is allowed. Come forth."

Another group of warriors charged from behind Aless and rode into the arena. She scurried to keep up with the man's long strides. "Thank you. My name is Alessandra."

"Indeed. I be hearin' of ye. And ye horse? Black mustang with white star?" He trudged down the narrow corridor of the extensive stables, as though he knew exactly where he was going. They passed stall after stall of horses. One stable boy after another stopped what he was doing and nodded to the older man. One combed the mane of a horse whose coat shone like flowing gold.

Alessandra paused to admire the horse too handsome to be real.

The man noticed her attention. "Akhal-Teke. Most beautiful horse in existence. One of the Crown Prince's favorites."

What had Tareq said about his horse being a faithful companion? It sounded as if he had his pick from any number of Arabian stallions and other breeds from all over the world.

"Me name be Perseus. Lowly groom, I am. But surrounded by me greatest joys."

Perseus looked like a wild man, although she could tell by the responses of the other stable boys and grooms that he was in charge. Something about the way the groom walked, touching first the mane of one horse, patting the side of another, marked him in a way that felt like home. She remembered Aiden, racing through open plains in search of wild horses, angling this way and that, seamlessly aligned with the gait of his horse.

Perseus turned into the last stall that stood against an exterior wall and opened to a view of a pasture outside. "I be here when the men brought her in. Kept her away from the stallions."

Orion whinnied at the sight of Alessandra, who dropped her pack and ran to greet her mare. She stroked the horse's nose, then her neck, brushed and clean. Her tack which hung on a nearby wall was oiled, free of the dust and muck of the long ride to Akkad. Even her hooves had been trimmed.

"Oh, my friend. You've been in good hands." She hugged Orion's neck and nuzzled her face into the horse's mane. Her throat swelled with relief and pure joy. Her mare was fine. And ready for their journey home. She turned to Perseus with a broad grin. "Thank you, sir. Thank you."

Perseus bowed deeply. "I be leavin' now. Enjoy yerselves."

"Wait." Now that she and Orion were reunited, there was only one thing left to ask. "The Crown Prince promised to take me home. Would someone be able to get him a message? To let him know that Orion and I are ready to go?"

Perseus looked at her quizzically. "Aye. That be possible."

"Could I ride Orion while I wait for him to arrive?"

"Only in the pasture. Ye'd be run over by the arena." Perseus nodded in that direction and ambled down the path before entering another stall. "There be a stand of trees at the far end of the pasture. Might get ye a bit of water and rest there."

Having her horse was another step closer to going home. Except a niggling sense of unanswered questions whispered beneath her decision to leave as she rode through the pasture. Still, even if the Stones beckoned her with mysterious warmth, they weren't enough to overpower a wall filled with venomous snakes. If the temple had defined her mother, it held greater horror than she'd imagined.

She'd finally recognized the truth. Coming to Akkad was a bad idea. She'd run from the very ones she loved to a place where children weren't even free to play outside. It had been weeks since she'd ridden past her mountain home. Surely, her family was safe now. The army that pursued her had left to search another area. Maybe even Akkad. That thought only confirmed that she needed to leave quickly.

After all, there were only two things that kept her here. A man who drew her like a fire on a winter's day and questions about a mother she already knew she abhorred. Neither was enough to make her want to do anything but flee this city as quickly as she'd run from the temple that morning.

Orion cantered through the pasture, ecstatic to be free. Aless felt the same way. They rode at a relaxed pace, stopping from time to time to let Orion graze on grass so scarce in this desert land. Alessandra peered around to get her bearings.

A road stretched out directly from the arena. Another battalion of war horses prepared to ride out. Stallions bedecked in flowing ribbons pranced and pawed anxious hooves on the dusty ground. Their riders, with faces painted in streaks of black, spoke in hushed tones, holding reins. Although richly colored turbans bounced on their heads, it was clear this was no leisurely ride.

A warrior who looked younger than the rest sat, his lithe body rigid against the saddle. His gaze darted around, as if in nervous anticipation. His horse snorted and pulled at lead. She remembered Tareq and his men when Rufus had charged their horses at the chateau. Only experienced horsemen prevented their steeds from bolting. This was a boy, and he was afraid.

Another warrior came alongside, growled a rough command, and then waited until the young man's horse steadied.

Aless looked around, unsure of what to do until Tareq showed up. Perseus had directed her to a stand of trees on the far side of the pasture. As she and Orion rode in that direction, an unexpected oasis beckoned. Unlike the desert all around, the clearing was surrounded by trees. A gurgling stream flowed on one side and birds trilled overhead. She ducked her head under low hanging branches and took in a breath of delight.

Water sprayed in mighty plumes as three cascading falls plummeted into a deep pool at the base of the cliffs. It was the waterfalls she'd seen with Tareq the first time they'd visited the temple.

A narrow pathway angled down the gorge, near its precipice, beaten flat from many treks up and down the mountain. It wasn't a broad highway, but it was a trail. She'd never seen it, not even as she gazed over the falls. It was a perilous route, although it proved there was a way out of Akkad other than the locked gate.

No one had told her she couldn't leave the city. Still, she'd had no way of escape except through a gate that defied an exit except by mysterious command. Not that she'd need the path anymore. Before long she and Orion would be riding away from Akkad with Tareq, happy to see the rugged cliffs behind them.

After a long drink at the stream, she and Orion headed back to the stables. Tareq would be there soon. She nudged Orion into a trot out of the secluded area and rode into the pasture, keeping her eyes on the perimeter. The arena was quiet and there were no more warriors in sight. Even Akeem and Basir seemed to have disappeared.

A gentle breeze stroked Alessandra's face and her body synced with Orion's rolling gait. It wouldn't be long, and they'd be on the open road, heading home.

The sound of thunderous hooves broke through her reverie. A group of black-clad warriors on massive war horses circled them. Orion reared in fear as Aless struggled to rein her in.

A wave of fear swept over her. Then indignant wrath. She wasn't doing anything wrong. She hadn't broken any protocol. Besides, she was no captive here. Straightening her shoulders, she mustered her strongest voice. "What do you want? I'm exercising my horse."

She studied first one of the warrior's eyes, then another. Each met her with blank stares from beneath the dark turbans. Their arms glistened with sweat, and they held scimitars at their sides, alert, as if ready to attack.

Aless remembered how Heydar betrayed her with the Hall of Justice soldiers. These men weren't guardians. Their eyes glistened as predators. When had she become the prey?

Chapter 16

Aless chilled in the noonday sunlight. She considered dashing through the enclosure of warriors, but they circled tighter, as if reading her thoughts. The war stallions' hooves were fixed in place, tethered by each master's command.

She was being kept at bay by unseen decrees, as well. This contingent proved that other eyes were upon her. And that she'd go nowhere without permission. At least until Tareq appeared to let them know otherwise. Where was he and why hadn't he answered her message?

A dappled stallion and its rider charged from the stables and toward the circle, ruffling the silence. It was Perseus.

The warriors glanced at him, then back to her. Their stallions pranced, then stilled as the men maintained the imperious wall around her.

"Oi! Are ye lost, girlie?" Perseus's voice and demeanor were calm. Peace seemed to interrupt the fierce tension. Speaking a low command, the man dismounted his steed. He walked past the horse's mighty haunches and powerful hooves. When his eyes met Alessandra's, he bowed slightly and grasped the reins from her hands. Then led her mare in a semi-circle and back through the stallions.

Once outside the warriors, he hoisted himself onto his horse with Alessandra at his side. His side whiskers ruffled in a slight breeze as he waited, poised, even regal. His intent was clear. He would not cower. And Aless was in his care.

The warriors stared first at Perseus and then Aless. A brusque order sounded. The dark company pivoted in unison and rode away.

Aless took in a deep shuddering breath. "What was that?"

The next moment, Perseus transformed from princely stature to protective grandfather. He leaned closer to Alessandra and spoke in a hushed, urgent voice. "That would not be yer welcoming committee. Where were you going, child? Leaving this place?"

Aless dropped her head, unsure of what to say. Disappointment surged in her belly. "I was waiting for the Crown Prince. Besides, what if I *was* trying to leave? Surely, I'm free to do so. Did you give Prince Tareq my note?"

"I am not yer servant, Miss." Perseus muttered under his breath. "And I'll not be knocking on anyone's door with a fool's mission."

"I'm no child, if that's what you think," Aless huffed. "The prince assured me of his escort when I was ready to go home. He's a man of his word. I'm sure of that."

"And he'll be leavin' today? At yer mere command?"

Aless felt stupid. Had she really believed Tareq would drop everything and lead her back to the chateau? She was hurt, too. Her gallant friend, Perseus, treated her like a petulant child. "Never mind. I'll talk to him myself."

Perseus only shook his head. He looked on grimly

as they rode back to the stables without another word.

Aless dismounted and handed Orion to a stable boy. She turned her back on Perseus and stomped away like a …well, like a sulky toddler. Still, she'd watched the man walk through the line of stallions without fear to rescue her. He understood the danger of being trampled in that circle. Why was he suddenly irritated at her for leaving Akkad?

Plodding toward the cropland and its laborers, she kept her eyes on the cliffs above, searching for Tareq. Movement near the entrance of the iron gate caught her attention. Black plaited hair bobbed, then disappeared under the bridge just outside the gate. What was Basir doing?

Another figure slipped from a large mesquite bush. It was Akeem.

They were hiding under the bridge.

Aless forced herself to walk at a leisurely pace back to the small oasis where she and Orion had rested. The trail up the gorge looked far less dangerous than the two bodyguards who lay in wait like a couple of trolls. Another proof that she was being watched, or worse, about to be snared.

The shady cover of trees greeted her like a friend. She stared up at the trail, grateful to be waiting for Tareq, instead of scaling its heights. Rustling sounded near a patch of feathery sage. Was it another rattlesnake? Downy feathers floated upward. Something large struggled on the ground, breaking branches, and spraying leaves. Creeping forward to investigate, Alessandra saw an eagle, bound in what looked like fibers of heavy thread.

She backed away. She and Rufus, a puppy then, had

been playing in the meadow years ago. A full-grown eagle had swooped down on Rufus and grabbed him in its huge talons, hoisting him into the air. Aless had screamed and attached herself to the dog's hind legs. She'd never forget the feeling of rising aloft as she yelled. "Let him go!"

Would she fly with Rufus to the top of the eyrie, only to become dinner? Or drop mid-air and plummet to the ground. Finally, the eagle released its hold, and she and Rufus fell into a patch of mulberry bushes that broke their fall. They were bruised, though not broken. And alive.

This eagle flopped vigorously on the forest floor. Alessandra stood back and watched its talons. The mighty beak rose into the air when she took a step closer. Its eyes were like tiny marbles of gold and black as it stared in her direction. She wasn't sure how to help. Still, she took another step forward. Then another. In time, the eagle grew tired of fighting. Aless untied Hildegard's shawl from her waist and dropped it over the bird, which sagged, exhausted, against the brush.

"Shhh. Easy now." Aless crept forward, advancing one careful step at a time.

She dropped to her knees and secured the shawl over the bird, so it wasn't alarmed at her presence. It lay motionless as she searched the undergrowth and found a network of fine rope wound around the eagle's neck and wings in a mass of knots. Where did the rope come from? It was thin, yet strong. Aless worked as carefully and swiftly as she could, but the tangles were hopeless mess of knots.

She backed away for a minute, remembering Suzette and her gift with animals. It was worth a try. She whispered a healing prayer she'd heard from Suzette, then went back to work. In moments, the last filament unwound in her hands and the eagle was free. Removing the shawl, she backed slowly away.

The eagle flapped its wings once and stood. It tottered, then righted itself like a proud statue as it gazed at her in silence. Finally, as if gaining strength, its wings flapped, and it rose from the ground. The eagle flew in a small circle, hovering near the brush. Then, gathered speed and soared away.

Aless waved as the eagle finally disappeared behind the mesa. The sun had begun its afternoon descent. Darkness came quickly on this, the east side of the cliffs. Still, no sign of Tareq. The trail was lit by the sun but wouldn't be for long. She considered a trek up its winding path. At best, it was an arduous climb. At worst, the path was wet and slippery from the spray of the waterfalls.

She waited, fidgeting, and brushing dust from her behind. Then studied the trail more carefully. Finally, she decided. She was used to mountainous footpaths. She'd be back to the top of the mesa in less than an hour.

****

Alessandra stood outside the cave-like dwelling, shifting on first one foot, then the other. Shema had invited her to meet her grandmother, she reminded herself. She was hot, dirty, and tired.

She'd survived the climb, which had taken two hours, instead of one. The ascent up the gorge was equally gorgeous and terrifying. The spray of the falls made the path slick in places. Some turns were so sharp all she could to was drop to her knees and crawl around a bend, praying that a strong wind didn't appear to blow her into the gorge. She'd leaned against the granite wall on the other side of the path, pressing into its solid strength.

Scrambling the final way to the top of the mesa, she collapsed on the ground with exhaustion. After a moment to revel in a broad, sunny expanse, she forced herself upright. That was the last time she'd use that trail.

She'd had plenty of time to think as she scaled the steep path. Her heart had been mystified, at first, with Akkad, a culture so foreign to her own. The warriors who surrounded she and Orion made it clear that she wasn't going anywhere. Perseus had arrived to defend her, and his presence averted anything worse than their unmistakable threat. But he hadn't been able to do anything except take her mare back to the stables.

She'd tell Tareq what happened and remind him of his promise when he arrived that evening. They'd leave as soon as possible. For now, she'd visit Shema's grandmother.

Smoke twirled out of the rooftop of Shema's grandmother's home. Aless took in a deep breath, willing herself to face the unknown, yet again. What could be so scary about an old woman? She'd ask her questions, then return to her room in time for dinner.

The arched door of Bethiah's home was low enough that Alessandra had to bow to enter. She stood outside, hesitating, until a quivering voice sounded from inside.

"Come, me dear. I be waiting for ye."

Startled, Alessandra almost ran in the opposite direction. Instead, she pulled her hands through tangled curls. She could do this.

Sunshine shifted into diffused light as she ducked inside the cave-like dwelling that greeted her into its stillness. Fire bounced from inside an earthen stove, piped for ventilation through the roof. Slats in the ceiling bathed the room in ribbony yellow light.

Fighting away shyness, Aless peered around until she saw a tiny woman sitting in a deep swing back chair woven in tree branches. She looked like a child with her legs swinging from a tree limb, her legs barely touching the earthen floor. That was the end of the similarity. A vibrant shawl covered a humped back and extended almost to brown weathered feet. The woman held a long stick that she stabbed into an oven.

Her bird-like hand motioned Alessandra into the room. Despite what appeared to be a frail body, Bethiah heaved a large piece of driftwood into the fire. A heavenly scent of roses and chamomile filled the room.

Roughly cut timbers were stacked beside the smoldering oven. A narrow table held a disordered array of pottery dishes, sprigs of dried plants and vials of oil. Earthen vases of every size and shape lined shelves along one side of the room.

A narrow pallet rested against the opposite wall, draped in rough burlap. This wasn't only a home. It was also a workshop.

The old woman glanced up with eyes the color of slate sky on a rainy afternoon. She lifted a strand of white hair from her face, as if to study her visitor. Her nose, hooked at the tip, wrinkled, and her burnished face gathered up in a small explosion of joy.

"Oi! It be you. Come, sit by an old woman on this luvely day."

Aless walked deeper into the room, aware that there was only one exit.

Bethiah grasped the arms of her chair, and stood for

a moment, as if finding her balance. Her frame was so tiny and so misshapen, Aless thought perhaps she was a mountain gnome, transplanted by magic to this arid place.

The old woman tottered, jabbing a cane in front of her as she approached the lowest shelf. With surprising deftness, she grasped a small pottery vessel with an ornate pattern etched around its perimeter. Rummaging through the shelves again, she chose two more pottery jars, and placed each one on the table. "Come, child."

Alessandra walked over, aware that she towered over Bethiah. Despite the difference in height, the old woman's presence filled the room as surely as the delightful scents. One fragrance overtook others. It was same aroma Shema used to anoint her for the feast. The one that had transported her to the chateau after a rain, where the undergrowth of fallen pine needles became part of the moist earth.

"I know that scent. Shema used it to prepare me for my first meeting with the chieftain. It reminds me of the mountains where I live."

"Aye. Its name is oud, most precious of all." Bethiah stroked a jar of polished stone. "What brings ye to me home, dear one?"

"I…" Something made Alessandra certain this tiny woman could see through any distraction from the truth. She dove in. "I came to see if you knew a woman named Lilith Gunter."

Bethiah gathered a bunch of dried flowers and placed them beside a wooden bowl and pestle. "And how would I've have known her?"

"I heard she once lived here."

"And this woman. Who may she be?"

Aless hesitated. "She was my mother. I never knew her, though," she hurried to add.

"And your pretty feet be ready to run at the sound of her name?"

"I'm not running."

"Indeed." Bethiah cackled in some unknown amusement. "Hard to believe, but I were a young woman once. Shema, she's me eldest granddaughter. She'll carry on me work after this old body finds its restin' place."

She plopped into her chair with a small groan. "Me lumbago," she muttered, stuffing a wad of her shawl between her lower back and the chairback. She motioned to the chair next to hers. "It'll hold ye. Sit."

Aless studied the tangle of tree limbs called a chair and wondered how she'd get up once she descended. She lowered her behind and held tightly to the arms as she sank with a decided plunk on the hard branches. Struggling to find her composure, she folded and unfolded her hands until finally, she ventured a tentative conversation. "These are interesting pieces of furniture." Although furniture was too strong a word for what felt like balancing on the limb of an oak tree.

Bethiah handed her a bowl of dried figs and pomegranates. "Eat, me dear. You be famished."

When Aless reached for the bowl, she was surprised how heavy it was and how easily Bethiah had held it. She took several figs and placed the bowl on a table next to an ornate goblet full of water. Aless wasn't sure how Bethiah knew she was parched and half-starved. She hadn't had anything to eat or drink since breakfast and her body trembled with fatigue. She ventured a long drink of water, then filled her mouth with the sweetness of a fig.

"Now," Bethiah said, settling herself against the chair and pulling out a clay-tinged handkerchief from her bodice. She spread the square of fabric on her lap and placed the flowers on it. "What be your name?"

"Alessandra." She wouldn't add her last name. Not yet.

"*Defender of the People.* Yer mama named ye well."

"What? No."

"She didn't name ye?" Bethiah's forehead crinkled. "Who did, then?"

"No. I mean. She did name me. But she never...knew me."

"Never?"

Bethiah's questions were so probing, Alessandra squirmed.

The old woman fingered tips of the dried flowers, separating them from their stems, forming a fragrant pile on the dingy fabric. A tear coursed down and filled a crevasse on one cheek. Her face seemed to descend into a weariness that traveled into her frail shoulders. "My job were to care for the little ones."

"Children? You mean when you were young?" Were these an old woman's ramblings? Maybe this conversation wasn't going anywhere, after all. She'd finish the water and fruit, then find a gracious way to escape.

An image of the little girl she'd seen on her first day in Akkad and how quickly she'd been whisked away came to Alessandra's mind. Shema's protective arm around Amira. And the company of girls who attended the cold, beautiful Laila.

"Aye. It were me job." Bethiah studied Alessandra with intent eyes. "When ye tilt your head like that? She did, too."

Aless drew back a little into the chair. "Who?"

"Yer mama."

Alessandra's body stiffened. Surely the old woman was wrong. "That couldn't have been Lilith Gunter."

Bethiah leaned forward, her black eyes flashing. "It were, indeed. I were there when she came up that trail. Black curls, torn purple dress, once so purfect. That one had been loved, fer sure. She spit, stomped that wee foot, and stabbed her finger. The girl had a will like none other. That I knew well. I loved her as me own."

Whoever the child had been, it was clear that Bethiah still grieved her. "Wait. I don't understand why she came as a child." She'd humor this old woman and be on her way as soon as she could. Aless tried to sip the water, but ended up gulping it, instead. Her legs once tired from scaling the mountain cliff, jiggled with nervous energy.

Bethiah pulled yet another tattered handkerchief from inside a sleeve. She wiped her face and blew her nose with loud honk. With a deep sigh, she looked back to Alessandra. "She didn't come to the city. She were taken."

"Lilith Gunter? I thought — she ruled here."

"That is what she became. Not how she began."

Alessandra placed her hand on her chest, willing her heart to settle. There had to be a rational explanation to all this. She wished Shema was there to help interpret.

Bethiah sat quietly, her tiny body tucked into the cavity of the chair.

Aless needed to say what she knew. If only to separate her from the image of a child taken from her home for some unknown reason. Whether it had really been her mother or not. "She did horrendous things. She killed her own family."

Bethiah nodded. "Indeed. The captive became captor."

"No." Aless protested, attempting to keep her tone measured. "She acted on purpose. She planned a massacre of men, women, and children."

Bethiah continued to pluck buds from each flower. She hiccupped once, then spoke again. "Yer hands. They be like hers."

"My hands are like Lilith Gunter's?"

"Aye. Her skin be lighter, but the power in them be the same. Ken I see them? Yer hands?

This conversation had moved from awkward to crazy. Alessandra's belly stirred with more than hunger. Bethiah's words were merely the confusion of an aged mind filled with hazy images of the past. Resentment threatened to spill out. This delusional old woman had no right to insinuate that she had anything in common with Lilith Gunter. There was no way she'd let herself be examined as some kind of nonsensical evidence.

Bethiah sat forward and extended her hands. The scent of honeysuckle in a summer meadow filled the air.

Aless shook her head. She had to leave. Now. She tried to climb out of the twig-woven seat. Yet, her body resisted the command, as if the branches held her tight.

Bethiah's kind gaze didn't waver.

Finally, with a determined burst, Aless hurtled out of the deep chair. She stood, wavering between staying or running without apology from this tiny woman, never to return.

Bethiah took her in, from top to toe. Her dark eyes were like a tiny bird that darted this way and that. "Tis the way ye stand. Yer hair, it be different. Yer eyes, though they be lighter...well, I ken read what your heart is shouting through them."

"I'm not like her."

"Ah." Bethiah patted a low stool at her side. "Come a bit closer."

Reluctantly, Aless approached. A tiny dread whispered through the stillness of the moment.

She and her aged hostess were at eye level when Aless took a seat. It was Bethiah who carried the fragrance of honeysuckle. It emanated from her presence and transformed into a bouquet of wildflowers in the lawn outside the chateau. A small groan escaped Alessandra's lips as longing for home became a flood, threatening to overtake her.

Bethiah reached under her apron and pulled out a finely crafted vessel, inlaid with precious stones. Then opened it. More sweetness, if that was possible, perfumed the room with frankincense, vanilla, and something else she couldn't name. If she'd been a child, she would've pulled her stool even closer, just to be near the refuge of that scent.

The old woman took Alessandra's hands in hers and studied them. Then massaged Aless's dirty, sore fingers with the ointment. It was expensive, lavish — still the woman slathered the oil over Aless's hands and through her fingers, rubbing its fragrance into her skin.

A blanket of warmth caressed first her hands, then journeyed as a healing stream eased over her arms and shoulders, releasing tension she hadn't been aware of in her neck. Even the muscles in her legs and feet relaxed as a swirling breeze kissed her cheeks. Peace Aless had never known followed. Tears flooded her face, dribbled onto her neck as something hard, something tormenting left. Goodness had arrived as a presence.

Aless looked at Bethiah in amazement. "What's happening?"

"Yer hands are receiving the promise they were created to carry. Rest, dear one. Ye've been trying so hard."

"I'm the daughter of a dreadful woman, Bethiah." Aless whispered.

"She did awful things, to be sure. What you've received from her isn't that part, though."

"How could she have anything else to offer?"

Bethiah placed her gnarly hand under Alessandra's chin. "Ye will see. Someday, ye'll understand." Tenderness softened deeply etched lines around her eyes, though her voice remained resolute. "You came with one mission, but anuther calling beckons. Look to the Stones, surrounded they be by evil, yet still untouched. They speak."

"I read a message this morning but didn't understand it. Tareq seemed afraid of them." Was Bethiah an interpreter of Akkad's mysteries? Or only an observer.

"And so he should. Be afeared, that is. The Stones carry a power greater than the temple. One he ken't understand. Tis easy to fear what is not understood. Especially in that place."

"There were snakes in the walls. The two stones got brighter as I held them, and I noticed what I hadn't seen before. The serpents seemed to be held back in some way by the Stones. At least when I held them."

Bethiah nodded. "And so, they always will. Especially in yer hands."

The aroma around them continued to comfort her. "I tried to go home today. Orion and I were waiting for the Crown Prince when warriors stopped us. I only came to visit. Surely, I'm not a captive. I haven't done anything to threaten this city."

"Not in a way ye know, perhaps. But threaten it, ye do." Bethiah placed the ointment on a table at her side, then returned her gaze to Alessandra. "What did ye come to discover about yer mother. Don't ye know her?" Bethiah spoke simply, as if this was a puzzle designed for a child and easily solved.

"Of course not."

"She knew you."

"No. She sent me away." Tears rushed to her eyes. Something about the woman's presence stirred emotions Aless had tried to bury. When she spoke again, her voice trembled. "Even my memories are blurred, there were so few."

When Bethiah reached for her hands, Aless felt another surge of peace despite the questions that persisted in her mind. Would she affirm the injustice of her mother's deeds? Of her abandonment?

"Yes," Bethiah said. "Her did send ye away. That I know. Away from the evil of this city. And what controlled her."

Panic rose in Alessandra, returning to overtake the sweetness she'd felt. She pulled her hands from the old woman's grasp. "She was strong. No one made her do what she did."

"Aye, yet the stoutest webs begin with only a strand."

"A thread that can easily be broken."

"If ye knew it were a web forming."

Alessandra's breathing became quick and shallow. Fury spilled out in her words. "You think it wasn't her fault. That her choices had nothing to do with the ogre she became."

"Choices always matter. If ye recognize when they appear, that is."

"Oh, so that's it. She didn't see any options. That excuses her behavior, of course." Aless didn't try to hide the bitterness in her voice.

"She didn't see no escape from them. Until the web were complete." Bethiah held both hands to her chest, as if she embraced Alessandra. "A voice calls from the Stones. Perhaps yer mother heard it, too."

"She sold herself to the same horror I felt in that dark temple. I don't want...I can't be..."

"Can't be like her?"

Alessandra jabbed a finger at Bethiah and shouted. "Do you hear me? She rises even from the dead to defile me. I won't let her. I won't."

Chapter 17

Entering the sanctuary of her room, Alessandra walked to the ledge and peered out over the vista of blue sky and mountains. Her breathing was ragged, and weeping trailed in a sticky flow over her dusty cheeks. One thing she knew. No matter how deep her mother's own pain, nothing would restore the lives she'd taken.

She'd journeyed with Tareq to a city she'd never known existed. He'd become so much more than a stranger. He'd protected her along the way, first from the soldiers in Sanctuary and then against Heydar's attack. Still, Tareq wasn't the reason she was here. Her determination to separate herself from the real Lilith Gunter had led her. She was too tired to fight images that filled her mind, though. Why had her mother been taken to Akkad, away from a family who loved her?

That night, Alessandra dreamed. Mountain air brushed her skin as she picked her way through underbrush up a steep hill. Muscles in her legs strained as she climbed, scaling rock, and struggling to make progress. The roar of a mighty river overflowing its banks and rushing over giant boulders came from hundreds of feet below. When a broad meadow beckoned ahead, Aless ran toward it. Grass tickled her feet, rustling as if by an unseen breeze. When she looked down, the grass became vines that inched up around her ankles.

She yanked her feet away, but the leafy vise only grew faster. It climbed her legs and around her hips. Hurtling her body forward, she strained to reach a nearby elm tree. If only she could scale its broad trunk. Instead of reaching the tree, she fell headlong onto the ground, where vines wrapped her chest, arm, and hands, until finally, dense foliage encased her.

She woke up, flailing, throwing covers and gasping for breath. Holding knees to her chest, she rocked back and forth. Her cousin, Maura, had held her after a nightmare when she was little, crooning songs of the Magi until she fell back asleep. Maura believed dreams carried a message. And Alessandra couldn't miss her more.

All night, she twisted and turned against the lush cushions. Finally, as darkness shifted into dawn, she put on her clothes, slipped on the sandals, and went for a walk across the mesa.

The temple rose as a black shadow, reflected in the dim light of an ashen sky. She refused to go back. Not after seeing the snakes, and knowing that they were there for a reason, restrained by a power she didn't understand.

Bethiah's words wedged deeply in a wound she'd hoped had disappeared in her quest. Would the Stones reveal another message? One that she needed now.

A faint echo of voices sounded from behind the temple. As Alessandra approached, she realized it was coming from the trail. Harsh commands and the slash of whips were nearing the mesa. Aless hid in an open crevasse, trying to discern commands from a language she didn't recognize grow louder

Torch light bobbed up the winding path. A man with scraggly black beard led the way, turning from time to time to lash his whip into the air at a small group huddled against each other, trudging up the steep ascent. A little girl stumbled, blonde curls damp against her face.

An older girl scurried from behind and caught the child's arm as she wobbled from side to side. With a swoop of her arms, the older one lifted the little girl and carried her. She held her in a tight embrace as a man, tattooed from the top of his head to the tips of his fingers, growled a low command and pushed them forward.

Children, some alone, others in twos and threes were tethered in fine rope, like the one that had bound the young eagle Aless freed. They trudged up the final ascent to the mesa, led by the black-bearded man. The tattooed man herded the last group onto the flat ground, while a stumpy man brought up the rear of the trembling crowd. One of the young girls tripped. She whimpered in pain when the tattooed man slashed his whip against her back, tearing the back of her gown.

Alessandra charged out into the open. For a moment, no one spoke. Suddenly, a brown-haired sprite broke free from the crowd and ran to Aless. She grabbed Alessandra around the knees and clung with tiny hands.

When the black-bearded man came after the child, Aless hugged her more closely. "Stop. You can't have her."

The trader smirked as he lifted his whip in one hand. "Be off with ye. Unless ye want the sting of my lash."

"What are you doing with these children?"

His lips curled in a snaggle-toothed jeer. "And I should explain to you?"

The two other slave drivers added their jeers. They surrounded her, separating her from the child, mocking her, tossing her back and forth with groping hands. She fought, scratched, kicked, still, they overpowered her and threw her to the ground.

"I'll teach ye a thing or two," one of the men leered. He grabbed her hair and yanked her toward his gaping mouth. Putrid sweat filled her nostrils, and the man's weight pressed against her chest. "Help me." Alessandra screamed before a calloused hand covered her mouth.

Screeching pierced the air over head. The slave drivers looked up into the rosy dawn of a desert sky. An eagle soared, then dove into the mob. Another, then another eagle rose from unseen aeries. They attacked the men, slashing with ragged talons, beating with massive wings. First one, then another eagle severed ropes that bound the children with one swipe of their mighty beaks.

The men lashed their whips at the eagles, only diverting them long enough to launch another attack with the men as their prey.

Aless shouted to one of the older girls. "Take the little ones. Go. Quickly." She crawled up to the edge of the mesa where she could watch the children's flight down the gorge. The oldest girls led the smallest ones down the steep descent, carefully weaving their way to freedom. What would they do when they reached the bottom? Would they be able to escape in the same vehicle that had brought them here?

Voices boomed and feathered headdresses of palace guards bobbed as they charged toward Alessandra. She rose to her knees, prepared to ward off an attack she had no strength for. The warriors split ranks as they reached her and headed toward the trail. Moments later, the traders were bound and driven into a single line onto the mesa at spearpoint. They disappeared into a back entrance of the glittering palace.

A familiar voice called. It was Shema, running across the mesa. She grabbed Aless into a strong embrace. "Come with me," she said. Supporting Alessandra with one arm, the young woman led her through the corridor of the small palace to the open-air apartment. She helped Aless slump onto her bed.

"What happened?" Aless asked, forcing herself to speak.

Shema touched her shoulder lightly and whispered a familiar blessing. "May the Lord be with you and with your spirit, from now and forever." She placed a pinch of white power into a pottery cup and filled it with water. "You saw something you weren't supposed to see."

Aless welcomed the drink against her parched throat. She felt like a sick child, cared for by her mother. That image would've brought comfort to many. But not to her. Instead, heartache groaned along with the pain in her body.

Shema helped Alessandra lie down on the cushions and covered her with a light wrap. She reached for two of the aromatic oils. The first smelled of lemongrass, fresh, soothing. The other opened to a fragrance of sweet almonds. Shema wiped away blood from a wound on her cheek. The aroma of the oils grazed the room, reminding Aless of Shema's presence, quiet, but pervasive against the stench of all she'd witnessed that morning.

She longed for Rory, for her family, for home.

First running feet, then shouting sounded outside her room. Tareq rushed into the room, filling it with his authority. "Leave us," he said to Shema. With a gentle touch, he examined the wound on her face. His eyes were dark, and hands shook. "Who did this?"

Suddenly, she was afraid. She looked at him as she

had the palace guards. Was he for or against her? She'd find out. "Young girls were forced into a procession up the mountain. Slave drivers herded them, lashing them with whips." The simple fact of what she'd witnessed filled her with fresh grief. And anger. "Why?"

The look on Tareq's face was ominous. He left the room without a word.

No time to ask about her capture in the pasture, Tareq hadn't stayed long enough to help her sort out yet another terrorizing event in the desert city. Her body hurt, though not as deeply as her heart. With a deep sigh, she closed her eyes and fell sound asleep.

Aless woke with a start and looked outside, disoriented. What time was it? The imprint of rocks pressed into her back reminded her of the man's body pressed against her own. Falling back into the cushions for a moment, she struggled to clear her muddled mind. There were children alone on the road somewhere. Unless they'd been captured by Akeem and Basir at the stables. She couldn't stand that thought. She had to make sure they'd escaped safely.

The oils Shema applied had healing properties. The bleeding had stopped, and her wounds no longer felt like swollen gashes. Grabbing Hildegard's shawl, she moaned as she stood and walked outside. Afternoon heat shifted into an evening breeze. Laborers returned through the ancient gate from their day's work carrying hoes and packs as they trudged up the gravel road.

Ever-present masked guards stood outside the palace as certain reminders that no one entered the sanctum of Dhamar Ghalib without their approval. A few white-robed servants scurried around, carrying platters of food and earthen vases, and placing them outside the palace entrance. Each one made hurried bows as she walked by.

Aless paused as she approached the temple. How could a building crafted by human hands evoke such terror? She made a wide berth around it, picking her way over desert grasses and keeping her eye out for snakes. The rush of waterfalls sounded ahead. Memories from that morning rushed in like an unwelcome flood. She couldn't do it. Couldn't take a step closer to the pathway.

The image of the determined face of an older girl hovering over a little one reminded her that she had no choice. She needed a closer look beyond the falls. Picking her way across native grasses she approached a craggy live oak whose branches angled like a fishing pole over the gorge. Holding onto its trunk, she looked down through the cascading waters. Vultures no longer circled overhead. Gravel shifted under her feet as she took a step toward an open area overlooking the falls. Crying out, she grabbed a sticky mesquite bush as she landed on her behind.

The stand of trees beyond the gurgling pool came into view and beyond it, the river. It wasn't a beautiful one like the rushing streams near the chateau, though it was usually clear. Now, the flow was streaked with red, as if clay trickled downstream. Vultures swooped nearby.

Alessandra shuddered in late afternoon heat. There was danger she couldn't see, even in broad daylight. Maybe it was a lurking slave trader, angry with her intervention. Songbirds no longer trilled back and forth through the trees. Something hung from the branch of a Pinion tree where she and Orion had rested when she'd first discovered the path up the gorge. A trail of red flowed from one branch, then joined a crimson stream from another tree, then another, meandered into the river.

She gasped and covered her eyes. Then uncovered them. A body dangled by the neck from a branch of a sprawling live oak. Blood flowed out of a gash in its belly. Another body hung from a higher branch, while one more swung in a ghastly breeze next to it. Three men, each with head snapped, hung as rivulets of blood streamed like a network of crimson thread into the river.

Chapter 18

Aless longed to run away but couldn't move. It was the slave drivers who'd attacked her. Three of them, necks broken, chests sliced open and blood dripping out of lifeless bodies. Like Heydar, vengeance in her behalf was swift and brutal.

She scrambled up an incline until her feet met the flat mesa. Then she ran, frantic and unthinking, dodging a servant who carried a platter of dried lamb and cheese. Back in her room, she dropped into the silken pillows and burrowed deeply inside their softness. If only she could hide. Better yet, be transported out of this hellhole of a desert city back to the home she loved.

A layered scent of woods and aromatic spices signaled Tareq's approach the second time that day. Alessandra sat upright. Akeem and Basir stood behind the Crown Prince, stone-faced. Had they been the executioners? Once again?

Tareq saw her eyes trained on the two warriors. "Leave us," he said. He sat, then reached out to her.

Pulling away from his touch, Alessandra tried to read Tareq's eyes. And her own heart. A vast expanse separated them, vying against the closeness she'd once felt. She hesitated, then spoke what they both already knew. "I went to see Orion today. I…I saw the men who attacked me. Hanging from the trees."

"I would've come sooner if I'd known."

"You…commanded their deaths?"

"Of course." He looked surprised, as if he wondered what else she expected.

"Why were little girls brought into Akkad?"

Tareq took a deep breath. He glanced away, then studied his hands.

"They were children. Herded captive into Akkad." Aless struggled to keep from shouting. She leaned toward him. "I have to know."

"They're here to be educated in temple worship." Tareq spoke in a careful, measured tone.

"In that horrible place?" She shook her head to erase an image of little ones peering up at venomous snakes that writhed inside temple walls. The brutal traders' presence uncovered a hidden reality. Children were taken as slaves to Akkad for some awful purpose. And Tareq seemed confused by her disgust.

"It is a century-old custom. You wouldn't understand."

She was sickened by truth she finally understood. She'd never known the prince. She'd followed an attractive stranger to an exotic land for what? Adventure in the guise of an ill-fated quest. Her heart was as far from Tareq's as home was from Akkad. Her voice filled the small room with outrage. "What is there to understand about enslaving children? What if one of them was your daughter?"

"My daughter would never…How can I explain this?" Tareq brought a hand to his forehead, as if he struggled to explain the incomprehensible. "Is it wrong? Yes. Trust me that we're growing beyond what has defined us in the past."

"Pretty words considering what I saw this morning.

Not enough, Tareq." Akkad's wickedness was like a cesspool bubbling to the surface. "You can change this. You promised to defend me after Heydar's attack. You'd make sure I was safe in Akkad. If you can do that for me, why not for these children?"

"I've done my best to honor my word, Alessandra. Those men hurt you. I understand that. I made sure it never happened again."

Aless sighed. "We aren't talking about me. This is about the children."

Tareq knelt on the plush carpet at her feet. "Remember our first time at the temple? The *Light of the Stars* responded to you alone. Perhaps your gift is to stand by my side, so that together we see Akkad come into a new day."

Had he said he loved her? "That's not why I came."

Tareq reached for her hand. "A mission led you to an unexpected path. One that must be obeyed for the sake of others. Your gift is far too great a calling to be hidden away in a mountain chateau. Your mother carried it well. Perhaps that is why an army seeks you.

"No!" Aless jerked away from his warm touch. She rose from the cushions and faced the prince with fire in her eyes. "I hate the temple. I despise the terror I saw in the children's eyes. And worse, the knowledge that they're taken captive from their families for some kind of perverse demon worship." She made a wide sweep of her arm outside. "All of this. The glittering palace, trappings of riches and honor. They're only a facade. There aren't enough jewel-encrusted bracelets weighing the chieftain's arms that can hide the truth. Children are captured like livestock. And you speak of mission?" Alessandra's exhausted body trembled with outrage.

"My home valued the gifting each child carried. Unlike Akkad that uses them. You speak of service to Gad El Glas. Service to a demon god, or to yourself?"

Tareq stood but kept his distance. His voice became an appeal. "The girls are orphans. They find family here. And are given an opportunity to minister in the temple, an honor sought after by many."

"What about this life would a child seek? To work in a temple with walls filled with serpents. You can't justify any part of this."

His chest rose as if expanded by something deep in his core. His shoulders squared and what looked like a shadow of rage glazed his eyes.

She'd seen those dark eyes grow even darker before, but they'd never been directed at her. Who was the real Tareq? Perhaps under that gleaming exterior, he, too, covered a heart that demanded what it wanted. No matter what stood in his way. No matter what it cost others.

In the next moment, his stance softened, and his words were calm and deliberate. "You came here, willingly. Did I force you?"

"Of course, I came voluntarily. Again, we aren't talking about me. Besides, you said I was free to go home. That you'd take me." Even though there was no way she could leave now, knowing what she did about the children.

"You came with a quest." His words were urgent, strong. "Perhaps the real one is an opportunity to shift a culture. Stay, Alessandra. Change it with me."

"What are you asking?"

Tareq knelt and extended one hand. "Marry me." He pressed his lips to her hand lightly. "My mother's last words were to watch for one who carried compassion like a garment. For a woman who had the capacity to rule beside me for a new future. You are the one I've sought, Alessandra Gunter."

Aless searched his face, his eyes, his stance. "I barely know you," she protested. "Or your culture." She remembered Laila's dance that first night. "Besides…there's something between you and Laila."

Tareq stood and drew her into his arms. He held her chin in one hand and his lips curled into a tiny smile.

She pushed his hand away. "I'm not a child. Nor am I blind. I saw her touch you…and how you reacted."

Tareq buried his head into her hair and spoke softly into her ear. "Alessandra."

Something about her name in his voice melted barriers inside, even the ones that shouted, *Step away*.

His grasp around her back tightened. His heart beat warm against her aching body. "I know you aren't a child. Believe me. We've felt the same desire. One assignment drew you here, but another beckons." Releasing her from his embrace, he looked into her eyes. "This city needs you. I need you."

Her mind raced with questions, though she longed to melt into the shelter of his arms. Neither part of her wanted to concede. Finally, she forced herself to speak what she knew. "I…can't."

Tareq studied her face silently. He brushed a strand of hair from her eyes. Then spoke with confident strength. "Come with me into the place you were born for." He stroked her hair and kissed her gently on the forehead.

Her resolve melted as he held her, as if she were a gift easily broken.

His arms caressed her waist. His lips pressed lightly

against one cheek. He stopped at her lips and whispered, "I want you, Alessandra. By my side."

Her fingers swept across his muscular back. She remembered a snippet of her dream as she ran to escape vines that grew up around her feet. When she looked up, Tareq's eyes were full of passion. Was it love that lay behind those dark eyes?

Chapter 19

Alessandra's mind whirled with Tareq's words that night as she fell into an exhausted lump on her bed. The man she'd called friend acted as though herding children as slaves into Akkad was a normal event. And so much as said that orphans being forced to serve in vile temple worship were somehow welcomed into a family. It was absurd on too many levels to believe from a man who'd just asked her to marry him.

His cure for this victimizing culture was to propose marriage on the basis of words from his mother, long dead and gone. What did carrying compassion as a garment mean, anyway? The prince had brutally avenged her once on the way to Akkad and today with the slave drivers. People were afraid in this desert city. It wasn't because Tareq was a benevolent ruler.

The electricity she felt at his touch was tangible. But not enough. His declaration was more like a business proposition than a vow to cherish forever. No promise of undying love. Only, *I want you by my side.*

Her body hurt. The gashes were healed, but the terror of the assault lingered. Sleep that night had been a fleeting moment. Her only comfort as she tossed against silken pillows was memories of everyday routines at the chateau, ones she once felt confined by.

Like parceling out cookies with a fresh pitcher of milk in hand to hungry children. Maura's voice above a child's cry and joy in Aiden's eyes as he called each horse by name. Lucy constantly underfoot, with her funny lisp and sassy disposition. And Rory, teasing a smile from her when she was angry.

She missed Rory, more with every day. She remembered her jab the night before she'd fled the chateau when she'd reminded him that he was a lowly teacher, not warrior. How blind she'd been.

Shema ducked her head inside her room and handed Aless a tiny leather pouch. Then she busied herself preparing a tray of breakfast, with figs, goat cheese and naan.

As Aless studied the pouch, a note scribbled on parchment fell into her hands. It was written in a familiar scrawl. She'd teased Rory mercilessly for years. How could one who read everything with print in the towering chateau library write like a toddler?

Rory. Her heart trembled as she read.

My eyes have been on you, Aless. Me, your pesky friend who beat you fair and square in every math contest, most spelling bees, sprints in the meadow, and climbs in our favorite sycamore.

To say nothing of other irritating qualities that stir your dander even now. How else would you know it was me?

Warmth overtook the chill she'd felt creeping over her since early that morning.

I have news of the chateau.

Alessandra's breathing morphed into a short gasp.

An adversary threatens on every front. Don't be deceived. The enemy's stronghold may be lined with eagle's down, but there are nettles inside. Be careful. Find the Stones and let them speak.

Yes. You can. I know you can.

Rory

Had he seen the eagles that had saved her that morning? She turned to Shema. "Did you see him?" She longed for a glimpse of his face, even if it was through someone else's eyes.

"Only the note tucked into my pack of oils."

"Why wouldn't he show himself? To me?"

"A wrong move jeopardizes the lives of many." Shema caught Alessandra's gaze and spoke, as if from memory. "Though an enemy builds its shelters on high and sets its nests among the stars, she who carries the light of stars will find and bring them down."

"You know the prophecy?"

"You may be the one called to carry that light, but you're not the only one who anticipates it," she answered simply. "These cliffs represent the very heart of Gad El Glas. The slavery, the treatment of children — all evidence of its wickedness multiplying even as we speak throughout Magi territory. Their assignment is no longer to enslave. It is to annihilate."

Shema kept her eyes trained on Alessandra. "What really brought you here? Your own will or the prophecy."

"I came to find out about my mother."

"And have learned so much more." Shema sat quietly beside her. "You were brought here on purpose, by those who know what you carry better than you do. You are lusted after, only not for your beauty alone. The gift you possess is the greatest treasure."

"I've never been aware of any gifts," Alessandra said, interrupting. "Only that I must separate myself from my mother. Hers was a legacy, all right. A despicable one. Other parents left glistening inheritances, while mine left devastation."

"Your mother came into Akkad as a child and as a slave."

"She massacred her family."

"Gad El Glas required utmost loyalty and obedience for the promise of power. It was all she had. What if the facts reveal a different reality? One that unravels your hatred?"

"She was a monster."

"I won't disagree. Though you don't know what she suffered in the temple." Shema took Alessandra's hands into her own and studied them, much like Bethiah had. "Has no one told you about your hands?"

"Your grandmother slathered on an ointment. I felt peace. Things I couldn't name."

"What you felt was a calling affirmed." The young woman paused, then spoke in careful, measured words. "There's something you need to know. An event is on the horizon. When Dhamar Ghalib dies, an immediate succession will take place in the temple. That ceremony begins with a human sacrifice."

"No. Why?" Never had a question required such dreadful revelation.

"Warriors dressed in black, who look like death itself, appear without warning. They'll herd everyone in the city into a procession up the mountain. When you see that happen, you must hide. Don't try to intervene."

"I don't understand."

"Gad El Glas requires blood. Your mother knew that."

A wave of nausea rushed from Alessandra's belly to her throat. She rushed outside and sprawled on the ledge.

She lay there for a moment, taking deep breaths and wishing she didn't know the very facts she'd come to discover. What kept hope alive that there was a shred of goodness in Lilith Gunter, when it was obvious there was none?

Shema helped Aless back into the coolness of her room and offered a sip of water. The two women sat, silently, on the cushions of the bed. Finally, Shema continued speaking with quiet intensity. "The sacrifice signals more than succession. It anticipates a transference of power — a multiplied one. That shift of power requires blood. A Magi's life will be sacrificed to honor the succession of Crown Prince Tareq into power."

"Magi — I didn't know there were any here."

Shema studied her. "My mother was sacrificed when I was a child. Dhamar Ghalib sought added power from Gad El Glas. His lineage is soaked with Magi blood."

"Shema. No."

"Gad El Glas lusts after the art of anointing oils. Only their fragrance can disguise its stink. The chieftain knows every lineage in Akkad. There are no secrets. Despite how we've hidden our children, he knows our treasures. And covets them."

"How could you live here?"

"We didn't choose Akkad. We were brought here."

"Why haven't you told me about these things before?"

"Living in Akkad is like being caught in a spider's web. When a network of strands is broken, new ones replace them. A cunning foe has crafted an unseen snare and you are its prey. That's why I'm telling you about the sacrifice. You can't stop it. You must hide." Shema was quiet for a moment. "Until then, go to the Stones of Promise. You alone can read them."

"I've been there. I can't go back. Even for a new message."

Ignoring Alessandra's protest, Shema responded with a gentle command. "Read them with your heart. You need their wisdom. We all do." She went to the ornately carved dresser at the back of the room and pulled out the midnight blue gown Aless wore her first evening in Akkad. "You're summoned to a private meeting with Dhamar Ghalib. The Crown Prince will be here soon. Remember the spider's web." Without another word, Shema turned and left.

A meeting in the morning? She'd never seen the chieftain except during one of the many feasts. Alessandra struggled to untangle the mystery of Shema's words as she dressed in the shimmering gown, then arranged her hair with trembling hands into a simple braid. *Soaked in Magi blood* echoed over and over. She couldn't pretend she hadn't heard. Shema's own mother had been sacrificed. The chieftain was very much alive and very much in power.

Memory of the day before rushed back. Fear in little ones' eyes. Older children holding younger ones in protective embrace, taking the lash of whips against their own tender backs. The filthy stench of a man's body pounding against hers. Grit of dusty clay in her mouth, gagging and choking her parched throat.

She remembered the little girl who had peeked out her first time on the mesa. And the girls who attended Laila at the lavish pool. Had they been brought up the same narrow trail with brutal slave drivers herding them like cattle? She had to find out.

What did that mean for a meeting with the chieftain today? Shema's warning about the spider's web frightened her. Swallowing dread, she bent to tie on leather sandals. She lifted her head when the Crown Prince appeared at the doorway.

Tareq bowed. "Alessandra, mon amour."

Aless curtsied, as if this were a formal meeting. "Come in." She stood inside and motioned to a pair of simple chairs. "I need to ask a question before we leave."

Something about his usual composure seemed forced. Tareq shifted from one leg to another.

"It won't take long. I promise," she said. Their meeting with the chieftain could be urgent. Still, only he could answer the questions that gave her no rest.

Tareq glanced at her, then to the ground, as if he'd rather be any other place. Very different than the night before when he'd embraced her with passion in his eyes. Now, a sea of something she couldn't define spanned between them.

Aless took a seat, ignored the distance, and jumped into the unknown. "I need to know about your god."

Tareq peered outside, as if looking for an exit. "Why?"

"By knowing my mother's god, I'll know her."

Tareq sat down, fidgeting his long legs first one way, then another. "It's an ancient religion," he began, speaking deliberately. "I don't believe in its so-called power, although its worship is central to our culture." His jaw tightened and fingers pressed into silken trousers. "A way to keep people compliant."

"And you worship this god?"

"It disgusts me. Fear is an effective control,

however." His face shifted into a look of deep sadness. "Again, I'm heir to this kingdom. It will, it must change." With that, he stood and held his hand out to Aless. "Our presence is required."

Chapter 20

They walked across the broad mesa, this time without Akeem or Basir following close behind. Brilliant morning light washed the plateau, signaling blazing heat that afternoon. Already, sweat ran down her back and the braid felt sticky against her neck. She summoned whatever strength she could find. Even though she had no idea what she faced in this meeting, she was determined to stand. If not for herself, for Shema, her mother, and the children.

Tareq's hand lightly grazed her elbow as they proceeded through a line of guards on both sides of the palace entrance. Feathered headdresses bobbed in respect as they walked into the palace. Coughing and muttered words sounded, and light dimmed in a narrow corridor that led to an opulent, yet hidden room obscured by the smoky haze of incense. Panther-garbed warriors guarded the chieftain who sat on a gilded throne, surrounded by rich fabrics and cushions.

A woman dressed in filmy black silk leaned over Dhamar Ghalib and offered him drink from a silver chalice. The etching of the serpent peeked through a slit in her gown.

Aless fought off a wave of alarm. Laila was only a woman, yet her presence shifted every atmosphere she entered. Aless fought the impulse to bolt out of this dank inner chamber.

Laila bowed languidly to Tareq with a slight smile. "My prince."

Seething rage grazed Tareq's face. At first, Aless thought she'd imagined it until his stance tightened. One hand clenched, then released at his side.

Laila's eyes sparked in a gaze that never left Tareq. She studied him, as if sizing up prey.

The spider web. Aless inched closer to Tareq with a sudden desire to protect him.

The aging ruler gazed up at the prince and placed one hand on his chest. "Only a moment, my son. Only a moment."

Tareq stood, unmoving. Then, he turned, and walked away.

Aless wanted to cry out, *Don't leave me*, but he was out of sight before she could beg him not to go. A wave of terror rose in her belly.

"Alessandra. Sit." The chieftain's words were a plea, instead of a demand. He motioned her to a cushion near his feet. "You have unanswered questions. About your mother."

A heavy, sodden odor battered her senses, as Aless sat beside the fierce tribal chieftain. Oily clay covered pock-marked jowls and settled into deep creases around his mouth. A jagged scar ran down one side of his neck and extended inside the silken robe.

He looked tired. And old. And sick.

How many cultures had he conquered? How many lives had been cut short at his command? She didn't have to wonder about one thing. She'd seen the children. And knew what Shema had said about his lineage.

Only Laila attended the chieftain, and her eyes were upon him alone. She didn't acknowledge Alessandra's presence in any way.

Aless searched the perimeter of the room. She half-expected to find herself bound in sticky threads as the kohl-lined eyes of a spider anticipated its meal. She jerked to attention as the chieftain's words broke the silence.

"I no longer believe I will live forever." The chieftain straightened his back against the pillows with a small groan. "At least not here, on this earth. The day will come when Tareq must walk in the fullness of his calling. Without me." The old man stopped for a moment and cleared his throat. His face twisted into a grimace that looked like a mix of pain and sadness. "My son was forced to face difficult things. Circumstances that, looking back, formed him. I don't want him alone. Promise me that you will reign, at his side." He cleared his throat, then coughed in spasms that shook his body.

He took a drink from Laila's hand, then lifted his head with a piercing look at Alessandra. "Tareq offers you a gift. Take it."

Laila's face became a careful mask as she wiped the chieftain's forehead and chin with a patch of lamb's wool.

This was no invitation. Tareq had talked to his father. It was time to know what really filled the old barbarian's heart. After all, he ruled Akkad. He knew about the children taken into the city. What other atrocities did his polite deference hide?

"I saw children taken as slaves into your city." Aless kept her gaze on the old chieftain, alert to Laila, who hovered beside him. "You and my mother traded in Sanctuary. What merchandise did you seek?"

A stench of rotting garbage filled the air and the

chieftain's visage changed. A thin crimson stream dribbled into a craggy chin. "Our transactions were varied. But all enriched by the world's most valuable resource."

Aless stared at him, refusing to flinch. No wonder Dhamar Ghalib coveted the art of anointing. Any personal warmth was like a perfume applied to cover a foul odor. He was a cruel barbarian. No less. "I know that treasure," she said. "You deal in children."

Dhamar Ghalib's watery black eyes held Alessandra's gaze. "Of course. Magi children."

Her family. The little ones she loved. Mere targets of a dark force that valued their gifting and spurned their freedom. Like the little girls she'd seen serving Laila. There was no regard for a destiny outside of service to a demon god, or more likely, to their own lusts. Although she'd come for another reason, what she'd discovered couldn't be tucked out of sight. The lid had lifted and decay inside spilled out, polluting everything around it.

She'd landed in the middle of her enemy's den. And was captive, not visitor, as she'd so innocently believed. No wonder she was anxious. There was much to fear. "Was my mother brought here against her will?"

The chieftain's obsequious veneer disappeared. "Hmph. What do children know? We gave her life. No less. She became what others longed to be."

"A witch?"

The chieftain drew his head back and chortled so hard an earring flopped from a sagging earlobe. "A woman who knew her dominion. And carried it well."

"She was already a gifted child. She was Magi."

The ruler's chest rose, then fell. He snarled like a wolf interrupted from its meal. "A pox on Magi. This is power you've never witnessed. The very supremacy my son invites you into."

Laila rubbed the chieftain's shoulders. Her languid hand floated down one shoulder and onto his chest.

Dhamar Ghalib straightened at her touch, as if it energized him in some way.

Aless felt her courage slip. Then took a deep breath. She couldn't wait to feel brave. "I'll never…"

"Never accept our god? Possibly not. Though given time you'll learn what they've all come to understand."

Aless grappled her emotions. She had to keep her reason strong to foil the old man's agenda. "What do you mean given time? I'm a visitor in Akkad. What is it that I'll come to understand?"

"You belong here. And here you will stay." The chieftain settled himself back into the cushions with a heavy sigh, as if the discussion had ended.

"No. I will not." Her voice exploded over the silence.

The warriors snapped to attention and in one motion, encircled her with spears extended like spokes in a wheel.

Laila almost laughed out loud. She turned to the chieftain, as if she hoped for swift retribution.

The chieftain seemed unfazed. He waved away the guards, then took a long drink from the goblet.

Aless planted her feet. No one was there to defend her. She'd stand for herself. "I will not stay. Certainly not as a captive." She took a deep breath to steady her nerves.

"Not as a prisoner." The old chieftain modulated his voice to an appeal. "As an invited guest, of course. One who will accomplish your reason for coming."

"I came only to know my mother."

Laila's hands tightened against the chieftain's chest.

The old ruler glanced up at Laila, then placed jewel-laden fingers over hers, as if in unspoken communication. "True. Though, a force stronger than that quest led you."

"I have a home. I must return. I *will* return." Incense filled her nose, trickled down her throat and threatened to strangle her. Aless rubbed her arms with clammy hands. She had to get out of this room.

"What of your calling to free the children?" The chieftain peered at her with a satisfied smile. He hounded her with what he knew, proving she'd been watched by more eyes than Tareq's.

Confusion drifted over her mind as musky incense clouded the air. A deep, numbing fatigue drifted over her being.

"You're one of us, you know. Just like your mother," Dhamar Ghalib said, leaning close. "You were called to worship here, at the side of the Crown Prince."

Laila dropped the chalice she'd offered the old ruler. Blood red liquid soaked her gown and spread out over the tiled floor. Her porcelain skin seemed to pale.

No one moved to clean up the spilled contents. No one spoke.

The chieftain looked to the ground, then to Laila. Was it amusement she saw in his eyes? This time when he spoke, it was to Laila who appeared chiseled in ivory. "She cannot escape her lineage, my dear Laila. She is her mother's daughter and therefore, destined for great things."

Laila spun around and stood for a moment with her back to them. Finally, she lifted another goblet from a tray behind the throne. Her hand hovered over it, only for an instant, then she turned and offered it to Dhamar Ghalib.

The chieftain and Laila had entered a world that didn't include Alessandra. But it did. "I will not...I cannot..." Aless cried out in frustration.

The chieftain crumpled in a flurry of coughing. Laila nodded to two warriors who gathered the slumped old man onto a richly embroidered litter and carried him away through another dark corridor. Laila stood, imperious, in front of the gilded throne. Without a word, she scanned Alessandra from head to toe, as if sizing up a potential foe. Or quarry.

Aless willed herself to speak without trembling. "What do you want?"

Laila's voice was matter of fact. "My servant Heydar failed to carry out his orders. A senseless loss in exchange for one like you."

Memory of the assault in early hours, and the vision of the panther filled Alessandra. "You hired Heydar?"

"Indeed. Still, perhaps he serves as a timely reminder." A chilling breeze wafted as the woman glided past and the same layered scent Heydar had carried lingered.

Laila pointed a long, manicured finger outside the palace. "My beloved calls."

Chapter 21

Aless searched the sky, as if it could somehow speak. It was too cloudy to see any of the constellations that tethered her to home. Pebbles below shifted and a dark form appeared on the trail. Alessandra felt the ground for a rock, anything to throw or pound against an assailant. A lanky form with a familiar lurch in his steps turned into Rory, who stood before her, smiling. He was dressed in black from head to toe like a Nayeli warrior, only without the feathered plumes.

"Rory!"

He scurried up the last stone and rushed to her side.

Aless looked into those firelit eyes that welcomed her home. She fell into his arms already stretched out to her. "What are you doing here? How did you find me?"

"I've been...keeping watch."

"How?"

"I'll explain later. We have to get you out of here." He ventured a small touch on the necklace around her neck.

"Nona gave it to me," Alessandra said, suddenly mortified. "She said it was okay."

"It is. Okay." Rory reached over and placed a strand of her hair behind her ear. "I'm glad you have it."

"The letter...The family. Is everyone all right?"

"I'll give you a full report as soon as we're out of this city."

"I can't leave, Rory. There are children here who were brought in as slaves."

"We can't help them alone. Not without the Stones."

"How? I can't steal them."

"They belong to the Magi. The Nayeli stole and hid them in their temple dedicated to Gad El Glas. We must get them back into our people's hands."

Alessandra shuddered. He didn't know what it meant to go back into that evil place. "I can try." She peered into Rory's face, streaked with fatigue and grime. "Yes. I'll get them."

"Good. I'll bring Orion from the stables to the stand of trees at the base of the waterfalls."

"How will you do that?"

"Friends in unexpected places. I'll meet you at dawn." With that, he was gone.

****

Hours later, it was time to leave. She had to get the Stones, then descend the trail beside the waterfalls in the dark. Impossible one and impossible two. Still, the thought of Rory and going home made anything seem achievable. She gathered her pack and steadied her heart.

A full moon shone overhead, illuminating the dark temple. She imagined opening those metallic doors, grabbing the Stones, and running to the trail along the gorge. She'd stash the Stones in her pocket and descend to the base where Rory waited with Orion. Over and over, she ran through the scenario in her head.

She changed out of silky trousers into her riding clothes and replaced sandals with her boots. The clothes she'd worn at the chateau were stiff and unyielding after the breathable fabrics she enjoyed in Akkad. Clothing that would never survive a rugged journey back home, though. She added naan, cheese, and figs to the other provisions she'd prepared the first time she decided to leave Akkad. Wrapping herself in Hildegard's shawl, she stepped out on the ledge.

The night sky was clear, revealing the constellation Taurus with its fiery red eye, Aldebaran. A cry like an injured animal sounded across the mesa. It wasn't unusual to hear the nocturnal scurry of a small woodrat, or hoot of a barn owl, but this was different.

A long, sorrowful wail sounded, retreated, then sounded again, sending shivers into Aless's body. On the heels of the dirge, a deep, powerful roar ripped through the night as drums began to pound. Boom, boom, boom. Alessandra peered around, trying to figure out what was going on and struggling to find a reference point. Splotches of light stabbed the darkness at the base of the mountain. Torches carried by ghostly figures of white-robed priests moved in a processional up the trail. As they approached, she searched for, but couldn't see Tareq leading their company.

She expected a crowd to gather at doorways of homes along the pathway. No one appeared. Not even a dog barked. Pulling back into the shadows, she held Rory's necklace in one hand, hoping to see the unseen. Nothing appeared.

Another roar sounded, this time louder as many voices joined as one. She pressed her back against the stone wall when a warrior appeared on the path wearing a bear's head, with teeth bared and face etched with war paint. Another followed dressed as a mighty bird of prey, complete with talons and narrow beak that extended over brilliant feathers. More animal-clad men followed, all howling in unison.

Aless couldn't take her eyes from the fierce procession that ascended the path behind the priests, jabbing torches into the air and bellowing, "Dhamar Ghalib, Dhamar Ghalib."

The bizarre parade formed a solitary trail up the mountainside, ascending closer to the mesa. What she saw next took her breath away. A white-washed, skeletal-faced man with a headdress of long black feathers that extended from his head and shoulders pounced onto the path without warning.

A woman screamed as he entered a dwelling and came out with her and a wriggling child in both arms. The mother looked back at the threshold of their home with arms held out in a plea. It was as if death had swooped in for prey.

Another warrior, just as silent and foreboding appeared. Then another. They thrust out men, women, and children, hurling them to the ground. With jagged spears, they prodded the people into single file and marched them up the trail. No one resisted the frightful specters.

It was the very scene Shema had described. A sacrifice at the temple was being held and everyone in the city had to be there. Shema had warned her to hide.

Alessandra glimpsed the shadow of an opening in the rock below she'd noticed the day before. Unlike Amira, she'd had no desire to investigate any place a desert creature might claim as its own. Until now. Aless slid down on her stomach until her foot caught its edge, then kept her hands gripped on the stone above until she could slip into the hole. Her heart pounded in erratic thumps. Only terror of what was going on above the ledge kept her pressing into what could've been a rattler's den or scorpion nest.

Shrill cries and harsh commands sounded in the darkness, but no one had come to her room. She pressed her body farther into the small space, thankful that she was its only inhabitant. Venturing a quick look, she saw people still moving up the mountain, herded by warriors with whips.

Drumbeats traveled to the top of the mesa and torch lights disappeared inside the temple. In moments, the massive shrine was lit like a glowering dragon from within.

An acrid, woody scent filled the air as footsteps sounded overhead. Furniture crashed and plates shattered as whoever it was ransacked her room. Aless fought to breathe evenly and not make a sound, until finally, it was quiet.

When she peeked out again, an aged woman trudged toward Alessandra's room. It was the woman she'd met the first day in Akkad. She carried a lantern and white dress over one arm.

Where was Shema who always prepared her for whatever feast or ceremony she'd been summoned for? Aless shrank deeper into the cavity and waited until the woman's shuffling steps disappeared. Wrapping the shawl around her waist, she grappled her way back up the ledge and looked around.

Her room was wrecked. The table of aromatic oils had been overturned. Broken vessels lined the floor, and a rush of fragrances filled the air. Had Akeem and Basir been looking for something? Or only for her. Cushions from her bed were strewn around the floor. The letter from Rory that she'd tucked underneath them was gone.

A familiar cry sounded in the distance. It was

Shema, struggling against her captors. A warrior slapped her and hoisted her over one broad shoulder. Then carried her up the jagged stairs to the mesa.

Surely, they hadn't taken Shema in Alessandra's place. The very thought caused bile to rise into her throat. She had to stop them. Wrapping the shawl around her waist, she dodged the open path across the mesa. The temple lit with a thousand lights, but no one else appeared on the broad plateau.

There was little shelter. How would she appear unseen? She wound around the pool area and ducked behind a thatch of mesquite when she heard a woman's voice. "Para!"

It was Laila, dressed in a white, shimmering gown and attended by a company of young girls in simple tunics. They, like the warriors with Shema, disappeared into the temple.

Everything was shadows and indistinct sounds. She jumped back as a jack rabbit bounded in front of her. Wrapping Hildegard's shawl around her shoulders, she took a breath and kept climbing. When she finally reached the top, she hid behind a large outcropping of sandstone and studied the mesa. A child and his mother were the last to be herded into the temple. He whimpered against her chest as she shushed him.

Alessandra crept in behind them with the shawl over her head. Inside the temple, the intense chill she'd felt before had turned into a blistering furnace. Drums kept their incessant pounding and the priest's chanting rose. *Dhamar Ghalib, Dhamar Ghalib*. She ducked behind a group huddled together along one side of stone benches. No one even looked at her. Instead, their attention was fixed on what was going on in front of them.

The huge fire pit she'd seen when she and Tareq had first visited the temple blazed with flames that licked the towering ceiling. Aless covered her mouth with the shawl, straining to breathe in stifling heat. She scanned the area first to find Shema. Unable to find her friend, she sought out Laila who appeared as a threat whenever they met. Although she'd only seen the woman in the palace, surely this malicious temple was her home.

Aless looked to the altar for the Stones and saw Tareq dressed in the white priestly regalia. He leaned over a large bier on one side of the altar with a censer, bowing and waving its incense. A body lay there, surrounded with flowers, fruit, and grains. Wiggling in for a closer look, Alessandra swallowed a gasp when she recognized the pock-marked face of the barbarian chieftain.

Dhamar Ghalib was dead.

She'd just seen him. What had happened?

Alessandra searched the crowd. Only a few seemed to take notice of her presence. They stared, some in recognition, others with distracted glances, encircling their families. Movement brought her eyes back to the bonfire where a small figure was tied to a stake beside its blaze. Her face was red with the heat and body slumped. As Aless elbowed her way toward the front, she recognized Shema.

In a moment she understood. Shema had known the sign. Had she known that it was for her? Running blindly through the tightly packed mob of people, Alessandra pushed and shoved as she screamed to Tareq. "Let her go."

A black specter pounced. Bony hands gripped her arms and she almost retched at an overpowering stink of rotten eggs. Staring into his ghoulish face, she wondered if he was human. Dark, empty eyes glared back, and his mouth stretched into a snarl.

"Bring her to me." Tareq's command sounded above the chaos.

Everyone and everything quieted, except the crackling of the fire. Even the drumbeats stopped. The priests stood, unmoving, on one side of the altar. The entire assembly watched and waited. The fierce warrior dragged her forward to the Crown Prince who stood on a low platform.

Questions raced through fear that demanded and yet, found no answers. Who was the real Tareq? The one who'd rescued her on their way to Akkad? Or the ruler who acknowledged capturing children and hauling them into the city like chattel. Aless searched Tareq's face, looking for any evidence of his affection.

Instead, a man with a countenance etched in stone spoke with chilling certainty. "Her life is offered in reverence for the life of my father."

A strange image came to her mind. It was from a story Maura had read to her as a child about a heathen king who'd demanded the interpretation of a dream he refused to reveal — on threat of execution. It had to be a message for now.

"Let me read the Stones!" Her voice was strong, insistent. The warrior shook her until her head flopped back and forth as she thrashed around, trying to get free.

"Let her go." Tareq's eyes had softened. Something rested in them. Maybe only curiosity. He stepped down from the dais to the altar and stood before her.

She smelled the scent of sandalwood and thought of his embrace. Bowing slightly, she looked into his eyes one more time, then walked to the simple oaken box where two white stones lay side by side. She picked them up and studied them. Words appeared on their smooth surface, like they had the first time she'd seen them.

Shema's words rang in her ears. *Listen to your heart.* Straightening her shoulders, Aless closed her eyes, determined to quiet her thoughts. Another image flooded her mind's eye. A child, bound to an altar. Her mother dancing before her.

"I understand the words," she said to Tareq, and then turned to the other priests. "They say, 'You shall not defile the land by shedding innocent blood.' " She returned her gaze to Tareq. "What happened here in the past? Who is the child on the altar and why is her mother dancing?"

The young prince seemed fixed in time. Nothing in his face or body moved. Until one hand trembled. Then his arms shook, and his body convulsed in giant quakes. All around them, Aless heard the sucking sound of a collective gasp as Tareq's once pale face turned scarlet.

"Tell me. I can't read any more until you tell me." She cried out, demanding an answer.

Tareq let out a loud wail. He pounded his chest and yelled, "You let them. How could you?" He jabbed his finger toward the body of his dead father. "My joy. My sister. Why was her life required? You knew," he said, ranting as though his father could still answer. "You knew my mother would die in grief. You killed her, too."

He spun toward the priests and extended the censer that smoked with incense. "You made her rejoice. You made her dance as she threw her daughter into the fire. You will pay. You'll pay now." A flame blazed out of the censer and hit the chest of one of the priests.

The man looked up in surprise, then crumpled to the ground.

Another blast hit a priest next to the one who'd just fallen. Tareq kept stabbing toward one after the other until finally, like a flock of egrets taking flight, the men dashed through the crowd, knocking people over in their attempt to escape. Flames hit another and another from behind, until a pile of white robes slumped in heaps on the way out the temple doors.

Aless looked around wildly. No one moved as the Crown Prince landed on yet another target of his vengeance. "Tareq. Stop!"

Tareq swirled in her direction, censer extended. He stared at her as if she were from another world.

Would she his next victim? She dropped to her knees. "Your sister," she said. "Let her go. No one has to pay. Not anymore."

Tareq had entered a zone of the past. Without a word, he stalked to Shema. Grabbing a sword from the hand of one of the warriors, he slashed the cords that bound her.

Shema fell to the ground, unconscious.

A loud hiss sounded from the back of the temple. An enormous white asp slithered through the crowd, scattering everyone in its path. "I will have my ssssacrifice," it hissed. "Who are you to ssssstop my offering?" The snake coiled toward Shema.

It was Laila. Or Gad El Glas. Or both. Alessandra cried out to Tareq. "Do something! Now!"

Tareq slowly rotated toward the snake and shuddered as it glided toward him and began a slow coil around his legs. He struggled for a moment, then stopped. His visage changed. "Come, Gad El Glas. Come to me," he said.

A force emanating from the snake's mouth curled along the ground toward Aless and Shema. It looked like smoke, but bone-chilling cold came with its advance. It whirled between them, separating Aless from her friend like a fast-moving glacier. In an instant, they were divided. The massive serpent appeared and wound itself around Shema, squeezing life out of her body as Aless looked on, with no power to defend the young woman. In moments, Shema lay motionless on the stone floor.

The fully lit temple became dark as an invisible presence separated the crowd and blew toward Alessandra.

Shema was dead. Alessandra's entire being filled with unthinking rage. Holding the Stones aloft in one hand, she screamed. "I curse you. Bring them down, Light of the Stars. Bring them down without mercy."

Raindrops fell from above as though the ceiling were only a canopy of darkness. Aless looked up in disbelief as the drops turned into sheets of heavy rain that penetrated temple spires. Flames mixed with rain sizzled and released an enormous cloud of steam. Burning drops of water fell through the air. A bolt of lightning landed in its center. Stones, smoldering coal, and ash spewed as another slash of electricity charged the huge edifice.

What had she done? Alessandra stood in the midst of a panicked mob of fleeing people, holding the Stones in one hand. Where was Tareq? The serpent had disappeared. The mass of people became a stampede out the narrow doors of the temple. Bodies fell, becoming lumps on the ground as fleeing inhabitants rushed over them, overtaken by blind terror.

Aless stood, frozen, as the crowd ran past. At the

back of the crowd, she saw Bethiah and Amira. The crowd had found another exit behind them. Bethiah placed Amira under her body and formed a tent over the child.

No one cared who they were. People stampeded the exits without looking back or being aware of anyone around them.

In moments, Bethiah lay, battered to one side, with Amira kneeling over her, kissing her face over and over.

Alessandra gazed at the stones in her hands and remembered a picture on the wall of her bedroom at the chateau. The hands stretched in front of her were her mother's hands. The woman she'd never known but despised. The woman she'd become.

Chapter 22

Alessandra ran outside and hid behind a thicket of mesquite behind the temple. Torrential rain stopped as suddenly as it appeared. Night was almost over, and dawn was on its way. Before long, morning would light the horrific work of that night. A frenzied stream of people swarmed over the mesa. Warriors charged this way and that, as if they were no longer sure of their mission. Or were looking for her.

The roar of the falls sounded ahead where the twisting path overlooked the cavernous gorge. It was her only way of escape. Aless trembled, knowing how slippery the trail had become in the rain. And how hard it would be to navigate near the craggy gorge.

She clutched the Stones in one hand. Their light pulsed slightly, then grew brighter, illuminating several feet in front of her. She stared at the two small rocks, then stuck them in her pocket. She couldn't afford being seen. Besides, why would they waste their light? Surely, they knew what she'd done.

She crouched lower, struggling to gather what was left of her courage, but finding none. If Rory hadn't been able to get Orion out of the stables to the bottom of the falls, she might as well quit running now. Her legs ached and drenched clothing stuck to her body with a clammy chill. She quaked as if she'd been soaked in ice.

A machete hacking through brush sounded. They

were after her. No surprise. No escape. She'd just lie down in the mud and die. But what if Rory and Orion waited?

Coarse voices carried in the night air. Noises morphed into a shadowy land with no sense of distance. Were the warriors getting closer? She took a deep breath and scooched down the trail, inch after inch. Her foot met the side of the cliff, signaling the first curve. Leaning against the cool granite on one side, she kept moving.

The Stones grew hot against her thigh. She paused and waited. Suddenly, a chunk of the cliff broke away from above and plummeted into darkness. Seconds later, it clattered on rock far below.

Taking a deep breath, she kept going.

A rustle sounded in a thatch of desert grass several yards behind her. She struggled to see in gray mist that descended like a wispy cloud. This time scuffling and the glint of a saber flashed beyond a precipice over her head. Someone had seen her. And was coming.

She steeled herself, keeping as much of her body on the ground as she could. Her hands gripped into mud on each side and her behind dragged the ground. She had to move faster, but pebbles that scattered on the path emptied silently into the gorge's abyss. A surge of cool air streamed upward. She was only a breath away from falling, like the gravel, into its wide abyss.

With steadfast accuracy, the Stones revealed a stray branch, an unexpected turn or steep descent as the falls thundered beside her. She ducked, almost smacking her head on a small overhang. Something skittered in vegetation above. Was it a snake? She shuddered and patted the ground. Maybe Laila had released serpents from the temple to prey on the terrified. Or to stop her.

Grief caught in her throat and threatened to take her down. She had no idea if Rory had been able to bring Orion to the base of the falls. Rory had counted on her, and she'd failed. She had the Stones in her pocket, although that didn't matter anymore.

Plumes of rushing spray glistened in the darkness. Someone stumbled. And swore. What had happened to Tareq and why had he disappeared? She moved faster, driven by someone's pursuit.

Finally, the rocky floor of the trail became sandy. A foaming mist swirled at the pool of water that signaled the base of the falls. She'd have to clear that last, furious pool. A dangling tree branch slapped her in the head. She hurtled forward with its force and ended up on her belly, staring into swirling water. Warmth of her own blood streamed through drenched curls. Gathering her last bit of strength, she inched back until wet grass replaced muddy stones.

She rose to her knees and saw Akeem, gold bangles clinking against his waist as he straggled down the cliff in the gloam of early dawn. Only yards away, Orion pulled against a lead that tethered her to a small tree.

Rory had done the impossible.

The horse danced back and forth in the semi-darkness as Alessandra ran to her, releasing the tether. Orion whinnied, then bent her head, as if positioning herself for Aless to mount. But her energy slipped away as surely as the night. She tried to lift a foot over her mare's back, slick with rain. And slid back to the ground. "Go, girl. Go without me."

A dim light appeared in the horizon. More warriors crawled down the winding trail with torch lights that slashed lingering darkness. She heard a shout, "Ala'!"

Still, Orion stayed, nuzzling Alessandra.

She had to get her horse out of there. With a giant lurch, Aless stood, hoisted her leg, and lifted her body over the mare.

Orion lost no time. She cantered toward the river with Aless barely hanging on. The water was rising. Fast. A deep roar in the distance shook the ground. Orion entered the water and picked up her pace until the river deepened.

Wild currents swirled around her as the mare couldn't touch the ground any longer. Her body lifted, then floated like a tiny craft in blustery seas. They were drifting downstream. Before long, they'd be off track, far from the road. Torchlight of Nayeli warriors neared the other side of the river. There was no going back.

In a herculean effort, Orion shifted to face the opposite shore and swam against the current. Her mare had to be exhausted, but she kept swimming forward. When her hooves found solid ground, Orion cleared the shore in a few bounds, then took off in a mighty lurch.

Alessandra tottered once, twice, and then tumbled to the ground. Her body slammed into the mud. She felt its spray as the ground molded around her body like a sodden blanket. She lay there, unable to breathe. Finished. Orion was free. Her beloved horse would be better off without her on this flight.

Thunder sounded. This time closer. Aless groaned with the thought of more rain pelting her body and chilling her to the core. Then again, maybe it was a sign, proof that it was time to give up. That escape was as doomed as her attempts to prove she was anything other than her mother's daughter. She'd chosen Lilith Gunter's path. The rest would follow in the downward spiral of decision after decision that wreaked havoc on the ones she loved. That couldn't happen. She'd die here, knowing she had no other choice.

Warriors stomped in unison, sabers raised over head, on the other side of the river. Soon, they'd find a way across. The massive iron gate would open, and they'd storm the bridge. It wouldn't take long. A deep rumble vibrated the ground, and something roared from the bend upriver.

Orion tried to nudge her, but she refused to get up. A dark figure who looked like a Nayeli warrior ran toward her from the stables. The end would come more quickly than she thought. She bowed, head-first into the dirt and prayed for a quick death.

"Aless. Get up. Now." Rory's voice was loud, urgent. He knelt beside her, wrapping his arm around her quivering shoulders. "I said. Get up. Now."

Aless shook her head and stayed curled in the dirt.

Rory squatted, then pulled her from the waist until she dangled like a sack of grain.

The thunder grew louder, though unlike the real kind, it continued as a rolling boom that headed closer and closer.

Orion screamed. She hadn't left. She still waited for Aless.

Torches jabbed the dawn, now on its way. Soon, nothing would hide them. What would death feel like? "Go. Away. Now."

"We're leaving. You're not staying here."

"You don't understand. I'm like her. I'm like my mother."

"No. You're not. Your family, Lucy — I need you." Rory pulled her face to his, hand lingering on her chin.

"Will you follow me, or will I carry you out?"

A deep orange lined the horizon, and the sky became gray instead of black. The ground shook with a raging torrent that Aless heard but couldn't see.

She struggled once, then melted into Rory's arms as he lifted her onto Orion and secured her body with the tether to her mare.

His midnight black stallion pawed at the ground as he mounted. "Fly, Star! Fly, Orion." Together, the horses charged away as an avalanche of mud, uprooted trees and rock barreled around the corner. Waves and waves of rolling crimson mud, trees, and boulders rumbled, expanding the river in a mighty rush that uprooted trees and devoured any obstacle in its path.

Away they galloped as morning light pierced gray dawn. Finally, on a crest beyond the city, Rory and Alessandra paused and watched in stunned silence.

Muddy, churning waters swallowed the once sleepy river and rushed to conquer more. The river overflowed fields behind them, threatening the stables. Frightened horses screamed. Some charged out of their wooden stalls, while others thrashed barriers with strong hoofs. As the pasture disappeared under water, majestic stallions broke free and raced away.

Warriors positioned on the cliffs scampered like fleeing spiders in a dash for safety. Muddy red waters spread out over the bridge, surging against its pilings until finally, the structure collapsed and joined the raging mass of debris.

Akeem and Basir were side by side, brandishing knives toward Rory and Aless. Which one of them had killed Heydar? Neither of them had forgiven her. She was the one who'd taken their comrade. And now, neither man was willing to stop his pursuit.

The river shifted its course toward the towering cliffs. Its immense force, powered by what surged behind it, hurtled over the rocks where Akeem and Basir stood.

Plaited braids of Basir swung back and forth as he tugged on Akeem, pulling him to higher ground. Not fast enough, though. The river captured first one, then the other. It tossed Akeem over a rolling boulder, and thrashed Basir in tangled tree limbs. Akeem bobbed to the surface for a moment. He grabbed a tree that floated by, hanging on as a raft. Until another boulder lumbered over its trunk, submerging him. Basir rose once to the surface, arms extended as if in a plea for help. Finally, both were gone.

Rory clicked his heels against his black stallion. "Ride, Star. Take us home."

Chapter 23

Ground quaked under Orion's hooves as another towering wave of mud, trees, and debris crashed from upstream. It joined the other flow like two mighty rivers merging into one. Rory led them away like a trusty sea captain, navigating the road ahead as certain as the North Star above.

Aless clung to her horse, her mind full of images of the night in Akkad. Shema crushed by the terrible serpent. Bethiah trampled by the crowd with Amira standing over her grandmother. Sorrow washed her as violently as the surging flash flood. The Stones tapped against her thigh, reminding her of their presence. Even though their light had come to her aid, she couldn't imagine why. Only one thing was clear. Their mystery didn't matter anymore. A test she'd never expected, one she hadn't recognized, confirmed her worst fear. Even after a journey to a devil's den to prove otherwise, in the end, she was still her mother's daughter.

Shema had warned her. Warriors had taken her young friend while Aless had done what she was told to do — hide. Rage she'd never known overtook her when she saw Shema crushed by the demonic serpent. She'd commanded the Stones to curse them all. She hadn't even separated the evil from the innocent. Before she could think or change her mind, disaster had answered her indiscriminate call. Everyone, including the blameless, had suffered.

She couldn't run fast or far enough to escape what she'd done. Weaving in and out of the cover of trees, she realized she should fear Nayeli snipers who lurked nearby. Instead, she was too numb to think about anything other than hanging on to Orion as her mare galloped beside Rory. When the cliffs of Akkad were no longer in sight and afternoon sun shone hot overhead, Rory slowed their pace and spoke quietly. "We need rest."

They stopped at a secluded stand of live oaks where Rory helped her dismount, then tethered the horses near a narrow brook. They sat, side by side, too tired to speak.

"Lean against me," Rory said. "I'll keep watch."

She was too exhausted to protest. Curling into a ball in Rory's lap, she slept.

In what felt like minutes later, a pair of mourning doves called to each other, interrupting dreams of raining fire and screams for help. Aless jolted upright, disoriented. How could morning sunlight appear in the eastern horizon? They'd arrived in this grove yesterday afternoon. She'd slept all that day and through the night. Her body ached, but she felt better. Until her mind woke up, too, and memories of Akkad arrived with it.

Rory offered her a drink from his skin of water. "Sorry. We'll get food as soon as we can."

Aless had forgotten her pack at the stables the day she'd expected Tareq to take her home. Now she and Rory had nothing to eat. Such a small mistake. Only an oversight. Yet another torrent of shame washed over her. She hid her face into her hands. "Go away. I'm dirty. You shouldn't be here. I might…"

"Hurt me?" Rory asked gently. "No. I won't leave.

I won't let you, either. Not again. Not ever.

"I can't tell you. What happened."

"I'm listening. Start from the beginning."

Alessandra wasn't sure how. Arriving in Akkad had been a descent into a web of deception, just like Shema had warned. She shuddered at the reminder of her faithful friend. Surely Rory's eyes would shift away as he tried to hide his disappointment. Finally, she managed to speak. "I failed. I proved I'm no different than my mother."

Rory was so quiet, she was sure he was appalled.

"I…Shema tried to warn me," she said faltering. "She…It should have been me. I hid, like she told me to. They took her, instead. It was my fault." She broke into deep sobs that shook her tired body.

Rory took her hands into his. "What else?" There was an urgency in his tone.

"The Stones. They…I don't know what happened. After Shema died, something came over me. This furious anger spewed out of me. I commanded the Stones to curse everyone." She ducked her head into her hands to hide her eyes from Rory.

He pulled away a lock of hair that dangled over her face and gently lifted her chin. "Look at me." It wasn't disapproval she saw in his eyes. It was empathy. "You can't imagine the evil that contended for you at that moment. Shema forgives you. She understands."

She curled up under his arm, like a child. "How do you know? She's gone."

"I know because of the land she entered the instant she left her body. She's safe now. And warring in our behalf, as always. This time from a different perspective. A perfect one."

"Aiden. And Maura. They'll never want to see me again. Now when they know…"

"That's not true." His tone was soft, then returned to a quiet intensity. "Did I tell you who she is? Laila?" When Aless shook her head, he kept talking. "She's the human form of Gad El Glas. Ruthless, demonic. She directs the Nayeli forces."

"How do you know?"

"I've done some resistance work for the Magi."

"A Magi army?

"You didn't know — All those warriors leaving Akkad. They were going to destroy Magi settlements. We had to stop them."

Aless felt stupid. "I should've known."

"How? You were in the center of the enemy's den."

"I didn't know Tareq was controlled by Laila. At least I hoped he wasn't. Until we faced each other in the temple. He let Shema go until Laila showed up as a snake. Something came over him. Like he lost himself in her. He forgot who he was."

"He's been under her influence for many years."

"So, why…Why would he pretend to care?" She choked on the words, then blushed to the roots of her head.

Rory spoke simply, belying a crinkle in his forehead. "Because he needed you. He hoped that in marriage he could access the Stone's power."

Aless looked down, humiliated.

"Look, you're called to carry the Stones. You failed a test, but you're not disqualified. You're out of Akkad. And we have the Stones. That's a lot." Rory looked her up and down. "Where are they?"

She pulled them out of her pocket and held them,

wondering if somehow the writing would appear now. Maybe Rory could help her understand their mystery. "There was writing on them that night. About shedding innocent blood. I saw an image of Tareq's sister being sacrificed to Gad El Glas." She stared at the two nondescript rocks and then held them out to Rory. "I don't want anything to do with them. Take them."

Rory studied them, then pushed her hands away. "I can't. They're yours to carry."

"Fine. I'll bury them." She stalked to a bit of damp earth, dropped the Stones to the ground, then dug a hole with her fingers.

"Stop." Rory bolted up off the ground. He picked up the Stones and placed them into her hands, curling her fingers over them. "Look. So, you messed up. It wasn't the Stones fault. It wasn't their power that commanded that disaster."

"You're wrong. I held them in my hands and cursed the whole crowd. That's when the torrential storm began."

"You don't understand the nature of the Stones — or the prophecy, for that matter. The Stones of Promise won't operate in vengeance."

"But they did. I saw them."

"No. Your anger tapped into the power of Gad El Glas. Yes, like Lilith Gunter. That doesn't mean you *are* your mother. Or that you're doomed to be like her from now on. You made a mistake. Forgive yourself. Your people need you."

"My people?"

"People who love you. Those who need the power of what you carry. Learn how to use the Stones. Like Shema said, read them with your heart."

"Shema...I don't know what I would've done without her in Akkad."

"She was there to help. She knew the Stones. And she knew you.

A stirring sounded in undergrowth outside the stand of trees. Picking up a branch on ground beside her, she scrambled closer to Rory. Another rustle in the dry brush and a figure appeared in the rose-lit dawn. She lifted the stick, ready to pound it on the person's head.

Rory whistled softly.

Perseus, gray hair flapping over aged shoulders and a lithe young woman rode into the clearing.

"Perseus!" It was her friend and advocate from the stables. "What are you doing here?"

"Here to bring ye a bit o' breakfast, me friend." Perseus held his arms out in triumph to Alessandra. "Good girl. Ye did it. Ye found the path, after all."

Chapter 24

Aless stood to embrace her friend as he dismounted. Even though it was like hugging a towering tree. "You showed me the way up the gorge. I wouldn't have seen it without you."

"Aye. Well, ye did. Glad to be of help." He unpacked several layers of naan, cheese, figs, and a skin of water. He handed them first to Alessandra and then to Rory as they sat in a protective circle, under the shelter of a row of scraggly mesquite bushes.

"What are you doing here?" Aless spoke with her mouth full of bread.

The two visitors were a study in contrasts. Perseus was as tall and rangy as she remembered from Akkad. He wiped away a slurp of water from his bushy beard and peered through gray eyebrows that listed here and there over watery blue eyes.

The young woman was dressed like a Nayeli warrior, entirely in black, including the turban. A long wave of auburn hair straggled out of one side of her head wrap. She stared at Aless with expressionless green eyes.

"Our work was done in Akkad." Perseus brushed crumbs from his lap and reached for a fig.

"Your work?"

"Aye. Lover boy, here. His eyes were trained on ye. When he couldn't see fer himself, we took over. Taking care of ye, we were. Makin' sure you made it out safe and with those Stones in yer hands."

"You were there to protect me? Because Rory asked you?" Aless remembered how Perseus burst into the circle of Nayeli warriors, as well as her terror. She'd never have to suffer what would have happened if he hadn't shown up. Aless turned to the young woman. "Wait a minute. I know you. You served Dhamar Ghalib."

The woman didn't reply, only glared back.

Rory saw the awkward moment. "Aless. This is Tara." He nodded at the girl whose emerald eyes were stony with an expression Aless couldn't read. No smile, no response from the achingly beautiful young woman. Nothing left for pleasantries. Aless felt a stirring in her belly. Maybe Rory was attracted to her.

Rory acted like he had no idea what was going on. His lanky body was already bent, preparing his pack. "We need to move quickly." He looked up at Aless. "Tara's got clothes for you."

Tara didn't look happy to share. She reached into her pack and tossed a wad of dark clothes her way.

Aless studied her riding clothes, stained with red mud, and tattered from her descent along the waterfall. The pants and tunic Tara tossed her way were not only a welcome change, but they were also designed for cover. Grabbing them, she went behind a tree to change.

"We'll prepare the horses," said Perseus. "And leave at your command." He bowed slightly to Rory, then went to the horses as Tara climbed a tree as a lookout. Orion whinnied as if to let Perseus know she was ready.

Each time Tara glanced Alessandra's way her expression proved she didn't like what she saw. Her face grimaced as if her very person brought a bitter taste in her mouth. Probably she saw Aless the way she saw herself. Worthless. Unlike Tara who appeared to be the picture of seasoned bravery.

Perseus and Tara had saddled the horses when Rory leaned over to kiss her. He spoke in a low voice. "Come out of hiding and join those to whom you belong." He mounted his stallion and led the way out of the stand of trees. Looking back, he addressed them all as he led the way forward. "We'll travel hard until nightfall."

Aless searched for a reference point as they rode. The cliffs of Akkad were no longer in sight. The plains were before them, which was both good and bad. Although bits of desert lingered in the foliage, they could be easily seen on this road where Nayeli troops traveled on their way to battle.

Alessandra searched towering pines for any signs of spies as Rory blazed a determined trail. There were only a couple breaks to water and feed the horses. And themselves. Perseus handed out an extra supply of dried figs and flatbread to her and Tara. They filled water skins from pools of clear spring water silently, then mounted to ride again.

Finally, days later as sunlight dipped in the west, towering birch trees and rolling hills replaced desert terrain. Alessandra's body ached all over. Orion, on the other hand, seemed glad to be back in the company of Perseus and the others. Patches of snow glistened on distant mountain peaks. Home. They were getting closer.

Rory slowed his stallion to a trot and led them into a grove of sycamore trees. "Time to break for the day. Tether the horses, then come back. One more watch before nightfall."

They led their horses deep into the forest where a

brook gurgled near patches of grass. After a quick drink and wash, they trudged back until the trail was back in sight. Without another word, Rory leaned against a tree and fell sound asleep. Tara crawled into scraggly pine and spread her body over a large branch, probing the vista outside the grove.

Just as Aless relaxed against a tree for a nap, Rory woke suddenly and held up one hand.

Tara scrambled down the tree and crouched low at its base. Rory pulled Aless to his side. They hid in a line of bushes, out of sight but able to watch the plains through the foliage.

Clanking amulets and brazen armor sounded first. Then, the brightly colored tunics and flags appeared. A smaller group of scouts followed. Their faces were painted like the angels of death she'd seen the night of the sacrifice. Dense clouds of dark smoke filled the horizon behind them.

Terror descended over Alessandra like a blanket. She had to run. Now. Before it was too late. When she tried to stand, Rory pressed his hand against her back like a heavy stone. She struggled against his hold until finally, he plopped his body over hers and covered her mouth with one hand. She couldn't move, could barely breathe. She wasn't going anywhere.

In what felt like hours later, all was quiet. Rory nimbly rose to his feet, releasing Aless from his grip.

"What were you doing?" Her words spewed indignant wrath. "How dare you. Don't ever…"

Rory turned and unwrapped a bedroll that was tied to his stallion. When he spoke, it was without apology. "They carry fear like a weapon. It works. People run, like a stand of birds scattered by a dog — so the hunter can shoot them. That's what you felt." He stood and brushed his legs. "Time to settle in," he said. "No fire tonight."

As if in response to their leader, Perseus and Tara unwrapped bedrolls and placed them near each other. Soon, the moon rose to full strength with cirrus clouds streaking over it.

Still mad and ashamed of the way she'd treated Rory — especially since he'd been protecting her, Aless carefully placed her own pallet a few feet from him. She avoided Tara's glare, as the young woman positioned her pallet near Perseus.

No one had words. Each of them lay on their backs and stared up into the sky. Even in dwindling light, it wasn't hard to discern Tara's gaze trained on her.

Rory pulled his blanket closer to Aless and held her in one arm.

She melted, and whispered, "I'm sorry." She curled closer, trying to sort out which question to ask first. And which ones could be asked in the presence of Perseus and Tara. Finally, she settled on the most obvious. "What led you to Akkad?"

"You. Of course. And we've suspected that the Stones were hidden there. Your presence proved we were right."

"What are you talking about? My presence."

"The Stones and their chosen carrier. We had to get you both out."

"We?"

"Magi forces surrounded you since you arrived. Perseus and Tara are Magi. Their eyes were on you in Akkad."

Alessandra's thoughts jumbled into a mix of gratitude and confusion. She rose from her mat, mustering courage to ask the unyielding Tara a question next. "What happened to Dhamar Ghalib? I saw him that afternoon. He was fine."

A cloud wafted over the moon, but the sound of Tara's voice didn't require an expression on her face. The young woman snorted, and her voice gravelly with scorn. "Poisoned."

"Who? And why?" Aless sat up, tumbling Rory to one side. Fatigue of the day lifted in a moment, and she hoped Tara had more than one word left for an explanation. "Laila turned her back when Dhamar Ghalib spoke of a marriage — between Tareq and me."

When she felt Rory stiffen beside her, Aless sat closer and grasped his hand with a squeeze. "She dropped a goblet he'd been drinking from. When she turned her back, her hand hovered over another chalice. One she offered a drink from." Aless said, remembering the moment. "He scowled and started coughing after he tasted it. Did Laila poison him?"

Tara exhaled loudly, as though Aless not only had too many words, but was too stupid to understand. "If the potion had been in my hands. I'd have shoved the vessel down his gullet. Gladly." Her breathing became sharp stabs.

Perseus rose from the ground and sat beside the young girl, venturing a long arm around her shoulders. His touch seemed to calm her. "Hush, now," he said, as if he comforted a child.

Tara choked away an almost sob. Abruptly, she rose, grabbed her pallet, and stalked away into the darkness.

Perseus peered over at Aless. His words were low and quiet. "She were taken from her home. As a wee girl…"

"Tara came in through the slave trade you discovered early that morning on the trail," Rory explained. "She was captured, stolen out of a Magi settlement."

The memory of those little girls, hurrying away from the slave traders returned. "I should have known. I couldn't…" No wonder Tara was untouchable. She'd been wrested from her home and family. That was only the beginning of what had been stolen from the beautiful young girl.

Fierce heat raced up Alessandra's neck and to the top of her head. She'd only given the women who served Dhamar Ghalib a passing glance, barely wondering where they were from and how they got there. They'd been taken from families as captives. Like the little girls. Dragged from homes, maybe even husbands and children. She couldn't ask, nor would the young woman tell her all that she'd endured.

Aless had been protected by Aiden and Maura. If she'd lived in another time and place, she might have been one of the women taken into the harem. Tareq had lied to her. But he'd never taken her as his own. She remembered the assault on her way to Sanctuary, then on the trail with the young slaves. Someone had stepped in each time, for whatever reason.

The loss Tara bore wasn't her fault. Or her family's.

As they settled down on thin pallets to sleep, Tara returned to their circle.

"I'm sorry. So sorry," Aless said.

Tara turned her back to Alessandra and curled herself into a tight ball on the pallet.

Rory hugged Aless tightly, then turned away as she tossed, seeking a place where rocks didn't jab her throbbing muscles. Or where memories didn't torment her battered heart. With a deep sigh and muttered prayer, she finally fell asleep.

Chapter 25

That night, the temperatures fell, and Hildegard's shawl was welcome. Tara looked over at her occasionally as if Alessandra had advanced one step away from enemy. They'd taken turns bathing in the spring. Tara had positioned her sleeping mat over the brush so they could have privacy. Aless had waited until Tara was done and dressed before she entered the small refuge. The water was so cold it took her breath away. Still, it felt good to be clean for the first time since she'd left Akkad.

After a quick breakfast, they saddled the horses and started the journey. Hours later, Tara perked up and pointed at something through the trees.

"It's her home," said Rory, nodding to Alessandra. "We're stopping."

They pulled the horses to one side and into a wooded area. Didn't he understand she was in a hurry to get to their mountain? She was tempted to remind him, then understood. Tara was returning to her family. Maybe for the first time in years.

Tara led the way up a small rise. They peered into a small basin where a village rested surrounded with mountains that towered over them like guardians. It was a tribe of nomadic Magi equestrians. Horses stood in a rough corral bordered by hewn timbers. The huts were rectangular tent-like structures with thatched roofs.

Gardens were cultivated and thrived at each home and smoke rose in gentle pillars from openings at the center of rooftops. Children played by campfires while men and women went about daily work. One woman stood over a staff, studying the mountains as if they held something she couldn't quite see.

Tara yelped. "Ma!" She nudged her horse to a gallop, whooping with joy. Reining in the steed, she leaped off and ran to her mother. They fell into an embrace, twirling, laughing, and gathering a crowd. It was like a warm fire had been lit on a cold day and drew everyone around it. Tara hugged first one, then another and another. This was family and she was home. At last, she beckoned to their small company.

"Aye, we be comin'," Perseus shouted. Rory, Aless and Perseus rode down the small rise, tethered their horses and walked into the village amid people's cheers.

Tara led the woman to them. "This is Ma. She…says thank you."

Aless ducked her head, but Perseus and Rory bowed like perfect gentlemen.

Rory turned to hoist a small child onto his shoulders and then stopped abruptly. Peering into the woods above the village, he held up one hand. Men appeared from every direction and formed a tight perimeter around the homes. Orion pranced an erratic dance of fear.

Aless looked around but couldn't see anything. Something had appeared as a threat, though. Not now, she hoped. Not when they'd just returned Tara to her family.

A screeching battle wail erupted behind the rise as Nayeli warriors, crests bobbing like evil banshees, barreled down the embankment.

Rory had a bow ready. Arrows flew from all around the circle. Some pierced the hearts of enemy warriors who fell to the ground, while others merely stabbed the air. Battle cries and combat took over the once peaceful village as men charged forward, armed with knives, clubs, whatever they could grab. Tara was there, blade in hand and slashing through the chaos.

Aless looked wildly around. Children and their mothers had disappeared into their tents. A flaming arrow hit one roof, then another. The thatch burst into flames.

More Nayeli warriors poured over the ridge and swooped into the basin. Rory, Perseus, and the other men held a strong defensive line around the homes but couldn't turn from the warfare to put out fires. Perseus dropped his bow and picked up a sword. He sliced one warrior, then another, slashing, dashing through the mayhem. Tara tossed a rope around a warrior's throat, yanked him off the horse and stabbed him in the chest.

Alessandra stood, frozen, only for a moment. She had no weapon, and no plan, except to somehow get the women and children to safety. Despite war that raged all around them. And rooftops going up in flames.

Alessandra pulled the Stones out of her pocket. Clearly, she'd been disqualified from using them. Still, pale blue light shone from within them. She looked at the battle around her and gasped. A path stretched out in front of her that seemed hidden from sight. Warriors dashed around it, some defending, others assaulting the equestrian village. Not on that lane, though.

Aless looked at the Stones again. Their light grew brighter. Grasping them in one hand, she crept into the first home. The smoke was so dense, she couldn't see.

239

Until a child cried out. A little boy and girl sat huddled in one corner. Their eyes were wide in terror.

Alessandra fell to her knees and held out her hands. "I'm here...to help."

Although the little boy looked at her as if she were crazy, the girl fell into her arms. "Come, Erik," she said.

Aless took each of their hands and ducked out. The path appeared before them and led to another tent. They walked inside as war still raged all around. There, a mother held a baby.

"Follow me," Aless whispered.

The woman stood for a moment with the child against her breast. Aless held the back of the tent up and the three became five as they headed out.

Smoke was everywhere. Mayhem, blood, cries flooded her senses and threatened to paralyze her. She remembered. The arborists spoke of burning trees. She and Rory had seen smoke behind the soldiers the night before. Even in Sanctuary the warriors had burned and pillaged. Flames that surrounded a serpent on the iron gate of Akkad. The insignia of Nayeli destruction.

The pathway appeared again. This time it led to another tent farther in the distance. When they entered, a mother stood in surprise with four little ones, crying and holding her skirt. She looked at Aless in disbelief.

"Trust me," Aless said.

Aless extended the Stones, and the way reemerged near a tent that was erected by a stream. Aless felt like the Pied Piper as the unlikely procession entered the tent. Again, children and their mother huddled into one corner. Aless entered tent after tent until the company of woman and children became a small battalion, walking unhindered and protected through fire and combat.

Finally, the pathway appeared over the stream flooded with snow melt.

When Aless held the Stones out, she almost whooped in delight. An opening appeared in the water with a wide enough gap that each mother and child walked across. Aless shook her head in amazement.

The passageway shifted, leading a way up a hill, away from the warfare.

"Do we have them all?" she cried out to one of the women.

The woman dressed in a simple brown tunic searched, as if taking a head count. She paused over one group of children and asked, "Molly?" A grubby little toddler appeared from the apron of an older girl and ran to her mother.

Aless kept the Stones extended as they climbed an embankment and down into a meadow. Smoke rose over the small incline, but they were safe. Aless sat down and shook. She peered around at what looked like thirty children, plus their mothers all in groups, holding each other and weeping.

One of the mothers nodded to Aless. "Thank you."

Aless didn't know what to say. It was the Stones. And her hands. How had they worked and what part did she have in it?

Hours later, Aless crept up to the rise with one of the other mothers. Sunset lit the sky with variegated shades of orange and crimson. It sunk low in the horizon beyond the battlefield where Nayeli warriors in bright tunics and painted faces lay dead on the ground. A few skirmishes lingered, until finally, the remaining Nayeli warriors leaped onto war stallions and fled the village.

The village was on fire. Aless signaled the women

and children. In a procession, they walked back up the hill and into the basin to their village. Without a word, they formed a line and passed bucket after bucket of water from the stream to put out flames that blazed over their homes.

Aless joined their company, determined to conquer every fire of the enemy. Women went in search of their husbands. There were happy reunions and despairing cries as a wife and her children huddled over a still form on the ground.

Aless looked around wildly for Rory.

A slender dark shape lay on the ground, her auburn hair splayed out. A woman knelt over her, dabbing tears with her apron, and wiping her daughter's face.

Aless rushed to the pair with water, offering each one a drink from a cup that had tumbled to one side of a tent. "Tara. You can't leave. Not now."

Tara's eyes cracked open. She smiled first at her mother, then gazed up at Aless. "It's your turn," she said. "Go. Take care of your family."

Aless touched Tara's hand. "I'll take some of that courage you carry. And remember where it came from."

Perseus ran to Tara and held her into a giant hug. He looked Aless up and down as if sizing up an untimely gift. Taking her hands into giant palms, he grinned a crooked smile under the gnarly mustache. "Grateful fer that light ye be carrying, Miss."

When Rory ran toward her, Aless fell into his arms. He smelled like smoke and battle. She should say something about his bravery, his leader's heart. She couldn't find words, though. For now, it was enough to be here. Together.

A man rode into the village from the main road. He

leaned against his horse's neck as he listed to one side. His clothes were the simple garb of a farmer, only singed with black soot and filthy with road grime.

Rory waved, as if he welcomed a friend. He rushed to the young man's side as he toppled off his steed. "Alaric. What happened?"

The young man was breathless. His face and hands were streaked with dust and his dappled stallion was drenched in sweat. Perseus hurried to lead the horse into a lean-to stable near the stream at the edge of the woods. Rory led Alaric into one of the thatched dwellings.

Tara and her mother carried in a pitcher of water and round of flatbread. Rory stuck his head outside and motioned Aless to join them inside.

"Alaric has news," Rory said, holding a skin of water to the man's lips.

The man drank and Rory helped him sit against a pile of kindling for support. "Nayeli warriors," he gasped. "They've burned every unarmed Magi settlement north of Akkad. And are heading toward Sanctuary." He took another shuddering breath. "The city's militia isn't strong enough to defeat their forces." He looked at Aless, then spoke softly to Rory. "There will be a bloodbath, unless…"

Rory spoke first. "Nona. I'll gather forces to defend the city. And get her out of there."

Aless leaned in beside him. "I'll come, too. Orion and I want to help."

Rory looked at her sadly.

And she knew. She had to let him go. Without fear for her. "We'll be fine." She mustered a small grin. "Orion and I can find our way from here to the chateau. Go. Take care of Nona."

Rory pulled Aless to her feet and into a quick hug. He turned to Perseus. "Ask a family to care for Alaric. We'll ride as soon as the horses are ready."

Aless and Rory stood outside the simple dwelling. The village stirred with activity. Men gathered the horses and led them to a nearby stream while women swept away debris around their homes. A child had found a stray puppy and played a game of fetch.

Aless held back tears. "Promise me you'll be back, Captain Rory."

Rory's starburst eyes flickered with his own grief. Pulling her close, he tilted her chin and kissed her, first deeply, then with lingering tenderness. For a moment, the world around them faded. Until brilliant sunlight broke through the clouds. Rory's embrace tightened once more, then released her.

"I promise."

Chapter 26

A single purple crocus peeked through melting snow. A lifetime had passed since she'd seen this mountain. And now it was late spring. The familiar scent of damp rot filled the crisp air. She was home. Almost.

Orion whinnied and pawed at the ground. Alessandra leaned over and hugged her mare around the neck. "Not much longer." She felt the horse's heart race as she rubbed one hand under Orion's jaw. "What is it? We're heading home. Can't you tell?" Surely, her mare could sense how close they were to the chateau.

"Come on, girl." She nudged Orion's side, but the mare pranced, unwilling to move forward. Aless crouched low. Nayeli warriors? Maybe Orion sensed their presence. She pulled the mare's lead toward the cover of dense pines. Orion, her friend who'd taken her through battle and rugged terrain, refused to obey her.

A deep huffing sounded in a small clearing. Two fat bear cubs rolled on the ground and then scampered toward her and Orion. Nearby, the enormous body of a mother grizzly hunched over winter kill, her mouth full of flesh.

Aless would've gasped but couldn't. They had to get out of there. Now. With as little noise as possible. She pulled on the reins, signaling Orion to back up as her heart raced. The fastest runner couldn't outpace a charging bear. Other than lurking Nayeli warriors, a grizzly with cubs and in the middle of a meal was the worst possible scenario. Everything inside her longed to spur her horse and crash through the woods.

She knew better, though. A noisy flight would enrage the grizzly into a full-on charge. What had she been thinking to ignore Orion's warning? She leaned back against the saddle, wishing she could retrieve the fragrance Shema said would hide her scent. There was no time, and she couldn't risk the noise of rifling through her saddle bag. She leaned back, pulling on Orion's reins as they retreated, afraid to whisper a command.

The cubs ran, bawling to their mother. In one gigantic shudder, the grizzly rose on massive hind legs. Aless stopped short in terror. The animal towered over a nearby boulder, nearly eight-feet tall. Teeth bared, it roared with a howl so ferocious that the ground seemed to quiver. Every scurry in the undergrowth stilled. Even birds silenced their songs.

Orion reared up. She took off in erratic leaps through the dense undergrowth as Aless clung on with all her strength. Aless shifted in time to miss a low branch as bark from its trunk scraped her leg from ankle to thigh.

If they'd been on the prairie, Orion would've galloped away. The woods were so dense, she charged, skirted trees, and then dashed again, over, and over. The grizzly ran toward them, sending shudders down Aless's already quaking body.

Orion kept plowing through brush and branches that tore Aless's skin and ripped her clothing. Releasing the reins, Aless leaned low over her horse and let her run. On and on, they zigzagged around and through the forest. Navigating through another stand of trees, they reached a clearing where Orion could run freely. Water bubbled from a nearby stream, flowing through the snow. The mare jumped over a fallen log stretched over their path with one graceful leap.

Aless took in a sharp breath when another log appeared, this one partly hidden by snow. Orion jumped again. The mare almost made it over when a branch grazed her back leg. Tottering only for a moment, Orion righted herself. Unlike Alessandra who fell, smashing her backside, and then her head against rocky soil.

A warm flow dribbled down her scalp. Aless shook herself, willing her body to stand. A wave of dizziness took her back to the ground where she tried to lift her head but couldn't. Minutes later, she forced her body into a crawl on the forest floor, feeling the icy ground leech warmth from her body. Her hands bled as she pulled herself up an incline and through damp undergrowth until her senses felt like the sun, growing dimmer with approaching dusk.

Orion, her friend, had left her.

She was so tired. No longer screaming for her to run, her body whispered, *Give up*. Cold seeped from her fingers and toes and traveled to her very core. It chilled her resolve to survive, to do anything but just lie there.

Footsteps of a horse padded on the forest floor.

Alessandra lifted her head expecting to see Orion. Instead, a young girl with long black curls appeared, dressed in an old-fashioned riding cape, and riding a pale, dappled mare. She looked only five or six years old. The little one slid off the horse and squatted beside her. An aroma of jasmine, with a note of citrus filled the air. Aless studied the child's porcelain skin and cheeks rosy from mountain chill. The girl held her hand out to

Alessandra. "Come. I'll take you home."

Was she an apparition? Aless tried to shake her head but couldn't move. She wanted to sleep, to never wake up.

The beautiful child crossed her arms and stomped one small foot. "Alessandra. Now."

Just as Aless wondered how the girl knew her name, the little one grabbed her hand and pulled. As she did, strength coursed through Aless's body. She sat up with the child close to her side, giving her head time to stop spinning.

"I'll help." The little girl positioned herself under Aless's arm and held her as they stood. Unnaturally strong, her small arms hoisted Aless onto the mare's back and then mounted behind her. Together they rode up the mountain. Aless looked up in terror at a flash of brown through the trees. The little girl patted her back with light taps, as a mother would comfort her baby.

"I have to get to the chateau. I have to…" Aless pointed to a path, beaten with use.

"Not that way." The child pulled the reins and rode in a steady pace in the opposite direction. Glimpses of a growling, shadowy figure wove in and out of the trees.

"Don't be afraid. I've got you."

"We need to turn…"

"Not here." The little girl spoke firmly.

They made long, languid circles up the mountain. A ribbon, faded blue and tattered, hung limp from a branch of a budding sycamore tree. She'd had a ribbon like that. Long ago. Was it hers from races through the woods or dashes up to the upper branches, determined to beat Rory?

Rushing water sounded in the distance. They kept

riding until they reached an outcropping of pure, foaming mist that plummeted from its high place. It was her waterfall.

Aless turned back in surprise. "I'm home. You brought me home."

The child helped her down from the horse. "Cross this stream. You'll find yourself right where you need to be."

"How did you know?" Aless placed her hand on Rory's necklace. The young girl became a woman with raven black hair that tumbled around her shoulders. She smiled at Alessandra, her eyes bright and amused.

Aless had seen that face before. In the picture Maura painted years ago that hung in her bedroom. "Mama." Aless stumbled toward her. She held her, smelled the layered fragrance she'd discovered in Akkad, felt the warmth of a living being. Her own mother. Finally, she understood. "You sent me away. To save me."

Her mother spoke tenderly. "I hid you as long as I could. And told Maura where to find you when I had to leave." She held Alessandra at arm's length as if to savor a child who'd become a woman she'd never known. "They did well with my beloved daughter." Her mother held Alessandra's hands in her own and kissed them. "Carry the Stones," she murmured. "Your family, your people — they need you."

"I don't know how."

"The Stones will teach you. Their wisdom is an open book to those who will listen. Its pages were closed to me. Not to you, though. Look around. Destiny speaks in unforeseen ways.

"And through one who carries the adventure you long for." Her mother's eyes danced with what looked much like joy.

"The future, Mama. What does it look like?"

"It looks like you. Full of promise. It looks like those who love you. Like the one who has chosen you as his own. Don't be afraid. Gather the goodness I failed to recognize on earth."

In the breath of a wind, her mother spoke again. "It's not time to join me, beloved. You have much to do. Much to enjoy on this earth. I'll see you in another life, for another journey that will never end."

"Don't leave me," Alessandra begged. "I need you."

"Forgive yourself." Lilith Gunter reached out her hands as her image grew fainter and her cloak became like leaves tussled by a gentle breeze. Finally, when she was only a faint glimmer of light, Aless heard what sounded like a kiss blown into the air that became a tender caress on her cheek.

In a swirl of mist, the fragrance of the meadow, and warmth of a sweet embrace, she was gone.

Alessandra's arms remained stretched out, embracing what had become fresh mountain air with a hint of her mother's warmth left behind. She felt the back of her head. There was no seeping wound. Her back didn't hurt. Nothing in her travel, battle-worn body ached. Love had come to help and healed her. All she felt was the lingering presence of the one she'd longed for all her life. Instantly, she knew.

She *was* like her mother.

She was loved. And forgiven.

Alessandra stood for a moment the bottom of the waterfall where she'd first seen Tareq. And been blind to the man who'd always loved her. The one she loved, as well.

Inside, she heard a voice whisper. "Go. Your family is waiting."

Picking her way through underbrush, she found the path back to the chateau. It had been a long time since she and Rufus had trooped up and down, only to peer over the edge of that waterfall and dream of faraway places.

Now, she couldn't wait to be home.

Alessandra read the position of the sun, just as she had every day she'd remembered at the chateau. It was suppertime. Her stomach growled as if in tune with the picture of home. The grove of trees planted by Magi arborists was still bare. Snow on the lawn that stretched out before the chateau glistened, untouched.

No footprints trampled fresh powder that had always invited mass snowball wars. Neither were there any snowmen, or snow women, as Lucy insisted on adding. Alessandra combed her hair back with one hand as she passed the trees to the front door. It was bolted shut. That was strange. The door was never locked except at night.

Rufus appeared as a sentinel once again. He barked at her coming up the small incline to the house from the window. He disappeared, then came back to the window. He acted like he wasn't used to a locked door, either. A little blonde head appeared beside him and in moments the front door swung open to Lucy and Rufus barreling down to meet her.

The dog arrived first. He knocked her down and they rolled in the snow. Aless laughed and held the dog as he licked her face. This was the chateau she remembered. Her journey had taken her through desert heat and now, back to her mountain. Chunks of snowpack sifted down her neck and turned into streams.

"Awess!" Lucy squealed in delight, running toward her as fast as her legs would go.

Aless sat up. "Lucy — you've grown! Look at how long your legs are!"

"Mama says I'll be tall as you." Lucy's little rolls of fat had disappeared, and her face was slender. She joined Rufus on Aless's lap.

Two figures glanced out the window. A moment later, Aiden and Maura charged out the door.

"You're home!" Maura cried out as they ran to meet her. Aless set Lucy aside, pushed Rufus away and stood up. Then fell into Maura's arms, smelling the scent of home. Aiden was next. She pulled her hands through his familiar red curls peppered heavily with gray. They both seemed far too thin. Maura stood on one side, with Aiden on the other, as if his presence supported her. "Oh, how we've missed you." She held Aless at arm's length, as if searching her niece's face for clues from her absence.

"Lucy," Maura said, "Aless is tired from her trip. Help me with dinner for a minute?"

Lucy went unwillingly with Maura while Aiden led Aless to the small sitting room where a dim blaze smoldered in the stone fireplace. "Come, sit. Tell me…tell me about…"

"About my journey?" Aless smiled sadly. "Terrifying, wonderful all jumbled up. I saw Rory. He left to check on Nona."

"Aye." Aiden had a crinkle in the middle of his brow she hadn't noticed before. He looked tired. And haggard.

"Where are rest of the children?" Now that she was home, she was ready to jump into the routines she'd known so well. She could help with the horses, the children, whatever they needed.

Aiden studied a small fleck on the floor. "We…" This was agonizing. Aiden spoke slowly at any given time. Now his words were like cold molasses that lingered in its vessel. He searched the room as if the walls had ears, then spoke softly. "They're in hiding.

"We had to," he added, as if he expected Aless to be indignant. "The arborists heard reports of a potential Nayeli attack. We sent most of the children with them into villages where they'd be protected. And where there was…enough to eat."

"I thought they were hidden here. At the chateau."

"That was the plan. However, these are not ordinary days. Magi children gathered under one roof became too dangerous."

"I don't understand. They were safe here."

"Not when the Nayeli found out about them."

Aless grabbed her chest at a pain so real it confirmed the truth. The Nayeli knew because Tareq and his men had come. They'd carried their information back to Akkad as she followed along, unaware. She remembered a lingering stench of smoke one morning after the warriors had arrived at the chateau. They were Nayeli warriors. Another generation of those who had massacred their Magi family many years ago. The walls of their home recognized what the inhabitants had not. "Aiden. I didn't…"

"You couldn't have known." Aiden brushed her chin with a gentle touch.

"If I'd listened," she said, her voice rising with frustration. "Clarion and Broc said I was targeted by the Nayeli. I never thought about the children being discovered."

"Peace, child. They're in good hands. And helping.

Marcella is teaching in one of the homes. She knows the trees, understands their signals. Invaluable information for Magi resistance. You know Louis and his mind for numbers. He shapes quadrants for the flow of battle plans. And, of course, Suzette's healing hands have saved many."

A catch sounded in his voice. "Lucy." Aiden's hands trembled a bit, as if he were cold. "Well. She's too little to go anywhere."

A pit formed in Alessandra's belly. "You're so pale. Have you been eating?"

"Aye. Though we're careful with supplies. Spring will help. No planting outside, though. Only in the few pots we have inside."

"Why?" That didn't make sense. Spring planting had always been a family affair.

"It's too dangerous. Certainly for Lucy."

Aless couldn't believe she'd ever followed Tareq and his men. "I've been stupid."

"No. Innocent."

"Maura tried to tell me. So did Rory. Their seer eyes recognized trouble."

"True, although we didn't know what to do. And when you left..." Aiden peered into her eyes, then looked away.

"I thought I was protecting you, my family — by leaving."

"That I understand. We're glad you're home." He hesitated. "If there was a place to hide you, we'd take you there, now."

Aless shivered with regret. She had nothing to say, no way to thank the man who'd been like a father since he'd dangled on a branch, inviting her into their lives.

Maura came into the room, wiping her hands with a dish towel. "Dinner's almost ready. I took some water up for a bath if you'd like. Not as much as usual, but still a bath."

As Maura walked upstairs with her, Aless struggled to find words to describe what she'd experienced on the mountain. Finally, the story spilled out in a hurried tumble. "I-I saw a little girl. At the base of the mountain. She was on a dappled mare and wore a green riding cape. She led me here after I fell and hit my head."

Maura held a hand over her heart and breathed out a puff of air. A sad smile lit her face. "My mother described that cape before her sister was kidnapped. It was her favorite riding gear. And she loved that mare."

They walked into Alessandra's room and stood side by side in front of the picture of the woman who'd appeared just in time.

Aless gazed at the image of her mother. "I thought you'd exaggerated her beauty. You didn't." She turned to Maura. "She told me to forgive myself. And that my family needed me."

Maura grabbed her into a quick side hug. "Aye. That we do."

Aless caught a whiff of herself and grimaced. "I'm so dirty. And stinky."

Maura pointed to the bathroom. "You've smelled better, but never have I seen a sweeter sight. I'll finish getting dinner ready. Join us when you're done."

Aless looked around her room after Maura left. It was unchanged, as if her family had awaited her return. The bed where she'd agonized over her decision to leave had been made. The chiffarobe was full of clothing that didn't seem like hers any longer. Grabbing her warmest pair of pants, socks, and sweater, she headed to the small bathroom.

There wasn't enough water to duck under in the claw foot tub, so she drenched herself over and over until the water turned brown. Shivering in the cool air, she dried herself and hurried to pull on the warm clothes. After digging back through the closet, she grabbed her riding boots and laced them. Finally, she placed the Stones in one pocket and headed downstairs.

She half-expected to see Rory in the kitchen, ready to tease her. But not even Mrs. Ransbottom was there. "Where is she?"

Maura stood over the familiar counter, gathering plates in one hand, and handing Aless a bowl of steaming potatoes. "She's so old. And wanted to be with the children who had no one. To be sure they'd be safe. She…"

So like the feisty woman with rolling pin in hand. A warrior with an apron.

Aiden joined them as they sat down to a simple meal of boiled potatoes with bits of parsley, green beans, and a few carrots.

"This is the best we can do, Aless." Maura murmured an apology.

Lucy broke in with her mouth full. "I likes veggie tables."

"Best meal I've had for many days." Aless nodded at Lucy who shivered in the cold room. "Let me stoke that fire a bit."

She glanced through the arched windows where the arborists' sanctuary was pristine in newly fallen snow. Was it a sudden wind that shifted the towering pine trees overhead?

A shadowy figure sat, perched on a branch of spindly needles. It was too large to be a raven or crow. She stepped back in alarm, almost tripping on the rumpled edge of a rug. It was a man, clad from head to toe in black. With an arrow poised in drawn bow.

Aiden came to her side. "Maura. You and Lucy. Go upstairs. Shutter the windows."

Maura held out her hands to Lucy. "Come, little one. We'll clean up later."

Lucy jumped into her mother's arms and waved at Alessandra as her mother scaled the winding stairs.

Whiz. A blazing arrow flew, landing with perfect aim into the center of the circle drive and sizzled in the snow. A man stood, full-length on the branch. Another arrow flew from first one, then another pine tree. One of them sent flames into a bare Tulip tree. Its sodden branches extinguished the flame. What looked like a singular flock of starlings were warriors. Nayeli warriors.

Aiden spoke in a low tone that Aless struggled to hear. "They're here."

Chapter 27

Aless peered outside from the cover of heavy drapery at the front window. The same arched window where she'd watched Tareq and his men arrive at the chateau months ago. She searched the trees, now full of snipers.

"What can we do?" Alessandra looked at Aiden and knew. There were three adults, and one child. Plus, an unruly dog. There wasn't much they could do.

"We've planned a few things — rocks wrapped inside socks, a catapult for flaming stuff." Aiden rubbed his brow and studied the floor. "The arborists were supposed to be here. They must've been diverted."

Aiden and Maura's plans were brave, but futile. They were tired and hungry, and the battle hadn't even begun. Aless wanted to scream, to cry. A few Magi gifts against an army of Nayeli. Insurmountable odds. They might as well give up now.

If not for Aiden and Maura. And Lucy. And Rufus.

Blindly marching to a battle line wasn't going to help. One scrawny woman didn't offer much in the way of bait *or* as a threat against the enemy. Except she had the Stones.

They'd cut an invisible path through the burning huts during the attack on Tara's village, bringing women and children to safety. She'd need more than a trail right now, though. Unless it led her family safely out of this mess.

Light snow fell, softening the image of doom in countless eyes that stared into the chateau.

"I have a plan. I can get us out of here safely." Aless pulled the Stones from her pocket. "Remember the Stones? The Stones of Promise."

"Of course," Aiden said, studying the two small rocks in Alessandra's hand. "They were lost generations ago."

"The Nayeli hid them in the temple dedicated to Gad El Glas in Akkad. I…brought them back."

The Stones nestled in her open palm. Like ordinary rocks. They didn't grow warm with blue light. Nor did any words appear on their smooth surface.

Aiden picked them up and rolled them over in his hand. "They aren't what I expected. What do they do?"

"I know. They don't look like much. Except, they led women and children out of battle on the way here — safely. They'll do it again."

Aiden placed the Stones back into Alessandra's palm. "We trust you, Aless. Except we must be sure."

She understood. She couldn't expect Aiden to risk the lives of his family without certain proof that the Stones would protect them. Even though there was no reason to believe they wouldn't. They'd brought an unseen exit through a raging battle. Surely, this wasn't any different.

"Let's try the back door." She hurried through the home that was usually full of children and noise. She pushed through the kitchen and stopped at the back door. Then searched for any response in the Stones.

Nothing. No light, no words.

"I don't understand, Aiden. They lit the way where

there was no way. Maybe if I go outside with them."

"Wait." Aiden leaned against a wall with a hand to his chest.

"What's wrong? Are you okay?"

Aiden's face was an unnatural white, his lips were colorless. He slumped against the wall and inched his way to the cold granite floor.

Maura appeared in the doorway and hurried to her husband. She knelt beside him with her arms around his shoulders. "Peace, beloved. I'm here."

Minutes later, Aiden pushed away from his wife's embrace. He tried to smile but only conjured the ghastly expression of a sick man.

Fear gripped Alessandra. Aiden had always been her hero. Since his arrival years ago when he'd led her out of that dark place, he'd welcomed her as his own. Even when she'd been angry and run from home, he'd never stopped believing she belonged to their family. And in her eyes, he'd never aged.

Yet, of course, he had. Was it his heart? Her mind raced from one awful possibility to another.

Until finally, she understood.

Aiden was afraid.

How could that be?

What a stupid question. Except, her foundation quaked as surely as Aiden's hands which he tried to massage into compliance.

Aless held her hand to the necklace and waited.

In a vision, smoke drifted in under the doors and up the walls. Its acrid stench crept into her nose and burned her throat. Battle cries screamed from every wall. Blood flowed down the hallway.

Alessandra's body chilled to the core. The massacre

at the chateau years ago. Aiden was there as a child. And the only one who survived.

Maura looked at Alessandra and nodded. "He remembers."

Her hero had scars. Like her mother. Like herself.

Aless studied the Stones in her hands, begging them to speak. To do something. To prove that this time she carried hope in her hands.

Maura peered up at her. Her voice was clear and strong, as if she'd heard an unspoken command. "You aren't the one who leads the Stones, Aless. They must lead you." Maura pointed at Alessandra's hands and nodded. "Your job is to follow."

Frustration threatened to boil over. She didn't have a strategy. Couldn't force her brain into any kind of submission. She had to think. Alone. "I'll be back. I need to find something in the library."

Aiden and Maura faced each other, forehead to forehead. Loving each other. And praying.

Aless jammed the Stones back into her pocket. She opened the oaken door and slipped inside the library. It was the room where the arborists first told her about Lilith Gunter. She fought a sense of betrayal. It was the same ache when she'd bolted in the middle of the night and run toward what turned out to be the enemy's lair.

Why had the Stones fallen short now when it mattered so much? She settled into a small nook beneath a window in the back of the room, grateful that Lucy was safely tucked away in her room. That spot, away from Lucy's eyes and constant search, had been Alessandra's indoor retreat for many years.

She pulled the Stones out of her pocket and studied them. "I didn't ask to find you. Yet, there you were in the temple. Like you were waiting for me." The Stones lay in her hand. She wasn't sure what she expected. "I need you. We need you."

Nothing. Except an impression. A knowing. *Will you follow?*

One thing she'd learned at Tara's village. The Stones weren't magic. Not in the way she'd thought. They worked by principle. As baffling as they were, they'd operated by love. Love that created a way where there was no way.

Alessandra finally understood the prophecy. The high place wasn't only Akkad. It was the lie she had to conquer. Love didn't come from perfect people in perfect circumstances. But no matter how flawed, it was strong. It bore the weight of terrible things and rose to overcome. She couldn't make the Stones work in her hands. She could choose love.

Aless searched outside the window. The focus of the warrior's attention seemed to be on the front of the chateau. She struggled to pry open the cold glass that refused to budge against its wooden sill. With one more tug, the window opened with a giant wrench.

Aless tied on Hildegard's shawl and climbed outside. Frigid air assaulted her lungs. Snow soaked the bottom of her trousers and sifted into the top of her boots. She was out of sight, only not for long. Leaning against the stony granite wall, she looked out over the army that had gathered in the meadow.

Dark eyes peering from black turbans still dotted the trees, with bows poised to shoot. Drumbeats sounded, boom, boom, as animal-clad warriors stabbing the air with flaming spears crowded the meadow. With a shrieking Ayyye, men dressed as death lined a path through the army.

Aless swallowed dread, remembering the gruesome invaders who had gone from house to house in Akkad, dragging out frightened people on the night of the sacrifice. The same powerlessness she'd felt then threatened to make her turn and run.

At the end of the line of death warriors, two people stood as if they expected her. It was Tareq and Laila, side by side.

Aless stared at the young prince and wondered if she'd ever been more than a pawn to him. Straightening her shoulders, she stepped toward the fierce army. A path had already been made. Only this one was lined with skeletal men, dressed as messengers of death. She straightened her shoulders and walked forward.

One of the black specters hissed as she passed. She couldn't help turning her gaze to the gaunt face of the warrior. It was the same man who'd pounced her on the temple the night Shema died. The one whose hands gripped her arms with unnatural strength. Once again, dark, empty eyes glared back, and his mouth stretched into a snarl.

Aless planted her feet and made a decision. She'd come without a plan. This time, although she didn't fully understand them, she'd trust the Stones. Keeping her eyes fixed on the Crown Prince, she walked through the line of warriors, brushing past the steam of hot breath and odd mix of sweat and aromatic ointments.

Tareq stared at the ground, unwilling to meet her gaze. He was as motionless as a statue, etched in bronze.

Laila pointed an alabaster finger as Alessandra approached. "Ah. She emerges from her hole."

Aless took a deep breath to still the fear, then the

anger that stirred inside. Laila had murdered her friend, Shema. She'd ordered the troops that had attacked Tara's village and led countless other atrocities against defenseless Magi. Laila's brutality and Tareq's weak acquiescence had been an effective alliance. Aless longed to call down fire from heaven again. This time, she'd target the woman behind all this destruction.

She couldn't, though. She hadn't forgotten Rory's words that the Stones never operated with vengeance. What would unveil their mystery now? She searched their pale grainy surface for words. Still nothing.

Snow drifted against the walls of the chateau and loaded tree branches with icy powder. An oak branch extended overhead like the hand of a giant protector. Aless had nothing to say to Laila. Tareq had been her friend, though. She'd begin with what she knew to be true. Bowing to the Crown Prince, she said, "Welcome to my home."

Tareq glanced away as Laila curled under the crook of his arm.

Alessandra took a step closer, keeping her focus on Tareq. "Laila needs you. Without your father. Why?" She pretended that the seductive woman wasn't there. That she and Tareq were alone, talking on the ledge that overlooked open sky one more time. "What do you have that threatens her rule?"

"How perceptive, oh failed daughter of Lilith Gunter," Laila interrupted with a taunting voice, draping her arm around Tareq's waist.

Aless straightened her shoulders and lifted her voice as unexplainable peace drifted over her heart. Was the calm she felt a work of the Stones? She lifted her voice, for all to hear. "My mother didn't fail. She disavowed

Gad El Glas in the end."

"Too late. Just as it isss for you," Laila drawled. "She was disqualified, as you are. As you were before."

Aless remembered the evil serpent at the temple and the way it had coiled itself around Shema. Aless refused to waver, determined not to be intimidated. "What do you mean as I was before?"

"You don't recognize the family resemblance?"

Chapter 28

Alessandra placed her hand on the colored beads that spun around a small opal. The next moment, Aless saw her mother at Laila's age, striking and defiant. It was her mother's stark beauty and regal stance in Laila. Her voice quivered. "You're her daughter."

"And what does that make you?" Laila cackled. "Hidden away, rejected as successor. You never knew your real father, did you? Anton Gunter? That worm? Hardly. Your father was a mighty Nayeli priest, killed by Magi warriors.

"Sad that I, alone, set my heart to avenge his blood. Sister? Never. Precious Alessandra. Too weak for the mantle only I received. A failure in the worst sense."

Alessandra wavered, stunned, at a revelation that made her gag in disgust.

A ghoulish soldier let out a low laugh, as if in derision. Another jabbed his spear up and down, muddying the snow, as others joined him. These agents of death acknowledged their true leader. It was Laila.

"Now that you're *home*, you'll be responsible for the deaths of those you call family. Small payment for defying the Nayeli." Laila placed a long, manicured hand on Tareq's shoulder.

Tareq jerked, almost imperceptibly, as if his body knew what his mind did not acknowledge.

Aless ventured a look back to the chateau. By now,

Aiden and Maura had realized that she'd gone to confront their adversary alone. She cringed, recalling the trauma that had marked Aiden. Surely, they'd tucked Lucy into a hidden nook where she couldn't be found. They'd do their best to shield her from an adversary once again intent on their destruction.

Laila's words pulled her back to the scenario before her. "Did you think you could win him?" she asked, with a jeer. "He is already spoken for. And has been from his birth. For he can only belong to her successor."

Laila had been appointed to carry out Lilith Gunter's evil legacy. She was unswerving in that goal. Trying to spar with the woman was only a diversion. Aless had to speak to Tareq as if he were the only one there. "You're worth more than this. She's only used you. She murdered your father to make you hers alone."

Tareq's composure shifted.

Laila mocked. "He never loved you. Nothing in you attracted him. You were only an assignment."

Suspicion charged the atmosphere. "Is that true? Did she send you?"

Tareq bowed his head and stayed behind as Laila strode toward Aless. Her fragrance, heavy and intoxicating, went before her like a shield. "Oh, my," she laughed. "You thought your meeting was only coincidence? Hardly."

The death warriors encircled Laila with their spears pointing outward. They stomped their feet against muddy ground, chanting a weird *Ahhhh, aiiii.*

Alessandra's heart plummeted with what Laila had said. Tareq's arrival hadn't been the hands of destiny. It was only a malicious plot driven by the cohort of Gad El Glas herself. She turned from the Crown Prince in sadness. Treachery had been his motive all along.

It was time to ask the Laila a question of her own. "Tell me something. Why do you hate the Magi?"

Laila's answer was abrupt. "I chose not to disappoint my mother." She curtsied, as if to mock Alessandra. "Unlike you."

Aless swayed a bit inside. She'd had one conversation with her mother as an adult. As real as it seemed, it was only a vision. What had really defined Lilith Gunter? Each part of the woman — what Aless knew and what she didn't — became the whole of a tragic life. Her mother had renounced the evil Gad El Glas right before she died. Was her final decision enough in exchange for a lifetime of hate?

Laila hissed a command. Whatever she said stirred the army into frenzied dancing and spears jabbed into the sky. "Ahhhh, aiii!"

Aless struggled to think. There was nowhere to hide, no quiet place to retreat. One thing was certain. Nothing could explain or deny what she'd experienced on the way up the mountain. A child had arrived on a pale gray steed and carried her safely to the waterfall.

The necklace Nona had fastened around her neck in Sanctuary that fateful day, truly allowed her to see the unseen. Aless had lain on a cold forest ground, unable to move. And a child had come to her aid. She'd witnessed her mother's heart in the form of a young girl. A child before slavery in service to a demon god, twisted by what she'd suffered.

Alessandra knew from Maura, the one who'd been with her mother the very moment that Lilith Gunter had left this earth free and forgiven. Loving her daughter.

Laila stood as an evil regent over a Nayeli army now

offering their frenetic worship with pounding drums and screaming mayhem. Aless understood the uproar was a staged distraction meant to avoid a simple question. "What about her decision at the end of her life?"

"An anomaly," Laila answered quickly, as if she'd anticipated the query. "A death-bed conversion. It meant nothing."

"It meant something," Aless said, calmly. She defended her mother. The one she knew she'd become. "She came to me at the base of the mountain in a vision. She isn't like you."

"In your imagination, you mean. How convenient. You and your precious Magi. She was your arch enemy. I saw you wield the Stones in the temple. My mother did the same thing — again and again — against Magi scum. Perhaps you're like her, after all.

"I *am* like my mother. I know when I'm wrong. She understood that, finally."

"It was too late for her. Just as it is for you."

Aless forced herself not to retreat or shift her stance as she faced her enemy. Her sister. Laila had embraced Lilith's trade in human souls. She, too, captured Magi and bound them in service to Gad El Glas. The young girls who surrounded her were proof of that evil work.

Aless shuddered to think what the little ones had witnessed.

In some ways, she'd been like Lilith Gunter, too. Her mother refused love because it had failed her. Blinded by bitterness, Aless longed to destroy any connection with her mother. True, she'd messed up in a big way at the temple. But, worse, she'd rejected the family who'd been her true north all along. The ones who knew her *and* loved her.

Like her mother, though, Aless never really lost them. Love kept looking for her, despite all she'd done to destroy it.

Aless pulled the Stones out of her pocket. They were warm to touch, though without a message she could see. She stepped forward until she saw Laila's breath turn to puffs of frozen droplets. "Take me."

Laila's arrogance wavered for an instant. "What makes you think I want you?"

"You pursued me to a mountain chateau. There are many other Magi families. What do you want?"

Laila's lips curled, although a small line appeared between her brows.

"I said." Aless spoke with authority. "What do you want?"

Silence. The skeletal guards glanced from Laila to Aless and back, perhaps unsure of their next move. Did Laila's once erect shoulders slump — only a little? Tension seemed to creep into the gathering.

The snow drove in heavy gusts, pressing pine branches to the ground with their weight. Snowflakes grazed Alessandra's neck and trailed down her back. They soaked through the shawl and saturated her hair. She stayed intent on what was going on in front of her, despite her body trembling in the cold. Something was happening, though she wasn't sure what it was.

Laila fidgeted from one foot to the other. Layers of snow gathered on the pelts of her chestnut mink coat and frosted her hair.

Tareq had moved away so gradually, that even Laila failed to notice. Dressed in a velvet tunic and covered with a robe of white ermine, he first glanced at Aless and then returned her gaze.

Lifting her voice, she shouted to the Crown Prince. "Your father was wrong, Tareq. His decision cost your sister and beloved mother. Will you side with a woman who makes hatred a legacy in your bloodline? So, the loss never ends?"

Tareq's voice pierced the air like an alarm sounding before battle. "You, Alessandra. She wants you. Can't you see? You asked if I was blind." The prince struggled for words, then spewed them out in a feverish rush. "Don't you understand? Lilith chose you, Alessandra. Your mother chose *you* to carry the Stones."

The guards stopped chanting. Their feet slowed, and weapons hung as if undecided.

In the center of a battleground, pressed beyond all Alessandra had to offer, a tiny thread of hope arrived. Her mother had known her daughter's destiny all along. Despite the evil Lilith Gunter had aligned with, she'd known. And acted.

The prophecy was true. *"Though an enemy builds its shelters on high and sets its nests among the stars, she who carries the light of stars will find and bring them down."*

She might not carry them perfectly. She'd carry them, anyway.

Laila hesitated, only a moment. Then she screamed. "Come, Gad El Glas. Come to me, your servant." She writhed with arms extended and legs swaying. Her body shifted and twirled, morphing into a coil that became a serpent. It was the white asp, sidling across the snow to Tareq.

Tareq's face shifted, and haughtiness descended over his face like a mask.

"Don't let her manipulate you." Alessandra begged.

Laila stretched out her serpentine head toward Aless as she coiled around the prince's feet. "He knowsss hisss destiny. Even if you don't."

Alessandra exclaimed. "Your heart doesn't belong to her. Be free, Tareq." With all her strength, she pleaded with her friend to hear, to know the truth.

Laila coiled at the prince's feet. "You. Are. Mine. Alwayssss mine."

Aless was losing him. Tareq had forgotten who he was, just like that awful night when he'd stood, powerless as Laila murdered Shema. The Crown Prince was disappearing as surely as the evil woman gathered vigor in her serpentine body.

The Stones became warm in her hand. Writing filled one, then the other. *Light. Completion.*

Aless grasped the Stones tighter. She finally understood.

Light always trumped darkness. Darkness and fear disrupted what was meant to be good, to be whole. She had been crushed by what her mother had been, never knowing what she'd become.

"Light, come," she said, upholding the Stones. "Complete what only you can."

A narrow beam glowed around her. It grew broader, wider, until even the warriors stared, slack jawed. The light grew like morning sun, brighter, warmer, and extending overhead into the canopy of pines. North wind shifted, and a southern breeze wafted in like a kiss, its tenderness brushing her face.

The snake bobbed its head and its black eyes narrowed. In the next instant, it let out a piercing screech, exposing fangs like scimitars. Every living thing in the woods silenced as the serpent rose to become an ashen dragon. It blasted an inferno into the forest, sizzling tree branches and exposing muddy undergrowth.

The ebony clad guards came to life. They jabbed spears into the air and shouted in unison as their pounding feet splayed mud and snow. This was the manifestation of their god, and they knew it.

"Light, you say? I'll give you light," the white dragon roared.

Flames sputtered in the melting snow, revealing bits of green grass that had endured through the winter. With another breath, fire scorched a stand of aspen just beyond the meadow.

"I know the real evil behind Gad El Glas," Alessandra said, crying out. "Far worse than a towering serpent, it twists the heart with fear — only to make you its captive.

"You don't have to bow, Tareq. Don't let it win. Not this time."

Like a mighty centaur in defeat, Tareq fell to his knees in the earthy sludge.

Chapter 29

The dragon blasted flames against Alessandra's beloved woods as it charged the chateau. The forest where she'd seen her first robin's egg and played afternoon games of hide and seek. One fiery breath scorched the sycamore she'd once climbed so high Aiden had to coax her down.

There was no way her family could survive this onslaught. And nothing Aless could do to stop it. She whirled around, placing her hand instinctively on Rory's necklace. A picture grew in color and detail. A little girl with auburn curls and green eyes bobbed up and down at Tareq's feet, holding small hands to be held.

Warmth flowed through her hand as she grasped the Stones. She peered down at the two plain rocks she'd first seen in the evil temple. They weren't magic in any way she'd ever heard in legends. They didn't cast a spell that descended over the unsuspecting. In fact, nothing about them had attracted her at first. At least not until they'd responded to her alone.

They offered no words this time, only a knowing. Tareq wasn't married, nor did he have children. His future had a voice that called to him, though. It was the cry of his own daughter, yet unborn.

Finally, Alessandra understood. Only Tareq could defeat the one sworn to destroy hope for a new beginning. Only he could stop the dragon.

His father had been a willing accomplice as Gad El Glas enslaved an entire civilization. Tareq was the next in line to either bow or to rise in courage against it. She had to tell him. Before it was too late.

The army's attention was diverted as they focused on the plundering dragon. Slipping the Stones into her pocket, she zigzagged through one contingent of soldiers and approached Tareq, who still knelt on the ground, alone.

She'd almost reached him when strong hands grabbed and swung her around. The stench of rotten eggs spewed from a warrior's gaping mouth and his face twisted in scornful triumph. As hard as she fought, the man's iron grip didn't budge.

Shifting her body in a determined pivot, she turned to face Tareq. Even if a ghoul held her captive, it wouldn't silence her voice. "I see her, Tareq. I see your daughter." She shouted, imploring him. "She stands at your feet, her green eyes loving you. Trusting you. Don't let Gad El Glas steal her. Not this one."

The dark warrior shook her until her neck ached. She donkey-kicked him in the shin and yelled louder. "The future is only secure if you have the courage. Stand against Gad El Glas. You're the only one who can defeat it."

The man held her tighter and repeated the shrill, "Ahh, aii, aiii!"

The rest of the army followed her captor's lead. Stomping their feet against the damp earth, they whirled and hooted battle cries. She couldn't tell if Tareq had heard what she said. He lifted his head from the ground and stared at her. He made no other move to respond.

"Pay no attention to the noise of the enemy," she

called out. "You have authority to end this."

Suddenly, the fiendish man who held her let out an unwarrior-like yelp. Aless peered around, wondering why the howling had stopped. Tossing Aless to the ground like unwanted garbage, the man scrambled back to the line of warriors.

Trees splintered and branches scattered into leafy fragments as a massive shadow hovered over the forest. Cool air became stifling heat. Aless pressed herself against the burnt skeleton of a once lofty oak. "Don't look," she whispered to herself over and over. "Keep your eyes on the prince." She had to convince him. Now.

"It was easier to bow to her, Tareq." She stretched a hand overhead. "This beast is Laila's true nature. You knew that in your heart all along. Confront the lie. Conquer what only you can."

She saw her own terror reflected in his eyes as the dragon dropped to the earth. It smashed through dense vegetation, crushing underbrush, and vibrating the ground. The army melted out of formation as its soldiers ducked into whatever cover they could find.

The dragon roared, "Tempt him, you will not! Finished! Finished!"

Aless pressed her body closer against the charred tree. There was no way of escape. She was going to die while Tareq stood, tottering back and forth as if he walked across a line of narrow hedgerows.

A familiar lanky frame appeared from a ridge that overlooked the clearing. It was Rory, sprinting into the meadow with long legs pumping. He charged through sentinels who made way for him without protest.

"No!" She'd longed to see him. Not now. Not this way. He kept rushing forward, ignoring her cries until it was too late to do anything but scream, "Stop!"

The dragon paused, as if deciding what to do with this man who kept plowing through the forest, dodging trees, and skipping over huddled soldiers.

Aless reached out her arms. "Rory. Please. Go."

Instead, he closed the gap between them. He dashed to Alessandra as the dragon lowered its mouth. Lunging, he grabbed her in one motion, threw her to the ground, and laid over her like a protective blanket.

Melting snow seeped around Alessandra's head and saturated her clothes. Mud crept around her ears and through her fingers as the warmth of Rory's weight pressed against her. The scent of the mountain in springtime filled her senses.

She struggled for an instant. "Rory, get off. We have to leave. Now."

An acrid odor of death filled the air. Aless tried to wriggle her way out of Rory's arms and legs that grappled and held her tight.

When a river of fire coursed over them.

Searing heat scorched her hands and rushed on both sides. Rory convulsed, then stiffened as he cried out in agony. Fabric, hair, and flesh smoldered in a putrid stench. With a low moan, his body collapsed against hers in dead weight.

Her dearest friend had come. Again. Just when she needed him.

Grief, regret, and longing poured out of her heart and wouldn't be stopped. She wept, longing to hold him, knowing she couldn't without hurting him more.

Rory's face lay against the mud, his chocolate hair black and burnt to stubble. His body was still against hers. Arms that had wrapped her in a hasty embrace were limp at her side.

Her friend. The one who'd warned her of danger before the journey to Akkad. Who'd never left, even when she'd rejected him. He'd followed her to the desert city and placed guardians like Perseus and Tara around her. When she'd failed and all she wanted to do was die, he hadn't let her.

Rory knew her. And loved her. Why had that seemed so small?

He lay lifeless against her, keeping her pinned. Exhausted and emptied, she crooned wordless comfort like a mother over a sick child. Over the boy who had become the man she loved. And now had lost.

The brush of a velvet and soft fur coat appeared at her side. Tareq knelt silently, tears streaming down his face. With the gentlest of touch, he lifted Rory and placed his blistered back onto a patch of scraggly grass and mud.

Aless cradled Rory's head on her lap, stroking his cheek, and wept. Knowing that, as always, he'd seen what was coming when she hadn't. And offered himself in her place.

A hush spread throughout the meadow. For a moment, nothing breathed.

Until a guttural voice sounded. The dragon thundered, breaking the stillness of that moment like an approaching storm. "Death to Magi filth."

Tareq drew himself up into the fullness of his stature. He faced the dragon, shoulders straight and chin jutted. Then stabbed his hand into the air.

That was it. A hand upheld in a now spring-like day with snow becoming watery streams and warriors who were supposed to deal out death but didn't know what to do.

The soldiers peered out from their cover in confusion.

"Death to you, oh, beguiling one." Tareq's words resounded across the meadow. "Death to you. Now!"

The dragon's mighty haunches wobbled once. Then again. It called out in a grainy voice.

"Help me."

Bones — Aless guessed dragons had bones. Whatever skeleton filled its bulk shook with a huge pop. There was a loud crack and another, like ice breaking in spring melt. The dragon's legs, then torso, collapsed from the inside out. Giant talons fell away, scattering the ground like discarded swords. Luminescent wings withered into wrinkled fingers. In minutes, a shrunken version of the once towering beast stood dazed under a soaring pine.

First one gaunt soldier, then another stood, as if to see more clearly what was impossible.

This time, with Alessandra at his side with the Stones, Tareq stretched his hand higher, and jabbed the air, over and over.

The dragon spun around wildly, as if seeking aid that refused to present itself. With another round of snaps and splinters, its body wasted away until it became the size of a large dog. With the whine of a pesky mosquito, it squeaked a command. "Help me. Now."

Instead of obeying an edict the warriors had no idea how to carry out, each one watched in amazement as the giant lizard buckled like a tower of hewn timber and fell into a heap.

"I said…" It rolled onto the ground, twisting and piping. "Gad El Glas. Come." In one spiraling motion, the dragon twirled into a snake that roiled against the ground.

"It's the power of your gift working, Tareq." Aless called, encouraging him. "Your gift to conquer what held your father."

The snake let out a strangled hiss and slithered closer. With every inch, its body shrunk.

The Crown Prince kept his hand extended. In a voice that first trembled, then became a roar, he yelled. "Go! Back to the one who controls you."

The serpent became a small asp that murmured at his side. "No, my chosssen one. Come to me. She lies. She liessss."

Tareq yanked a jewel-encrusted sword from his side and slashed it across the serpent's body. Green ballooning smoke erupted, then dissipated in an overpowering stench of decay. The asp shriveled into dry, lifeless skin. He looked in wonder at Alessandra. Then to Rory who lay motionless on the ground.

No one spoke.

Instead, the army of plumed warriors came back together as one and bowed. All except the grisly savage who'd stood over Aless as a personal vendetta. The man's face paled under slashes of white paint that had once formed a hellish ghoul, now subdued.

Sunlight grew brighter.

Rory lay motionless on the ground.

Chapter 30

Alessandra tucked Hildegard's shawl tenderly around Rory's body. His breath became tiny puffs that barely moved his lips. His skin was cool to touch, despite the terrible burns that melted any remaining snow around him.

"No," she pleaded, caressing his face. She kissed his eyelids, willing the starburst eyes to open. "Don't leave me. Not when I'm finally home. Not before I tell you that I've loved you forever."

She pulled the Stones out of her pocket and begged them. "Save him. Save him now."

A small cry sounded from the same ridge Rory had entered. A little girl ran, fearless, through the barbarian army. Muslin dress flapping in the breeze and arms swinging, she dashed, intent on Rory's still form.

"Suzette!"

The child headed straight to Rory. Hair the color of burnished copper bounced as she plopped beside him. She nodded once to Aless, as if to say a quick hello. Then turned her attention to Rory.

She knelt beside him and laid petite fingers on his belly. "It can't have you, Rory. You belong to us." She lifted her voice into a song that filled the air with its fragrance of hope. "The Lord bless and keep you. May His face shine upon you and give you peace."

That was it. Suzette rested her hands on Rory a

moment longer. She kissed his cheek, and then wrapped Alessandra into her freckled arms. Together, they sat at Rory's side.

A blush of color traveled from Rory's neck to the top of his head. He shuddered and took a shallow, hiccupping breath. His hand quivered. With a deep gasp, his chest expanded, and starlit eyes opened.

He took a breath, then another. And another. His body shifted against the ground.

What was happening?

He cleared his throat and moved his lips, as if checking to see if they still worked. "Hot. So hot."

Was he dying? His body had been cold minutes before.

His cheeks flushed and body quaked. Once. Then again.

"I...pain...It's leaving." He took another long, rattling breath and touched his face. "I...I can..."

He sat up and felt the back of his head. Tiny sprouts of new hair appeared from a pink, flawless scalp. The stink was gone. He held a hand to his nose. "I smell the forest."

As he rubbed the back of his head, then his arms, charred remains of skin and fabric fell away like dust. He reached to his legs. Black ash dropped into the mud, and fresh skin appeared.

Rory searched and found Aless. "I'm new. All over me," he whispered.

Suzette and Tareq danced and whooped beside them as Rory's muscular arms enfolded Alessandra. In one swoop, he drew her into his lap, pressing her against his chest that throbbed with each heartbeat.

Aless stroked his sinewy back that peeked out of

tattered remains of the tunic, grateful for what every touch revealed. Rory was alive. She reached for his lips and kissed him. Her body leaned into his until he toppled over. Joy traveled back and forth as they giggled, then laughed with each embrace and each kiss, together in this moment.

Then she remembered.

They weren't alone. And Rory didn't have much in the way of clothes on. He was healed, but his garments hung in shreds. And she'd been lost in the delight of his brand-new body. A once grim soldier hid an almost grin and scuffed his feet against the dirt. Tareq smiled as he draped his long ermine cloak around Rory's shoulders.

The warriors — well, they were a mess. Not doing what gnarly barbarians were supposed to do. Several wept openly. Others fell to the ground, as if in reverence of the moment.

In the midst of burnt pine needles and singed trees, Rory rose to his feet. He stood, regal, acknowledging the wild assortment of bowing soldiers. Tareq stood beside him, arm wrapped around Rory for support. For that moment, side by side, Magi and Nayeli reigned together in peace.

Suzette saw her mother emerging from the chateau and bound after her. "Mama!"

Maura rushed through the Nayeli army holding one arm out for Suzette and the other to Aless. Together, they tumbled to the ground laughing and crying.

"You did it," Maura said. "You heard the Stones. And they led you."

Aless hugged her tighter. "You were there. When the weight of my gifting grew heavy…"

Mrs. Ransbottom waddled into the meadow, her

aged legs struggling to keep up with a horde of children returning to their family. "Oi, girl. We missed you. Something terrible."

"We're here, Awess! We're here," cried Lucy, tearing out of the chateau, and making a beeline to her siblings and the small company of Magi children.

The children jumped around Alessandra, demanding hugs. Then noticed the army of warriors and went to chat. One of the guards removed his crested helmet and stooped to study a smashed crocus bloom in Lucy's hand.

Rory gathered Aless into his arms. "We're here, indeed. And going nowhere soon."

"Where's Aiden?" Aless panicked. "Is he alright?"

Maura nodded and pointed to a small army who approached the meadow.

Aiden rode, leading a troupe of arborists behind him. There was Clarion on the mottled gray stallion and Brocagni who swayed on the back of the dogged mule. Sunlight reflected on the cygnet of ivy encircling Clarion's head. Broc hulked over the mule, surly as ever, glaring this way and that through the crowd of Nayeli. Swathes of white hair bobbed in a warm breeze and stubby fingers clenched his sword.

Aiden dismounted and held out his arms.

Aless looked to Maura who stood beside her. "Your hero husband is here — with reinforcements."

Lucy spun in a cartwheel in the muddy grass. When she came upright, she pointed at Aless. "It's you, silly," Lucy said. "Daddy wants to hug *you*."

Aless lost no time running into the familiar refuge of Aiden's arms. She felt his heart pound and knew. He'd left the chateau during the showdown, amid snipers and a Nayeli army to gather the arborists. She whispered against his chest. "If I crafted a father from the stars and brought him to earth, he'd never be as perfect as you."

Aiden gathered Maura into the circle, along with Lucy and the other children who chimed in. "Move. It's my turn."

Finally, Rory stepped in. "Avast ye timbers and blunder-butts. Out of the way." He pulled Alessandra out of the small mob and nestled his face into her hair. "I heard your vow of unending love, by the way. And am holding you to it."

Aless rested her head against the softness of the fur cloak. Every trace of smoke had disappeared from his skin, swallowed in the scent of a meadow in springtime. "How did you know what was going to happen?"

"Silly girl," he said, mimicking Lucy. "Don't think I haven't had my eyes on you. I was there that day in Sanctuary when all was burning around you. I watched you on the ledge in Akkad, longing to hold you." He took a breath and held her tighter. "Besides, I know when a dragon is ready to spew. Never pretty."

Aless brushed her lips against his now healed neck. "You think you're so smart." She leaned in for a kiss, then looked up with a question. "Wait a minute. Where's Nona?"

Rory pointed in the direction of a small group gathered around the front lawn of the chateau.

Nona waved as she trotted their way. "Oi, couldn't miss this moment, Alessandra," she said, out of breath by the time she made it to the meadow. It was the brogue and the woman Aless loved. "Besides, I hed to see how you and that necklace were faring."

"It unveiled the unseen…over and over. Protected

me in more ways than I knew. Best of all, it showed me my mama's heart."

"Ah. That's what it were for. Of course, ye didn't know the whole story." She smiled and nodded to Rory who hadn't left Alessandra's side. "Tell her, me boy."

Rory blushed and knelt in the mud with one hand offered to Aless. "The necklace was for you. All along. Set apart for a time like this." He looked up with his starburst eyes. "Marry me, Alessandra Gunter. Be mine. Forever and always."

Aless studied the face she'd adored since he'd beat her at the first race down a mountain trail and finally knew what she saw. It was love.

"I will." It sounded like a promise.

And it was.

Chapter 31

Ribbons dangled from the hawthorn branches in the front lawn of the chateau. The two trees had been planted in honor of Maura's parents. Their branches merged and became a leafy portico that welcomed each person to the refuge of the chateau.

Rory waited under the arch, dressed in a white shirt, and pants the color of evergreens. The children formed a path from Rory to the front door of the chateau. Lucy, Suzette, Louis, Marcella each held a branch from the flowering trees on the front lawn. They poked each other and squirmed, ready to get this event moving so they could play in summer sunshine.

Alessandra stood at oaken door with Aiden on one side and Maura on the other. She gazed down at the simple cotton whisp of fabric and ribbons that trailed to the ground and seemed to float in the gentle breeze. Nona had brought the fabrics from Sanctuary. Maura had spent hours at night, when the house was finally quiet to craft a dress that was Alessandra's alone.

Rory's necklace was her only jewelry. Vibrant threads outlining the tree of life in Hildegard's shawl covered her shoulders. It gleamed fresh and clean after a good scrub in the claw-foot tub upstairs. The Stones that rested in her right hand pulsed with warmth, as if affirming the event.

"Are you ready?" Aiden asked with a crooked grin.

Aless swallowed and looked at Rory in the distance. He was smiling, nervous. Just like her.

Maura was dressed in a gown that looked crafted in wildflowers. Wisps of hair dangled from a wreath of dandelions the children had made. She pulled Aless into a quick hug. "Your mother knew this day would come," she said. "And celebrates with us."

She and Rory had planted a Japanese maple near the meadow. Somehow her mother knew Rory would be the one. That he was part of the plan, part of the love that never failed.

Life hadn't been some generational evil lurking, waiting to overpower her at the worst possible moment. Instead, the very ones who knew the truth about her mother also chose to believe a new future for her daughter.

"Thank you," she said to Aiden and Maura. "For coming to get me that day."

"Aye," Maura laughed. "These arborists — always proclaiming their love from a tree branch."

Aiden reached out and grabbed them both into a hug. "We knew you were ours. From the beginning."

Perseus stood beside Rory, ready to officiate the ceremony. Aless half-expected to see a curry brush in one hand. He still looked other-worldly — grown and nurtured by the mountains, carrying their strength. His shoulders stooped, as if he bowed to care for an imperfect world. His keen eyes searched with the air of authority that no one had conferred but remained none the less.

She remembered his words, "Hullo, lass. Ye be in the wrong neck of the woods, so to speak." And yet, she'd been sheltered even when she didn't know she needed it. Thanks to Rory.

Tareq entered from the meadow, looking more like a visiting relative than royalty. On one arm, he supported the tiny bent form of an old woman. A vibrant scarf of blue, red, and purple covered a humped back and she held a long stick that stabbed into the ground.

A young girl with black hair that shot out in sprigs held his other hand. Even from a distance, Aless recognized her crooked smile and springy stride.

"Bethiah! Amira!"

Amira waved and danced as Bethiah tottered on her cane and grinned. Aless lifted her dress and ran toward them in an undignified, unbride-like dash.

"Oi! Come back!" Mrs. Ransbottom shouted in her quavery voice, bossy as ever. "Ye must walk like a queen while we toss flowers on yer path."

"Too late," Aless called back as she ran to greet the three special guests from Akkad. She grabbed Amira into a hug, then embraced Bethiah with a gentle touch.

"It be good to see ye, dear one." Bethiah patted her cheek and kissed Alessandra's hands.

Tareq stood patiently as the three females chatted as if teatime had arrived. It was the same place where a dragon had been conquered and her beloved Rory had been healed.

Aless turned to Tareq and curtsied. "Welcome to our home. We salute the new king of Akkad." She felt awkward, unsure of what else to say.

The king shifted this way and that. His usual royal poise turned to awkward young man.

She blushed, until a giggle traveled up through her belly. For minutes, she and Tareq laughed, bridging the expanse between them. Without warning, Tareq knelt at her feet.

She pulled away, embarrassed. "No."

"This isn't a proposal, Alessandra. You already have the best." His handsome face turned somber. "This is an apology. And a thank you." He paused for a moment. "Akkad is changed because I am changed."

Amira lifted her hands to Tareq. He hoisted her into the air and spun her around. "Did you know? I've claimed these two as my own. They're helping me clean up the city."

Aless smelled layered fragrances she'd learned to define. It was frankincense, orange, and sage. The aroma of a fresh start.

Bethiah spoke in a voice much larger than her stature. "Aye. The slaves, they be released. Sent home in good Magi hands. And that temple? Couldn't be denying it's presence. Don't ye know?"

Tareq rushed in to explain. "We were together that first day back in the city — Bethiah, Amira, and me."

"I sed use that kingly authority for somethin' useful." Bethiah's hand rested on her hip, as if she was accustomed to commanding Akkad's new ruler.

"So, I did," Tareq stopped for a moment, as if to relish the memory. "I held my hand toward the temple and commanded it to fall."

"And we's watched it shake." Bethiah looked pleased to be part of what came next.

Amira wriggled her way out of Tareq's arms. She flapped and twirled in a circular motion, then chortled her toneless laugh.

Tareq clapped his hands. "That's exactly what happened. An earthquake. Though only on one end of the mesa. The hated walls quaked. They waved as if saying good-bye and collapsed right into the gorge. Every snake went with it."

"Gone, gone, it is. Fitting end, it were," Bethiah said.

"The temple was only an empty shell," Tareq continued. "Gad El Glas had already bowed. The gorge had plenty of room for its ruins."

"Good riddance." Bethiah spat on the ground for emphasis. "Besides, t'were a picture of a new day fer our king. The joy he has comin' will make sadness crumble jest as certain as that pit o'hell fell into ruin."

Aless offered quick hugs and hurried to the arbor where Rory stood, waiting. What had begun as a mild breeze became unruly gusts. Her curls that Maura had carefully entwined with fragrant lily of the valley spilled out in escaping strands. Plans for perfection fluttered as surely as the wind shifted over the happy crowd. Rory offered a quick kiss, amid cheers from the little ones.

Perseus combed his mustache away from his lips, along with a fine line of spittle that traveled down one edge. He peered around silently, until everyone was quiet. Except a magpie, that chose to be heard on this momentous occasion. Turning his attention to Aless and Rory, Perseus spoke as if this was an evening chat by the fire.

"Aye, you two. Ye be in love and all that. And learned a thing or two. Especially you, Alessandra. Like how the adventure you found mebbe wasn't the one ye planned. But it were the one that called you. Not fer yerself, but fer those who needed what ye carried.

"Between these two hawthorn trees there be a door. Tis one that leads to a new path. Like the trees, this way is grounded, though it never stops reaching fer heaven. It stands ready for you to take, beeloveds."

Perseus scanned the crowd. "These two must go, don't you know? Can't be holdin' them, even if you long to." He opened Alessandra's right hand and placed one of the stones into her palm. Then did the same with Rory. "They be called Stones of Promise fer a reason. Stronger than weapons of war, and a far sight more valuable than rubies. Anything ye desire can't compare to their worth."

Perseus peered up into the sky as a rain cloud blew in overhead and pelted icy drops. His tone that had begun unhurried became urgent as he charged Rory and Alessandra. "They'll guard ye in the darkest of places and present ye with a crown ye cannot see. For whoever finds their words, finds light for their way. Even out of deepest captivity."

Rain answered with sprinkles that became torrents. The children squealed in joy and danced as adults raced across the lawn to the chateau and its shelter.

Fitting, since it was the same towering granite walls that remained after a fiery dragon and all that had raged against its refuge. It had survived the worst. And now welcomed the hope of yet another beginning.

Chapter 32

Rory and Alessandra stood at the waterfall. Their horses were saddled, and bags packed. Orion whinnied and pranced, ready for their journey. Aless stroked her mane and offered her an apple from her pocket.

They weren't sure how long they'd be gone. Good-byes at the chateau were full of tears, but giggles, too. Bethiah and Amira stayed. There was plenty of room for a new workshop where they'd teach Maura and the children how to craft healing balms.

Tareq had returned to Akkad, ready to release freedom from the heights of the mesa to the river below — and everywhere his travels took him. If his wisdom fell short, he had Perseus at his side for guidance. Tara was there, too, as Tareq's wife. Their green-eyed baby girl had arrived only weeks ago.

The reign of Gad El Glas had come to an end as surely as the temple crashed into the gorge. And as Bethiah had said, joy had come to take its place.

Rory pulled Aless close, burying his face in her hair. He murmured in her ear. "What's next?"

Peering back at the cascading waters, Alessandra smiled. The waterfall still spoke of liberty, even if it wasn't the kind she expected. This freedom had opened her eyes to love. And charted a path through the impossible.

Aless pressed her husband's warm lips with a kiss

before she answered. "Let's find out.
   "Together."

A word about the author…

Laurel Thomas crafts stories of ordinary characters who achieve the extraordinary. History and the fantastic mesh with daring adventures in her fantasy novels, When Stars Brush Earth and Stones of Promise, published by Wild Rose Press.

Through Write Your Heart Out! and WriterConOKC, she teaches and supports other multi-published industry professionals who equip writers for success through national conferences and weekend intensives.

https://www.laurelannthomas.org/

Thank you for purchasing
this publication of The Wild Rose Press, Inc.

For questions or more information
contact us at
info@thewildrosepress.com.

The Wild Rose Press, Inc.
www.thewildrosepress.com

www.ingramcontent.com/pod-product-compliance
Lightning Source LLC
Chambersburg PA
CBHW051142030726
47504CB00004B/1003